THE YOGA SUTRAS
for Children

Roopa Pai, a Bengaluru-based writer, columnist and speaker, is one of India's best-known children's authors. Many of her books are bestsellers, enjoyed as much by adults as by children. Among them is the award-winning, much-translated *The Gita for Children*, listed by Amazon India as one of '100 Indian books to read in a lifetime'. Her TEDx talk 'Decoding the Gita: India's Book of Answers' has received over two million views to date.

When she isn't writing, Roopa leads heritage walks around her city with BangaloreWalks, a company she co-founded.

Sayan Mukherjee is a multidisciplinary illustrator and passionate storyteller from Kolkata. His work includes paintings, book covers, animated frames and children's picture books drawn using various mediums. Sayan is also a muralist and has created expansive feature-scapes across India. You can know more about his work at www.sayanart.net.

OTHER BOOKS BY ROOPA PAI

The Taranauts Series

The Gita for Children

Ready! 99 Must-have Skills for the World-Conquering Teenager (and Almost-Teenager)

The Vedas and Upanishads for Children

THE YOGA SUTRAS for Children

ROOPA PAI

Illustrations by Sayan Mukherjee

hachette INDIA

First published in 2023 by Hachette India
(Registered name: Hachette Book Publishing India Pvt. Ltd)
An Hachette UK company
www.hachetteindia.com

1

Photographs: Wikimedia Commons: Page 15: CCA-SA 3.0 Unported license;
Page 19: Public Domain; source: http://www.columbia.edu/itc/mealac/pritchett/00routesdata/bce_500back/indusvalley/protoshiva/protoshiva.jpg;
Page 22: Wikimedia Commons/Wikidata
Back cover: Photograph of author by Rohan Pai

ISBN 978-93-5731-195-3

Hachette Book Publishing India Pvt. Ltd
4th & 5th Floors, Corporate Centre
Plot No. 94, Sector 44, Gurugram – 122003, India

Typeset by Manmohan Kumar, Delhi

Printed and bound in India
by Thomson Press India Ltd

FSC
www.fsc.org
MIX
Paper | Supporting responsible forestry
FSC® C010615

Y oung ’uns, you will herein find
O ld wisdom to calm a jumpy mind;
G et ready, go! Let faith be your guide –
A ll the bestest, enjoy the ride!

CONTENTS

Right. Let's Kick This Off, Shall We?

Hello there! How wonderful, that of ALL the possible books you could have picked up, you chose THIS one! Congratulations! And now that you're here, rest assured that you are in for a fun, exciting, very unusual, and ultimately happy-making ride.

Yeah, yeah, yeah. That's what they always say, right? But this one's *different*. No, seriously.

Still sceptical? Tell you what, let me give you the 'elevator pitch'* about the Yoga Sutras. Let me tell you, in very few words, and using bullet points (because according to all the marketing and advertising and education and social media gurus out there, the Instagram Reels generation – that means

* Originally, the term 'elevator pitch' applied to the monologue that eager-beaver Entrepreneurs (people with ideas) launched into, whenever they found themselves sharing an elevator (place of no escape) with super-busy Venture Capitalists (people with money), to try and get the latter to invest in their businesses. Nowadays, it simply means trying to sell a proposition to someone in a very limited time – which necessarily means keeping the pitch short, smart, somewhat vague and very exciting.

YOU – has a VERY short attention span), the things you might expect to gain once you've read this book.

First off, as a title, Yoga Sutras sounds suitably venerable and hoary, but it also, let's admit it, sounds unfamiliar, possibly boring, and more than a little scary. Here's the alternative click-bait title to get your attention: Maharishi P's* Ultimate Handbook of Mind Control. Ooooh.

Now for the rewards waiting for you at the end of this book, assuming you have followed its instructions well:

* A mind like a still, clear mountain lake (like in those screensavers);
* Some v. cool Asanas for the mind (and none for your body – because those are just so mainstream, amirite?) that will help it make your body listen to you – *every* time;
* A comprehensive list of the things that muddy our mind lakes and make us miserable (so that we can then go about eliminating them, and get to point 1);
* An ability to see things *as they are* and not *as they seem* (very useful when you're checking out the number of likes and comments and heart emojis on your friend's Instagram reels compared with yours, and dying inside);

★ Maharishi P? Who's that? What does the P stand for? Patience, young 'uns – no, his name wasn't Patience – all will be revealed in good time.

* The explosive secret of lasting happiness (PS: It isn't cooler friends or more money or unlimited free pizzas or getting the top rank in an exam or India winning the Cricket World Cup); and
* Mystical powers (Not even kidding. But since most of us will probably get to that Sage Vishwamitra-Durvasa-Vashishta-Agastya stage only a few dozen lifetimes hence, it's best not to put too much hope in that direction).

And those are just the highlights. I. Mean!

Thank you for your time.

***

So, did it work, the elevator pitch about the Yoga Sutras? You're nodding, some of you. And some look as yet unconvinced, but quite intrigued. Whatever. We have your attention, and that's what counts. Hurray!

Have to admit, though, that Maharishi P would have mightily disapproved of the word count of this pitch. The man believed intensely in keeping things crisp and concise – if he'd been around today, he would have totally trended on Twitter for his ability to put a deep, luminous truth about the human psyche into a three-word, way less-than-140-character sutra. In other words, he was the patron saint of your very-limited-attention-span generation, hundreds of years before you were a thing.

Right. Are you all set to dive into the shining, shimmering depths of a whole new world – the crumpled, layered, confounding, topsy-turvy, hall-of-mirrors expanse of the human mind? Do you have the courage it takes to explore a dazzling place you never knew? Are you possessed of the open mind and heart required to take in a new, fantastic point of view without bias or judgement? Can you muster up the commitment needed to undertake the long, arduous, rewarding journey towards absolute fearlessness and freedom that Maharishi P promises all dedicated travellers along this path?

Yes? What are you standing about for, then? Let's go!

Note: Now's a good time to look at the Pronunciation Guide on page 290.

So What's the Big Deal About the Yoga Sutras?

(Plus, can we please finally spill the tea on the P – in the mysterious Maharishi's name, i.e.?)

Uh-hunh. You will have to cool your heels a wee bit longer before we spill the tea, sorree!* To keep you engaged and entertained in the meantime, here's a fun quiz. All you have to do is pick one of the answer options and hope that it's the right one. Actually, it doesn't even matter if your answers are wrong – there are no prizes to be won here if you're mostly right, and no shame if you're largely wrong. Everyone taking the quiz wins the 'prize' of knowing a lot more about the Yoga Sutras by the end of the quiz than they did when they began, that's all. And that's the hallmark of the best kind of quiz, right?

Right. Let's go.

1. Had you ever heard of the Yoga Sutras before you came upon it in the title of this book?
   - (a) Vaguely, somewhere, maybe in a history lesson.
   - (b) Never heard of it.

* Oh, allll right, if you simply can't wait, hop on over to page 29 and check out the box 'Maharishi P, Man of Mystery'.

(c) Yes! And I also know what P stands for (but don't worry, I'm not telling)!

2. This question is for those of you who picked option (c) as the answer in the previous question – and for everyone who didn't. What, in your understanding, are the Yoga Sutras?
   (a) A fat text describing every yogAsana in the world (I hear it has some great illustrations too, of ancient human pretzels who could fold themselves into all kinds of shapes).
   (b) A slim text describing the 10 Original and Authentic Asanas (Did you know that most of the postures everyone contorts themselves into these days in their yoga classes are not the 'real deal', in the sense that they have nothing to do with the Yoga Sutras?).
   (c) A fat text describing ways in which to control your mind, among other things (This one, surely! Did you think I wasn't smart enough to make some intelligent deductions from the alternative title you provided in the previous chapter? – *Reader of this book*).
   (d) A slim text describing ways in which to control your mind, among other things (Ha! Did you think I wasn't smart enough to bowl you a googly? – *Author of this book*).

3. What does the word 'yoga' mean?
   (a) The most boring period in a schoolday.
   (b) Different things, depending on whom you asked in ancient India.

(c) The most fun period in a schoolday.
(d) A class my mum goes to and swears she lurrrves (although I suspect what she really lurrrves is the fact that she gets to hang out with her friends after).

4. What does the word 'sutra' mean?
(a) It's the same thing as a shloka (Or is it the same thing as a mantra? Actually, aren't shloka and mantra identical?).
(b) I know it's a word that gets added on to a lot of fusty old Indian texts, but I've never thought about what it means.
(c) A thread.
(d) I have absolutely no idea.

All done? Have you picked your answers? Now let's see what the correct answers are.

Of course, Question 1 has no 'right' answer. You either knew about the Yoga Sutras (YS) or you didn't. If you chose option (c), hurray for you! If you chose option (a), that's great too (although the mind is such a trickster, it may be fooling you into thinking you've heard the name before even if you haven't, because it can't bear the thought of picking option (b) and admitting it doesn't know something). If you picked option (b), there's absolutely no shame in it. The YS aren't very well known at all among the general public. (If you had said, for instance, that you had never heard of the Bhagavat Gita or the Quran or the Bible or the Guru Granth Sahib, that would be somewhat concerning, but the Yoga Sutras are definitely not what you would call 'popular ancient literature', even in India.)

On to Question 2, to which the right answer is... option (d)! Yes, the YS make up an ultra-slim text, its 195 (or 196, depending on whom you ask) sutras, each with an average length of six words, adding up to no more than 1,200 words. IN ALL!

You heard that right – 1,200 words. That's about the length of a school essay – it can't surely be the length of an ENTIRE ancient text! It is, though. There's more. Consider this. If you wrote the sutras out, in run-on sentences, on lined A4 paper, they would just about cover ONE A4-size page, back-to-back! Just as a comparison, the Gita has 700 four-line verses, and a word count of close to 21,000 words. Yet the Gita is considered to be a concise little text, especially when held up against the Great Indian Family Saga it is embedded in, the Mahabharata, which has 100,000 verses, and – hold your breath – close to 1.8 million words!

No wonder the YS never made the bestseller cut, you're thinking – they certainly didn't have the physical heft that their competition does, and maybe not the literary or philosophical one either?* Not true. The very fact that the YS have survived for hundreds of years, and, despite ups and downs over

★It's easy for the Bible or the Quran to be eternally in the bestselling category within their respective faiths – they are the only texts that contain, according to their adherents, the Word of God. In that sense, they have no competition. There are so many texts sacred to the Hindus, on the other hand, each for different reasons, and to different groups of people, that it is a tussle for any text to stay perennially in the Top 10. Or 100. Especially since so many of them are less about a conventional 'creator God' that you are supposed to believe in, and more about YOU. Specifically, about how you can find the God-spark within yourself.

the centuries, are still being talked about and studied and exalted in the twenty-first century, not just by Indians but by passionate scholars and followers all over the world (in fact, the YS and the Gita are arguably the best-known ancient Indian texts outside of India), tells us something about the strength and staying power of their content.

And what is that content? The most mind-blowing content of all! The YS give you the answers to humanity's oldest, most existential questions:

1. Who am I, really?
2. What is this universe around me, really?
3. What is the point of life, really?
4. Is death, that scary, scary point of no return that we are ALL hurtling towards – from the very moment we are born – yup, NO ONE and NOTHING gets out of here alive – the absolute 'THE END'? Really? (Please say no, please, pretty please!)

Oh-kay, you're saying. But don't the Upanishads and the Gita also answer the very same questions? They do (smart of you to catch that!). And very lucidly at that. Let's pause for a moment here to quickly summarize their answers.

1. You are not your body or your mind, you are something deeper than your deepest feelings, wiser than your wisest thoughts, you are that which is unchangeable, invincible, perfectly blissful, and eternal.
2. The universe – or the universe as it appears to you – is as real or unreal as you want it to be, given that YOU are constructing it, constantly, in your mind; it exists

because YOU are conscious of it, it has no independent existence apart from you. (Wait, what?)

3. The point of life is to understand what is *really* real and what only *appears* to be real – when you do, you will see that, at the very core of your being, you are no different from anyone or anything else in the world, and that no one and nothing in the world is different from you. Then there will be no more fear – because we only fear the 'other' – and when fear doesn't guide our actions, bliss, which is our original and true state, will automatically result.
4. As for death, refer to Answer 1. The last word of the answer, in particular. Now quit hyperventilating.

Right. Are the YS's answers to these questions very different, then? Is that what makes them a must-read text? No. As long as we don't get too technical about it, the YS hold much the same opinion as the earlier texts.

What makes the YS so different and so important, the real reason their content is so explosive, is that they don't just *tell* you this stuff, they also give you the step-by-step lowdown – through processes and practices – on how to *experience* it for yourself (short answer: by controlling your mind)! I don't expect you to believe what I'm saying, Maharishi P seems to say in the YS, I know some of it sounds really, like, *out there*. That's why I'm inviting you to undertake this most marvellous journey for yourself – here, I've even put it all down on this A4-size paper for easy reference.

Except, the sutras are anything but 'easy' to comprehend. To make them easy to memorize, the good Maharishi P made the sutras so short that they ended up being very cryptic as well.

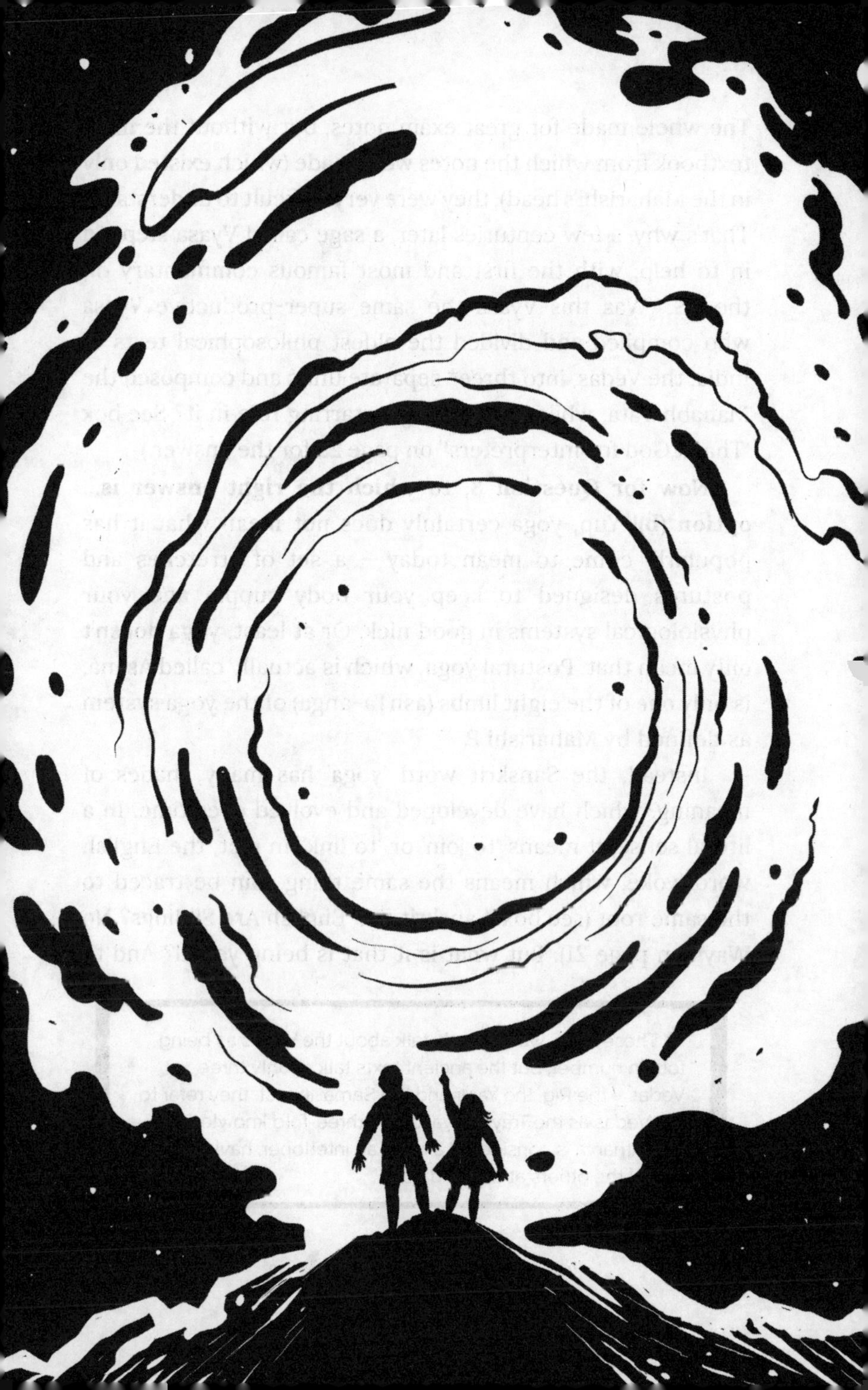

The whole made for great exam notes, but without the main textbook from which the notes were made (which existed only in the Maharishi's head), they were very difficult to understand. That's why, a few centuries later, a sage called Vyasa stepped in to help, with the first and most famous commentary on the YS. (Was this Vyasa the same super-productive Vyasa who compiled and divided the oldest philosophical texts of India, the Vedas, into three* separate units and composed the Mahabharata, while also playing a starring role in it? See box 'Thank God for Interpreters!' on page 25 for the answer.)

Now for Question 3, to which the right answer is... option (b)! Yup, yoga certainly does not mean what it has popularly come to mean today – a set of stretches and postures designed to keep your body supple and your physiological systems in good nick. Or at least, yoga doesn't *only* mean that. Postural yoga, which is actually called Asana, is only *one* of the eight limbs (ashTa-anga) of the yoga system as defined by Maharishi P.

Instead, the Sanskrit word 'yoga' has many shades of meaning, which have developed and evolved over time. In a literal sense, it means 'to join' or 'to link'. In fact, the English word 'yoke', which means the same thing, can be traced to the same root (see box 'Sanskrit and English Are Siblings? No Way!' on page 21). But what is it that is being yoked? And to

★ These days, we routinely talk about the Vedas as being four in number, but the ancient texts talk of only three Vedas – the Rig, the Yajur and the Sama. In fact, they refer to the Vedas as the Trayi Vidya, or the three-fold knowledge. The Atharva is considered a bit of an interloper, having joined the others at a later date.

O Maharishi, What the Deuce! Why Were You Being So Abstruse?

Why, indeed? After all, like any great teacher, the Maharishi would surely have hoped that his painstakingly composed compendium of the ancient practice of yoga, the first of its kind, would serve to enlighten several generations to come, on the subtle art and science of mind control. Why make the sutras so concise, then? And so mystifying? Here's a fascinating, and perfectly plausible, theory about that.

But first, a little detour to the *Phaedrus*, a dialogue between the great Greek philosopher Socrates and his interlocutor Phaedrus, as recorded by Socrates's most famous student, Plato, circa 370 BCE. While narrating an ancient Egyptian myth about the creation of writing to Phaedrus, Socrates talks of how the god Thamus, the king of all Egypt, reacted when the god Theuth arrived to present to him his latest, greatest inventions for humankind – numbers, arithmetic, geometry, astronomy, draughts, dice and letters of the alphabet.

When it was finally the turn of the letters to be presented, a justifiably proud Theuth was fairly shaking with excitement. 'This invention, O King,' said Theuth, 'will make the Egyptians wiser, for I have discovered the elixir of memory!'

To this, Thamus, shaking his head sadly, replied, 'Oh, my dear Theuth, how your affection for your invention has blinded you to the truth! This invention will produce nothing but forgetfulness in the minds of those who learn to use it, because they will not practise their memory. You have invented an elixir not of memory but of reminding; and you offer your pupils the appearance of wisdom, not true wisdom, for they will read many things without instruction and will therefore seem to know many things, when they are for the most part ignorant, since they are not wise, but only appear wise.'

Neither Thamus nor Socrates were alone in their unease about the letters. A similar concern over the introduction of writing as a means of recording and passing on knowledge was shared deeply by our own ancient seers, who, for thousands of years, had passed on the great wisdoms only through oral instruction.

Was it this conviction, that future generations would first outsource their memories to books, and 2,000 years later, even more comprehensively and frighteningly, to their smartphones, that prompted the Maharishi to keep his sutras cryptic? Did he deliberately keep them mysterious so that they could never truly be understood without instruction from a good teacher? Did he keep them to 1,200 words in the hope that future generations would still have the mental capacity it took to memorize them? There's a thought!

Who Was the First Indian to Say, 'I Want It in Writing'?

Very likely someone from the Indus Sarasvati Civilization (ISC), which is, as far as our knowledge goes, the subcontinent's oldest civilization. Artefacts excavated from ISC cities show clear evidence of a 'script' (new work has revealed that this script isn't made up of the letters of an alphabet, but of pictorial characters, where each character represents a word instead of a sound), but no one has been able to decipher it yet. Somewhat inexplicably, writing seems to have gone underground or disappeared entirely in India after the ISC began to slowly decline some 4,000 years ago.

Until, some 1,200 years later, the written word began to show up again, this time on rock edicts of the Mauryan emperor Ashoka, who ruled from 268 to 232 BCE. This script, which has been deciphered, is called BrAhmi. Unlike the ISC script, this

This inscription from the Ashoka Pillar in Sarnath, Uttar Pradesh, shows us what the BrAhmi script looked like

was an alphabetic script, and it was mostly used to write edicts in a language called PrAkrit, popular in north and central India. Ashokan edicts in the south are in Tamil, but the script is still BrAhmi, with a few new letters introduced to accommodate uniquely Tamil sounds.

Even though we haven't found hard evidence for BrAhmi before Ashoka's time, scholars think it is likely it had been around for at least two to three hundred years by then. In other words, BrAhmi was around at the time of Socrates, Plato and Maharishi P. Although it is impossible to know exactly when the Maharishi lived (see box 'Maharishi P, Man of Mystery' on page 29), writing was certainly becoming popular in India by the time he arrived on the scene.

what? Simply put, yoga is a practice that yokes together body and mind, mind and spirit, your human self with your divine self, the little, fearful, selfish, egotistic, individual 'i' that we believe we are, with the vast, universal, fearless, everyone-and-everything-embracing, the-world-is-my-family 'I' that is our true nature. Once that union happens, the yoke itself disappears, allowing us to soar free and unfettered.

Here is a popular shloka from the Maha Upanishad about the difference between the two I's. So dear was this ancient and deeply Indian sentiment to the founding fathers of our country that they even decided to have it carved into the entrance hall of Parliament, so that everyone who walked in was constantly reminded of it. Write it out, hang it up in your room, say it out loud, and hold it in your heart – not just its words, but also its spirit.

अयं निजः परो वेति गणना लघुचेतसाम्।
उदारचरितानां तु वसुधैव कुटुम्बकम्॥

ayam nijah paro veti gaNanA laghuchetasAm
udAracharitAnAm tu vasudhaiva kuTumbakam

This is my own, that one is the 'other', so quibble the small-minded;
The large-hearted declare – why, the world itself is my family.

But back to yoga. The word is found extensively in both ancient texts like the Vedas, the Upanishads, the Gita, and the Yoga Sutras (duh!), and more recent ones like the *Hatha Yoga Pradipika*. It is also part of various Indic* traditions, including YogAchAra (Buddhist), ShramaNa (Jain) and Tantra. Each tradition

☆ Anything that pertains to India, its languages, culture or people.

and each text interprets the philosophy of 'yoga' differently. For instance, every chapter of the Bhagavat Gita is named for the particular kind of yoga, or 'path to union', that is described in that chapter. In the Katha Upanishad, which is older than the Gita, young Nachiketa is given the knowledge and rules of something called yoga, defined as 'the control of the senses', from Yama, the Lord of Death, himself. That knowledge, Yama promises Nachiketa, will free him from death. As for 'yogis' – fiercely solitary practitioners of yoga, with their matted hair, emaciated bodies and ascetic lifestyles – they are a vital part of the forest landscapes of the Ramayana.

Can we conclude, then, that yoga originated in Vedic society, which arrived on the world stage after the decline of Meluhha,* a 'country' often identified with the ISC? Not necessarily. A tantalizing clue that yoga predates the Vedic civilization, and was well known to the ISC people, comes from a tiny seal retrieved from the excavation of the sprawling city of Mohenjo-daro in the 1920s. Only about an inch square in size – and not even entirely whole – this seal shows a cross-legged figure, surrounded by animals, seated in the classic yogic posture of meditation that is practised to this day! Does India have an unbroken connection with yoga, then, that goes back 5,000 years or more? Very likely! Hold that thought for at least as long as the goosebumps last.

★ The records of one of the oldest civilizations in the world, Sumer, which flourished on the banks of the Euphrates and Tigris rivers in Mesopotamia (part of today's Iraq) 7,000 to 8,000 years ago, mention a prominent trading partner called Meluhha. Most scholars associate Meluhha with the Indus Sarasvati Civilization.

The Ancient Yogi – or Is It Yogini? – of Meluhha

Take a good look at the famous ISC seal below. Many of the animals that surround the figure – elephant, antelope, tiger – are associated with a very popular Hindu god of today. The horns/three-pronged headgear the figure wears could very well represent a trident, a weapon associated with the same god. Plus, this god is often referred to as Adiyogi – or the primordial yogi – and, what do you know, the ancient seal shows a figure in a meditative yogic posture! Excited historians who noticed all this gave the figure the name Pashupati, Lord of the Animals, which is also one of the names of this god. You know who we are talking about, don't you? That's right – Shiva!

Let us pause a little here to wonder why animals are called pashu in so many Indian languages. The word comes from

An impression made from the 'Pashupati' seal

pAsha, which is Sanskrit for noose. The pAsha is no ordinary noose, however; it is an 'astra' or divine weapon – Ganesha is usually shown holding it (to signify his power to 'lasso' any obstacles in our paths and remove them), and so is Yama (to extract our souls from our bodies when we die).

It isn't just animals but also humans who are pashu, for we are all bound, according to Indic philosophy, by the pAsha of samsAra, or the cycle of rebirth, doomed to return to the world over and over again.

Now that you know this, do you see how the name Pashupati can also be read to mean 'Lord of the noose of samsAra', which in turn means someone who has mastered his senses, overcome his fears, and is therefore superhuman, divine, eternally free? That's the ideal, the scriptures tell us, that we all can, and must, aspire to.

Right, back to the little Meluhhan seal. Observe it again, closely. Hmm, could the seated figure be, in fact, female? The bangles it is wearing go all the way up the arms, very similar to the ornamentation displayed by the 'Dancing Girl of Mohenjo-daro' (look her up on the internet). Plus, new excavations at Harappan sites like Rakhigarhi in Haryana have revealed that women were buried at the centre of cemeteries and with rather more paraphernalia – pots of food, ornaments, decorative plates – than the men, which seems to indicate that they (women) may have had a higher position in society. Add to this the fact that other Harappan seals show female figures with animals, and that the cult of the mother goddess has always existed in India, and it begins to seem quite plausible that this is a female figure in a yogic pose.

Which theory is your favourite?

Sanskrit and English Are Siblings? No Way!

Yes way! Sure, when you are first introduced to the idea that many, many words in English and Sanskrit have the same root, and in fact, sound similar to each other, it blows your mind a bit. That is because, in India, we are used to thinking of English as the foreigner's/colonizer's/modern/'scientific' language, and Sanskrit as its exact opposite, a deeply Indian/most ancient/sacred/'religious' language. The truth is, though, that both Sanskrit and English – along with many, many other European and Indian languages – are descended from the same, roughly 6,000-year-old, Proto-Indo-European 'mother language'. Today, close to 46 per cent of the world speaks a language derived from this mother language, and a vast number of those speakers are in India.

Sanskrit – especially its earliest version, Vedic Sanskrit – arrived on the scene well before English, or even its predecessor, Latin, did. Scholars and linguists of every hue have raved about the 'wondrous structure' of what is called Classical Sanskrit, which is the Sanskrit we are taught today. Classical Sanskrit was derived from Vedic Sanskrit, but unlike the latter, it was bound by the rules of grammar, syntax and metre. All these rules – no less than 3,996 of them! – are contained in the sage Panini's famous book of linguistics, *Ashtadhyayi*. In fact, the word 'Sanskrit' itself is the anglicized and abbreviated version of 'samskrita bhAsha', which means 'perfectly constructed language'.

If Classical Sanskrit, taught and used only by scholars, became the language of literature and scripture, PrAkrit, which means 'natural', was the language of the common people. Without rules to constrain it, PrAkrit, also derived from Vedic Sanskrit, morphed into many PrAkrits, which eventually developed into languages such as Hindi, Urdu, Bengali, Odia, Assamese, Punjabi, Gujarati, Kashmiri, Marathi, Sindhi and Nepali.

Here are some sets of words, in Sanskrit, English and Hindi respectively, that sound very similar to each other: mAtr, mother, mAtA; nAma, name, nAm; trINi, three, tIn; samartha, smart, samarth; manas, mind, mann; samah, same, samAn; sevA, serve, sevA; bandha, bond, bandhan; prashansA, praise, prashansA; patha, path, path; sarpa, serpent, sarp; bhrAtr, brother, bhai; sthiti, state, sthiti.

And this is just the tip of the iceberg! Start putting together your own list now!

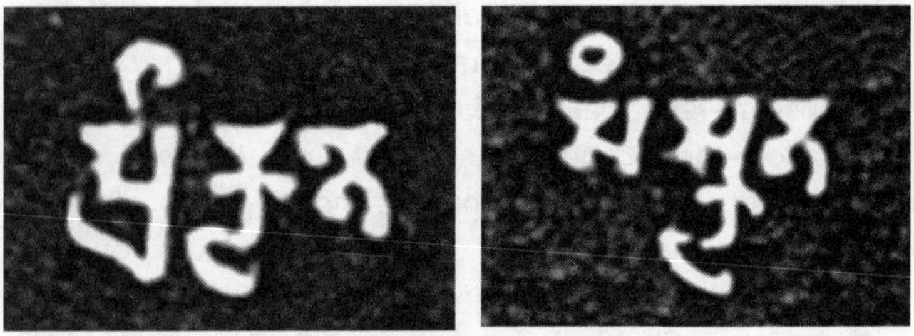

The words 'PrAkrit' and 'Sanskrit' written in BrAhmi on the Mandsaur stone inscription of Yashodharman Vishnuvardhana, 532 CE

Which brings us, very neatly, to question 4 of our quiz. And the answer to that is... That's right, option (c) – the Sanskrit word 'sutra' indeed means 'thread'.*

With reference to yoga, how can we understand 'sutra'? We can read it as the unbroken thread of practice and philosophy that connects us, the current inhabitants of the subcontinent, to its most ancient inhabitants. We can read it as the shining, life-giving river-thread that flows through the many-hued, many-layered, ever-changing but, somehow, beautifully harmonious fabric of India's civilizational history, affirming yet again our commitment to the idea that we are each of us only a part of the whole – no different from and neither superior nor inferior to anyone or anything else; and that our individual welfare lies in yoking ourselves and our efforts to the welfare of everyone and everything else. (For real-life examples, look no further than the climate crisis and the successful, pan-global quest for the Covid vaccine.)

Specifically with reference to Maharishi P's Yoga Sutras, we could read 'sutra' simply as a 'string' of clearly laid-out

★ You may be familiar with the word 'sUtradhAr,' or 'thread-wielder'. Often, the word is used to describe the impartial, non-judgemental narrator, or witness, of a play or story At other times, the same word is used to describe a puppet-master, the Machiavellian genius who controls the movements and, indeed, destinies of everyone around. Quick question: If you believe in God, who is also often referred to as the 'sUtradhAr' of our lives, do you imagine Him (or Her or It) to be the first kind of thread-wielder, or the second?

steps – unembellished by elaborate 'pearls' of explanation – to help us achieve control of our minds, creating in the process a strong, unbreakable link with our highest selves, so that we become the very, very best version of ourselves.

Now then, ready to explore some ancient Indian 'string' theory? Come on!

Thank God for Interpreters!

Maharishi P, for various reasons, some of which we have discussed, chose to keep the sutras of the YS compact and cryptic. Future generations might have lost the great wisdoms of this marvellous little text entirely if it hadn't been for the interpreters of the YS, who took it upon themselves to expound and elaborate on the sutras as they understood them. The earliest and most authoritative commentary, the *Vyasa Bhashya* (bhAshya is Sanskrit for 'commentary') dates back to around the fifth century CE.

Was the sage who put together this commentary the same Veda Vyasa who is believed to have compiled the Vedas and dictated the Mahabharata to the divine scribe, Ganesha? Many people believe that is so. Others say it could not be, since the texts were composed hundreds of years apart. Maybe the author of the *Vyasa Bhashya* used Vyasa's name to give his commentary more credibility. Maybe 'Vyasa' was a title, an honorific, given to (or adopted by) great scholars in the centuries following the original Vyasa.

By the way, the original Vyasa's given name was not Vyasa but Krishna – Krishna Dvaipayana, 'Krishna of the Island'. He was so named because he was born on a river island, to the beautiful fisherwoman Satyavati (who was also called Matsyagandhi, the fish-scented one, because, quite naturally, she smelt strongly of fish). Krishna Dvaipayana, or Veda Vyasa, was the father of the three princes of the great Kuru dynasty – Dhritarashtra (whose sons were the Kauravas), Pandu (whose sons were the Pandavas) and Vidura.

Whoever the Vyasa of the *Bhashya* was, his wonderful commentary has been considered the 'official' version for so long that many scholars have speculated that it was in fact Maharishi P himself who wrote it, under a pseudonym. This isn't likely, though, given the difference in the language of the two texts. Plus, all the other commentaries on the YS that were written in the centuries after, while they differed from the *Bhashya* in small ways, never countered the original interpretation in any of its fundamental aspects.

This is quite unusual in the Indian knowledge tradition. For example, even though Adi Shankara, the eighth-century Vedic scholar and teacher, was such a towering genius, the basic philosophy of his commentary on the Upanishads – Advaita – was challenged by other great commentaries that followed, like the ones by Ramanujacharya (VishishTAdvaita) and Madhvacharya (Dvaita), each of which has its own committed set of followers in India today. For any one person's view on anything to stand for centuries, like Vyasa's has, and not to be roundly challenged by someone or, more often, by several someones, is very rare. Why do you think we are called the 'argumentative Indians'?*

Among the other commentaries on the YS, the best known are the *Vivarana*, dating back to the eighth or ninth century

* Just to be clear, there's no shame in that moniker – it just means that we are part of a culture that allows the space for questioning, a culture in which no human-generated wisdom, whether it is about God, life, electrons, viruses, or diets, is ever considered complete, final, or set in stone. Anyone and everyone, whatever their race, religion and gender, is allowed to have a shy at challenging it or adding to it, as long as they are being respectful.

and believed, by some scholars, to have been composed by Adi Shankara himself; the *Tattva Vaisharadi,* by Vachaspati Mishra of Mithila (present-day Bihar), also circa ninth century; and the *Raja Martanda*, composed in the eleventh century by that greatest of philosopher-kings of medieval India, Raja Bhoja, after whom the city of Bhopal is named. Around the same period, another commentary on the YS was written by a rather unexpected scholar in a rather unexpected language. The language was Arabic, and the author, the medieval Arab traveller, scientist and polymath, Al-Biruni! Clearly, the best literature has always transcended borders of every kind.

Although the YS have been around for close to 2,000 years, if not more, they have gone through their own ups and downs through the millennia as far as their popularity is concerned. While a good many commentaries on them continued to be composed right up to the sixteenth century, the British, when they began to rule India and take a more than casual interest in her ancient texts in the eighteenth century, found no living tradition of the YS, no teachers around who were teaching this particular text. In the intervening 200 years, the YS had inexplicably gone underground.

Fortunately for us, the YS were rescued from relative obscurity and vibrantly revived by the charismatic Swami Vivekananda, who is also credited with taking Indian philosophy to the Western world, in a most emphatic way, towards the end of the nineteenth century. The baton was then picked up by the great practitioners and teachers of yoga such as Tirumalai Krishnamacharya, the HaTha Yoga* (see next page) pioneer, whose students included modern masters like B.K.S. Iyengar and Pattabhi Jois, and Sivananda Saraswathi, whose disciple, Vishnudevananda, founded the yoga system known as Sivananda Yoga in 1959. Today, it is these, and similar other forms of Asana-based yoga, that have taken the world by storm.

Phewww. This box is a serious data-dump, packed to the gills with names and dates. If you are feeling a little overwhelmed at the end of it, don't. This is not a history class, and you are not expected to commit the facts to memory. Plus, as you can see, none of this information is part of the YS themselves. It is just part of what is called 'setting the context', to let you know the YS's place and progress in history. You can permit all of this info to vanish from your head this instant – *Poof! It's gone!* – and come back to it only if and when you are preparing for a YS quiz or presentation or something. Okay? Okay.

✪ A different branch of yoga, involving mainly the body and the breath, that has its own lineage dating back to the eleventh century. Versions of haTha yoga (including ashTAnga yoga), mainly involving Asanas, became popular in the twentieth century thanks to teachers like Krishnamacharya. This is what the world – and most of India – today knows simply as 'yoga.' (PS: Could it be that haTha yoga, mispronounced by a Western tongue, was the forerunner of what is popular in the West today as 'hot yoga'? Haha, just kidding!)

Maharishi P, Man of Mystery

It is time. Here we are, *finally*, to spill the tea on Maharishi P. But since it would be somewhat anticlimactic to do this in a straightforward fashion, especially after holding out for so long, here's a challenge for you: find his name in the shloka below! This, by the way, is a shloka that's probably familiar to some of you who take yoga lessons, because it is often chanted at the beginning of each class, as a prayer to the Maharishi.

योगेन चित्तस्य पदेन वाचां मलं शरीरस्य च वैदिकेन ।
योपाकरोत्तं प्रवरं मुनीनां पतञ्जलिं प्राञ्जलिरानतोस्मि॥

yogena chittasya padena vAchAm malam
sharirasya cha vaidyakena
yopAkarottam pravaram munInAm patanjalim
prAnjalirAnatosmi

Thaaat's right! Maharishi P was none other than Maharishi Patanjali! And now that our veil of ignorance has been ripped off, he should stand before us, revealed in his full glory, right? Wrong! As often happens with personalities from ancient Indian history, very little is known about the Maharishi. Hang on, you're saying, doesn't the shloka above itself contain information about him? Yes and no. Let's do a rough translation of it and see, shall we?

I bow to that exalted sage Patanjali, who cleared the impurities of our minds through yoga, of our speech through grammar, and of our bodies through Ayurveda

* Now, it is true that there was a Patanjali who wrote a book on Sanskrit grammar. This book, *Mahabhashya*,

is, in fact, a commentary on the famous linguist and grammarian Panini's *Ashtadhyayi*, which is the definitive text, to this day, on Sanskrit grammar. The *Ashtadhyayi* is also the world's earliest work on linguistics, given that it has been dated to the fifth or sixth century BCE.

* According to commentaries on the *Charaka Samhita*, one of the foundational texts of Ayurveda that is believed to have been authored (or edited) by the famous physician Charaka in the first century CE, there was a Patanjali who wrote a revised version of the *Samhita*, called *Charakapratisamskrita*, and a Patanjali who wrote a different medical text called the *Patanjalatantra*, centuries apart from each other. Neither of those texts, however, has ever been found. (*Fun fact*: It is one of these two Patanjalis, presumably, that a brand of Indian Ayurvedic products, Patanjali, is named for.)
* And then, of course, there was our Patanjali, who composed the YS, and lived somewhere between the fourth century BCE and the second century CE, depending on whom you ask.

We have no idea whether it was the same Patanjali or many different ones who wrote these very different texts.

Where does the shloka itself come from? From the *Raja Martanda*, the eleventh-century commentary on the YS by Raja Bhoja (remember him from the box 'Thank God for Interpreters!' on page 25?). We cannot be sure whether the Raja composed it or if he was just quoting an already existing prayer to the Maharishi, but that's where we first come across it.

There is a second shloka about Patanjali in the *Raja Martanda*. It follows the first, and gives us a little more 'information' about the Maharishi.

आबाहु पुरुषाकारं शङ्ख चक्रासि धारिणम्।
सहस्र शिरसं श्वेतं प्रणमामि पतञ्जलिम्॥

AbAhu purushAkAram shankha chakrAsi dhAriNam
sahasra shirasam shvetam praNamAmi patanjalim

I bow to that Patanjali, who by his actions has become one with his true self, who bears the conch and the chakra, and who has a thousand heads, pure and white

Eh?

Hold on. Does the 'conch and chakra' reference ring a bell? Which Hindu god is often depicted holding the same two objects, along with a lotus and mace? That's right, Vishnu. Who or what, associated very closely with Vishnu, has a thousand heads/hoods? Right again – Ananta Shesha, the cosmic serpent on whom Vishnu reclines as he floats on the ocean of milk.

What could this verse be telling us, then? That its composer believed that our Maharishi was an incarnation, an avatar, of none other than Ananta Shesha himself? Right answer! In a cool plot twist, in the Tamil Siddha tradition, which worships Shiva, not Vishnu, as the premier Lord of the Universe, our Patanjali is considered to be one of the 18 siddhIs, or enlightened souls.

That's it. That's *all* we know about Maharishi P, really. But if there's one thing we can say with some conviction about him, it is this: with his talent for yoking together disparate entities – Shiva and Vishnu, grammar and medicine, human and divine – in himself, Maharishi Patanjali was clearly one of the most 'well-connected' people of ancient India, which makes him the perfect yoga guru!

◀ Maharishi P, as imagined by our illustrator, Sayan. Did the Maharishi really look like this? Who knows? But given that our ancient rishis usually did not bother with trimming their hair or beards, had few opportunities to load up on carbs and sweets (they lived in forests and subsisted on what the jungle provided), and owned little by way of clothes, finery or mobile phones (seriously, who needs the stress!), this calm-faced, fit-looking yogi is probably pretty close to the real thing!

Just a Couple More – Okay, Eight More – Clarifications

Remind me again – how exactly does yoga help me to lead my best life?

Good question. It will require a rather involved answer. Here we go.

The point of our human life, according to Indian philosophy, is darshana – seeing. Seeing what exactly? The truth about ourselves – and everyone else.

And what is that truth exactly?

That, despite what we see when we look in the mirror, we are NOT the things we can see and hear and feel, like our bodies or our breath.

That, despite how deeply we suffer in our minds because of emotions like betrayal, anger, jealousy and grief, or how much joy other emotions like love, happiness and heroism bring us, we are neither our mind, nor the thoughts and emotions it generates.

With me so far? Great.

So, if we are not our bodies or our minds or our ideas or our feelings, what *are* we?

We are, each of us, a consciousness, an energy, an awareness, that simply stands by and watches the never-ending roller coaster of thoughts and emotions trundling by in our minds, taking us alternately to Himalayan heights of ecstasy and Mariana Trench lows of misery. The consciousness that is us is aware of the roller coaster; in fact, it is because of that awareness that the roller coaster even exists, because what we are not aware of simply does not exist for us. The roller coaster itself, however, *has no power* over the consciousness. What happens on the roller coaster, in other words, stays on the roller coaster.

If I don't know it, does it even exist?

Is it true that what we are not aware of does not exist for us? Think about it – until Dutch merchant Antonie van Leeuwenhoek made a microscope powerful enough to see bacteria and similar creatures in the seventeenth century (it must have been a real shock for the poor man), organisms not visible to the naked eye simply *did not exist* for people. Until Spanish explorer Christopher Columbus set off west from Spain in the fifteenth century to find the spices of the East (the earth was spherical, he reasoned, so he would eventually hit the Spice Islands) and bumped into the 'New World', where strange and unknown fruits and vegetables like potatoes, tomatoes, cocoa and chillies grew, the Americas (and those particular fruits and veggies) *did not exist* for the people of the old world – Asia, Europe, Africa.

Taking a different tack, we are all guilty of sometimes being entirely unaware of the needs of certain groups in our communities. Take the physically challenged, for instance. When we design an event or a building or a pavement, we often design it without the tweaks and additions necessary to accommodate the needs of the physically challenged, not because we maliciously want to keep them out of those spaces, but because they – the physically challenged – simply *do not exist* for most of us. That is why it is so important to 'expand our awareness' – through reading, observation, conversation, reflection. When we listen to a point of view different from ours with an open mind, when we make the effort to become aware of those whose voices are not often heard (people, animals, trees, rivers), when we make the other 'feel seen', we get closer to darshana – the understanding that beneath all our external differences and wildly diverse ideas, we are all channelling the same cosmic energy that sustains the world.

Let's make this easier with an analogy. The REAL you, say our ancient texts, is similar to the light of the projector bulb which enables a film – in this case, the film of our lives, to play on a screen – in this case, the screen that is the world. In other words, the film 'exists' because of the light. The film itself, however, has no impact on the light. Think about it. Does the light of the bulb die when the film ends? Nope. It continues to shine, now illuminating a blank rectangle of screen. Does this light only allow certain genres of films – fantasy, drama, slasher – to play? Nyet. The light has no preferences – it illuminates whatever film the projector is loaded with. Does the light feel hurt when the villain insults the hero or excited when the heroine agrees to go out with him? Lol. Of course not. Can the same light enable another film to run (in other words, cause another film to exist)? Suuure!

The problem is that – focus hard now – *we forget that we are the light*, and imagine that we are the film. We get so involved in the film – and it's ALWAYS a mega-action-thriller-melodrama film – that we never take a moment to step back, take a breath and remind ourselves – 'You are the light, silly! The LIGHT! Chill – that stuff on screen is not happening to YOU!'

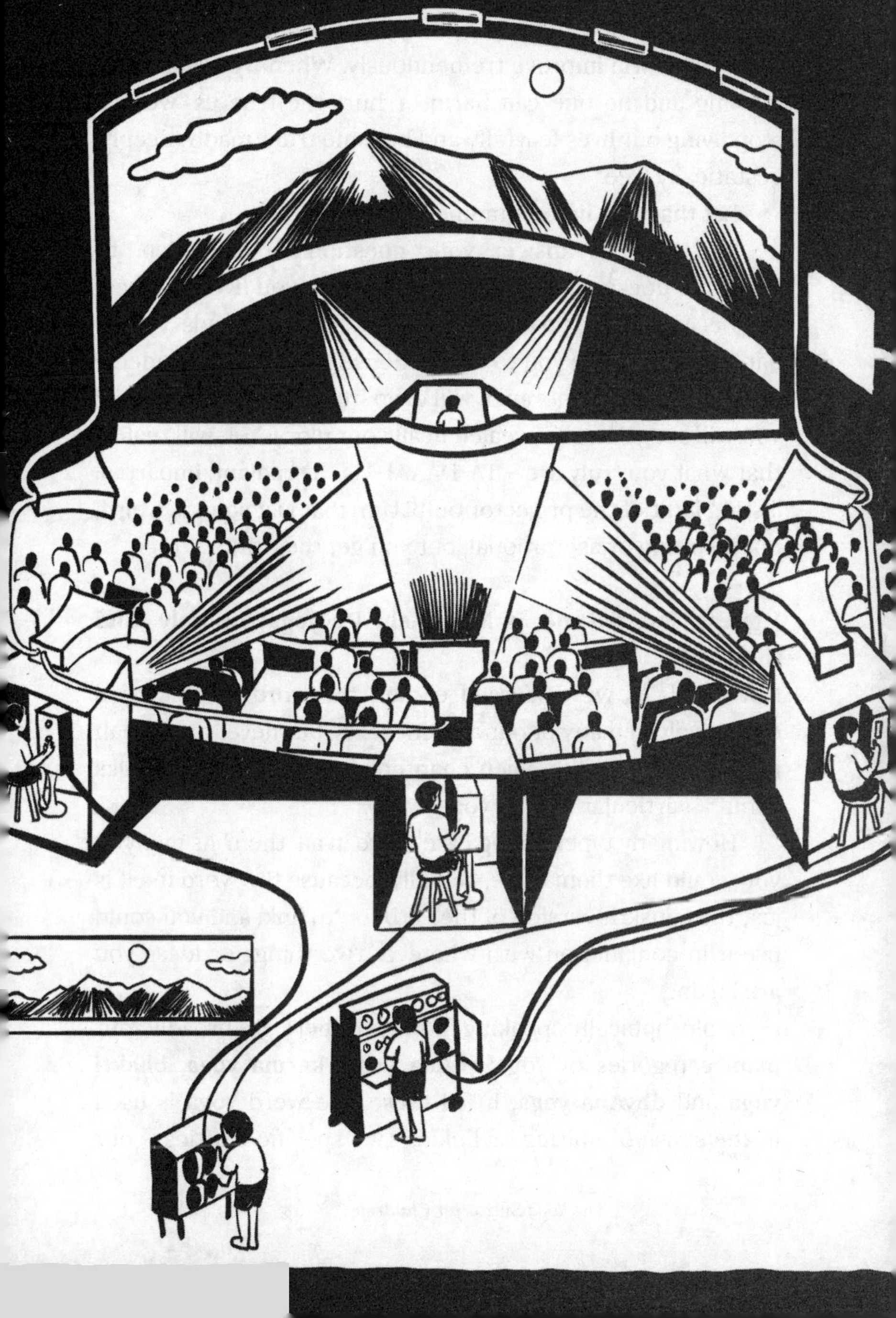

Once we 'see' this truth, the sages promise, the quality of our lives will improve tremendously. When we realize that nothing and no one can harm or hurt the true us, we will stop living our lives fearfully and become truly, madly, deeply, ecstatically free.

Let that sink in for a moment.

And now to answer your question. Yoga (which, to reiterate, doesn't just mean 'Asana'), helps you live your best life because yoga takes you by the hand and leads you to darshana – it helps you to 'see'. Practise yoga single-mindedly and the scales of ignorance will drop from your inner eye, and you will see yourself revealed in all your glory. You will realize that what you truly are – TA-DAAA! – is the radiant, impartial, lasting light of the projector bulb. Um, that just sounds weird, not inspiring or aspirational, but you get the drift.

I guess. But tell me, is Maharishi P's yoga the only kind there is?

Not at all. As we discussed earlier, the word yoga is used extensively in many of our ancient texts, but never more than in the Bhagavat Gita. Each chapter of the Gita, in fact, talks about a particular kind of yoga.

How many types of yoga are there in all, then? As many as you would like them to be, actually, because the word itself is just the Sanskrit version of the verb for 'to link', and you could use it in conjunction with whatever two things or ideas you are linking.

Philosophically speaking, however, there are broadly four main categories of yoga: **jnAna yoga**, **karma yoga**, **bhakti yoga** and **dhyAna yoga**. In all these, the word yoga is used in the sense of uniting or linking two specific entities – our ordinary, human self (which is mainly concerned with bodily needs like food, reproduction and survival, and eternally embroiled in thoughts, emotions, confusion and anxiety) with our extraordinary, divine self. Every other kind of yoga is a subset of one of these four, or a combination of one or more of them, in different proportions.

Okay, you've made a halfway decent pitch for yoga. I'd like to give it a shot. Which kind should I pick?
The one that fits you best! Easy-peasy!

Ugh. I hate making decisions. What if I make the wrong one? Why don't you just tell me and put me out of my misery?
Ah, there lies the rub – you, and *only* you, can make that decision for yourself. You see, if there is one thing that all ancient Indian texts recognize, it is that every single person is unique.* (You will never hear the rishis say that we are all equal, although they *will* say, over and over again, that everyone and everything should be *treated* equally – equally well, equally

★ Didn't the rishis say that our differences were only on the outside and that we were all the same energy? Now they're saying we're all not only different but also unique, i.e., that there is NO ONE who is exactly like us? How can two absolutely opposite-sounding things be true at the same time? Here's how. Yes, we are all the very same energy at our very core. But as long as we live in the world, we function through the bodies and minds we inhabit, which are very different from *anyone* else's. That's why each of us needs to find our own way to our core, by understanding the unique strengths and challenges of our bodies and minds.

respectfully.) That is why there is no one-size-fits-all yoga. You need to do the work to understand yourself first, and then pick the path that you believe most suits your nature, or svabhAva. Here are some tips to help you along, though.

* If you are the sort of person who enjoys reading stuff, listening to experts, taking classes, trawling the internet for the best videos on whatever subject you are trying to master, and if, once you've gathered a sufficient amount of information, you proceed to reflect on the data and come to your own understanding of the subject – in other words, if you are the sort of person who comes to grips with a topic via your mind and intellect – it would make sense for you to use the same two instruments to understand the truth about yourself. The path best suited to you, then, is the path of knowledge, **jnAna yoga**. This kind of yoga gets us to the truth by solving the problem of ignorance – you think, because of your ignorance, that you are the body and mind; jyAna yoga will teach you, will help you 'see', through sound logic and rational argument, that you are not.
* If talks and lectures bore you stiff, and you find it difficult to process abstract, theoretical ideas, much preferring to go out and do stuff – create apps, start a company, join a protest, cook dinner for the family on Mum's busy night at work, and so on – the path of action, **karma yoga**, may be for you. Most of our actions are essentially selfish, however – we do them because we want to

be successful, or rich, or famous, or popular, or admired – and that's what puts our minds in turmoil ('How dare that person not acknowledge my contribution!' or 'Now that I've invited her to my birthday party, she will invite me to hers. Right? Right??'). Karma yoga gets us to the stillness we need for darshana by teaching us to act unselfishly. It urges us to take the 'I' out of our actions, and do something simply because we believe it is the right thing to do, not because it will give us something in return.

* Are you the sort of person who suffers because you feel you are carrying all the burdens of the world on your shoulders? Do you find yourself unable to reach out for help from your friends or family even when you need it, because you either 'don't want to trouble them' (when the true reason may be that you do not believe you are worthy of their love), or because 'they will ruin it/they won't do it right' (when the true reason is that you find it hard to trust other people)? Maybe the path of devotion and surrender, **bhakti yoga**, is for you then. Bhakti yoga gets you to darshana by teaching you to put your faith in the universe and offer up your actions to it, believing that something far wiser, more powerful and infinitely more compassionate

than you has your back and will guide you towards right action. Once you have transferred your burden, you can put your head down and work, with very little fear and stress.

* Maybe you are the sort of person who says, 'Sure, I'll read the books and listen to what people have to say, but I'm sorry – I won't, I can't, take what others have said as the gospel truth. As for believing that something 'out there' is looking out for me – that may be a comforting thought, but I simply cannot wrap my head around it. I only trust the evidence of my own personal experience. If I can actually 'see' that I am not my body or mind, that I am something different from my thoughts and emotions, then, and only then, will I believe that that is the truth.' If you're nodding just now, saying, 'That's me!' then maybe the path of meditation, the path of looking inside your own mind to find the truth, **dhyAna yoga,** is the yoga for you.

The good part about all this is, as Krishna assures us in the Bhagavat Gita, that no one path is better than any other to get you to the truth. Even better, these paths are only entry points into your journey. As you progress down whichever path you have chosen, you will notice that one or more of the other paths will intersect yours at some points, and converge and diverge at others, until, somewhere along the line, they will all come together to create a superfast highway towards the truth.

Sounds v. cool. Now where do the YS fit into all of this? Which kind of yoga are they a portal to?

We already know that the basic promise of the YS is to give us practices and processes that help us still our minds and become mind-control ninjas. And therefore, it is very likely to be a text about...that's right – dhyAna yoga!* (JnAna yoga, the other yoga that involves the mind, will do the opposite of stilling it – as you take in information and your neurons begin to fire, classifying things, storing facts away, making connections and arriving at flashes of sudden comprehension, more and more thoughts are created, not fewer. At least in the beginning.)

Does that mean that the YS aren't meant for those who are more inclined towards the path of jnAna, karma and bhakti yoga?

Not at all – dhyAna yoga is for everyone. Here's why.

- **If jnAna yoga is your jam:** When your mind is overheated from too much jnAna yoga-ing (think of the night before an important exam), a spot of dhyAna yoga is a good way to give it some well-deserved downtime so that it is nicely refreshed and ready to function at its highest level on exam day.
- **If you're more the karma yoga type:** When you're feeling physically overwhelmed from too much karma

★ dhyAna yoga was referred to as RAja Yoga – or the royal path to yoga – by Swami Vivekananda in his nineteenth-century book of the same name, in which he gave us his (very popular) interpretation of the YS.

yoga-ing, or feel you are losing sight of whether your actions are selfish or unselfish ('if I started my newspaper collection drive because I wanted to raise whatever money I could for the Blind People's Home, I should not be worried whether I raise 50 rupees or 500, right? Why then am I feeling so low that my friend has collected more newspapers than me?'), dhyAna yoga will help you cut out the noise and simply focus on your task.

- **If bhakti yoga floats your boat:** When you are assailed by anxiety and despair because of something happening in the world – a war, a terrorist attack, communal hatred – or closer home, at school or within your family, and find your bhakti wavering, there's no better remedy than to still the mind. Sit down somewhere quiet, breathe long, deep breaths, understand that there are some things you cannot control, surrender those things up to the universe, and ask for grace and guidance. That process – of turning the spotlight away from whatever's going on outside and directing it inward to find solace – is nothing other than dhyAna yoga.

You see? Maharishi P knew what he was doing when he picked dhyAna yoga to expound on!

What was good enough for Maharishi P is good enough for me. Let's get on with the 195 sutras!

Super! Just a little more detail about the sutras before we go on. The 195 sutras are divided into four chapters – samAdhipAda, sAdhanapAda, vibhUtipAda and kaivalyapAda.

pAda in Sanskrit means 'foot' or 'quarter'. One way to look at the chapters, then, is that they are the four quarters that make up the whole of the YS. Another is to look at them as the four feet on which the YS stand. Pick your favourite angle!

Given that 'becoming a yogi' is a process that could take several lifetimes, we are only concerning ourselves, in this book, with the ideas and hot tips contained in the first two chapters of the YS. But it wouldn't do to not know at all what the others are about, so here's a brief intro to all four.

1. **SamAdhipAda: And Now for the Lowdown on Yoga**
   Like every good handbook, the YS's first quarter, with its 51 sutras, begins at the beginning, with some essential definitions. What is yoga? Why yoga? What or who is God (if there is such a being, that is)? How the heck – in theory – do you get your monkey-mind to be still, for ONE teensy-weensy second? Every answer to these questions is a building block of the magnificent edifice whose shining pinnacle is samAdhi, a state when the mind is absolutely clear and still, which is the goal of the yoga practice taught by Maharishi P. But how does one scale the edifice and reach the pinnacle? Read on.

2. **SAdhanapAda: Readying for Ascent**
   Learning definitions by heart is all very well, but translating them into action so that you can get to a higher, freer, happier place? Ah, there's the rub. But Maharishi P has set it all up for us in the 55 sutras of this chapter, in eight neat steps of a 'ladder to freedom' (because the goal of life, according to ancient Indian philosophy, isn't happiness or success or wealth, but

freedom, or moksha) that he calls ashTAnga. He deals with only the first five 'essential prep' rungs in this chapter, however. The sAdhanapAda is also where we meet 'kriyA yoga,' a three-step preparation *for* ashTAnga yoga. Most of us cannot even hope to get to any level of stability on the first rung of the ashTAnga ladder, but the Maharishi wasn't thinking only of amateurs like us when he put the sutras together, so there are two more chapters, meant for more advanced practitioners.

3. **VibhUtipAda: Three Last Steps to Woahhhh!**
   Calm down – those last three steps are not little itty-bitty ones, nor metre-long strides, nor even Olympic-record-beating 10=metre long jumps. They are GIANT leaps into a whole different plane of existence, entirely executed by the mind – a mind made razor-sharp and laser-intense by the absolute mastery of the first five. Maharishi P, in the 55 sutras of this chapter, guarantees all kinds of superpowers to those who can make these leaps – the ability to read minds, move things without touching them, walk on water, recall past lives, become invisible, predict the time of your death... Whaaaaaaa?? I mean, good to know what you're working towards, right? But not so good to obsess about, warns the good Maharishi, for these superhuman powers are no more than traps, meant to keep you from your *real* goal. While you strut around on top of the ladder, crowing over everyone else struggling below, you are in danger of forgetting what the top of the ladder really is – a launch pad for your own glorious solo flight into true freedom.

4. **KaivalyapAda: Flying by Your Own Light**
   How wonderful is the thought of being entirely self-reliant, depending on no one but yourself! How comforting to know that you will never have to be alone, never have to fly blind, never have to fear the darkness, because you carry all the equipment you need – a wise friend who always has your back, a compass that always points true north, and the light of a thousand suns – within yourself! Maharishi P assures us that it is possible to live life this way – unchained, fearless, soaring – simply by clearing our minds of all kinds of devious monsters that lurk there, whispering the worst kind of stories about ourselves and the world, determined to keep us crawling, eyes to the ground, quaking in fear. The important thing, says Maharishi P, is to raise our heads, at least for long enough to grab the ladder he is so generously offering, and begin to climb. Let's go!

One last, last question – ancient texts are always somehow about God, but I'm an atheist. God, in a sense, is against my religion, haha. Will the YS work for someone like me?
Actually, most ancient Indian texts are not about God at all, they are about YOU. The oldest among them, the Rig Veda, actually has a popular sUkta (hymn) that questions the existence of an all-knowing Creator God. And the Upanishads make declarations that would be considered blasphemous in many religions of the world – they unequivocally state, for instance, that there is no difference between God and you.

Scholars are divided on whether the YS is a theist (God-focused) or atheist (the opposite of God-focused) text. What neither side can deny is that only five sutras, out of the 195, talk of an entity called Ishvara (Maharishi P's catch-all name for the great cosmic energy that gives everything life, which could be equated to God). Patanjali recommends 'Ishvara praNidhAna', or 'surrender to Ishvara', as one of the ways to get to samAdhi, or stillness. What the Maharishi is saying is that however hard one works towards something – samAdhi in this case – it is very, very hard to get there unless one's efforts are also blessed by Ishvara. By humbly accepting that we need the universe as our ally to bring our efforts to fruition, we have a better chance, he reckons, of getting to where we're headed.

If that seems like more God than you can handle, then maybe the YS aren't for you. But if you feel that you agree in general with what the Maharishi is saying (except that you would like to use the word 'grace' or 'destiny'* in place of

★ Do you know what the word for 'destiny' is in Sanskrit and many other Indian languages? – adrishTa. Now, drashTA means something, or someone, who sees, or bears witness; a-drishTa is its opposite – something that happens without a witness . By calling one's destiny 'that which happens without a witness', Indian languages, and Indians themselves, acknowledge that it is a force not of the visible universe, and we have no control over it. Religious people call that force God. Patanjali calls it Ishvara. Hamlet, in the eponymous play by William Shakespeare, says simply – 'There are more things in heaven and earth, Horatio, than are dreamt of in your philosophy'. You can call it destiny, or grace, or simply adrishTa. Whatever name you pick, there is no denying that THAT is often what differentiates two people who begin life with the same advantages, come equipped with the same amount of talent and put in the same effort, but end up with different results.

'Ishvara' – i.e., you would rather say 'however hard one works, one needs that X-factor called luck to crown his efforts with success'), then maybe they are. Even if you are simply willing to set aside your reservations for the moment, because you are most interested in finding out what the other 190 sutras that have nothing to do with Ishvara have to say, you may discover some very cool stuff in the YS.

The choice, as always, is up to you.

I'm in! Let me find a mat and a quiet spot, and you can press 'Play' on Maharishi P's guided meditation app and I can become a mind-control ninja. That's what the YS are about, right – meditation?

Errmm...love your enthusiasm, but unfortunately, there is a tonne of prep to do before you actually sit down to meditate. As we mentioned earlier, Maharishi P's version of dhyAna yoga centres around his eight-step process, ashTAnga. In ashTAnga, meditation – and that too, a very basic version of it – only comes in at Step 6. Also, no app. So why don't you just sit back, relax, and let the Maharishi himself lead you from one step to the next instead?

Here he comes now – get ready. No, no notebooks – he *hates* those. Just listen, and connect. Only connect.

And Now for the Lowdown on Yoga

TEN DAZZLING SECRETS FROM THE SAMADHIPADA

SECRET 1:	There's no time like the present!
SECRET 2:	Stay off the vritti train!
SECRET 3:	You are not the storm, you are its calm centre
SECRET 4:	Rip off the labels – you can be anything, everything, nothing
SECRET 5:	Know your thought-buckets, and empty the unhelpful ones regularly
SECRET 6:	You can change your nature – simply redesign your chitta!
SECRET 7:	Find joy in the present, inspiration in the past and purpose in the future
SECRET 8:	Top hacks for success: long-term commitment, steadfast practice, great reverence
SECRET 9:	For a clear, steadfast mind, start with faith
SECRET 10:	A four-ingredient recipe for calmness (garnished with a most vital fifth ingredient)

CONVERSATION

Hi there, Maharishi P!
Now, what's it going to be?

अथ योगानुशासनम्
atha yogAnushAsanam
Now, it's the lowdown on yoga.

We're all set! But erm...what exactly is yoga?

योगश्चित्तवृत्ति निरोधः
Yogashchittavritti nirodhah
Yoga is the stilling of the churning, changing mind.

Really? That's it? And why is that important, anyway?
What does it achieve?

तदा द्रष्टुः स्वरूपेऽवस्थानम्
tadA drashTu swarUpeYvasthAnam
Then, you see yourself as what you truly are.

Eh? What do I see myself as, otherwise?

वृत्ति सारूप्यमितरत्र
vritti sArupyamitaratr
Otherwise, you see yourself as the churnings and changings of your mind.

Right from the get-go, from the first four 'aphorisms' (a cerebral-sounding word for a short observation that contains a scientific principle and/or a philosophical truth) of the YS themselves, it's easy to see what a good teacher Maharishi Patanjali is. There is a logical flow to the sutras, and so much information – the content of the text, the definition of yoga, and the outcome of the practice – is contained in just *nine* words. When translated (somewhat loosely, as we have done) into English, the word count shoots up to thirty-six!

It must be said, though, that the 'nine words' part is a bit of a trick – the ancients, when they composed in Sanskrit, were wont to smoosh a whole bunch of words together and present it as one word. That kind of thing is allowed in Sanskrit – it's a very 'efficient' language, apart from being an elegant one.

If you are going to chant something in Sanskrit, or set a Sanskrit poem to music, therefore, always make sure to check what the individual words that make up the compound word are. Otherwise, you could end up breaking the word at the wrong places and either have it make no sense at all, or worse, change the meaning of the verse entirely!

PS: *As you read this chapter and the next, you will find that the sutras being discussed aren't always in numerical order. That is deliberate, to help you get a better understanding of the YS's lessons.*

Secret 1

There's No Time Like the Present!

अथ योगानुशासनम् ॥ १.१ ॥

atha yogAnushAsanam

Now, the teachings of yoga (1.1)

The very first sutra of Maharishi P's text is as straightforward as it gets – atha means 'now', and yogAnushAsanam, which is made up of the words yoga (yoga), anu (continuing) and shAsanam (teachings), may be translated as 'the continuing teachings of yoga'. Essentially, Maharishi Patanjali makes the intention of the text that follows very clear – in it, he will expound on the teachings of yoga.

But let's take the disarmingly simple phrase a little further, by looking at each word a little more closely. We have already talked about the various meanings of the word yoga, but one piece of info we haven't touched upon is that, in this context, Yoga – the capitalization is deliberate – was not just a word or verb but the name of a particular school of Indian philosophy.

What does that mean, though – 'school of Indian philosophy'? To answer that, we will need to start with the Vedas, which are India's oldest texts.

What the Vedas do, like so many other scriptures, is try and provide answers to humanity's existential questions (i.e., questions that are about our existence itself – Where did I come from? What happens after death? Where did the universe come from? That kind of stuff.). It is really entirely up to each of us to either accept the answers or theories they provide, or come up with our own. In ancient India, there were some sages and philosophers who believed that the Vedas had all the answers, and others who did not. The ones who accepted the authority of the Vedas were called Astikas and the ones who didn't, nAstikas.

Among the nAstikas were Gautama Buddha and Vardhamana Mahavira, who came up with different answers to the same existential questions, and founded two nAstika schools of philosophy, which came to be called Buddhism and Jainism respectively. The other two nAstika schools were AjIvika, whose followers believed that everything was already predetermined by 'fate', and chArvAka, whose followers were the original YOLO (You Only Live Once) champions. The chArvAkas were like modern scientists in their approach. They only believed in what they could perceive and therefore verify (if I hang wet clothes on a line and see them fluttering in the breeze, completely dry, a few hours later, I can verify that the sun's heat, combined with a good breeze, helps in drying clothes), and rubbished ideas like the indestructible soul, the afterlife and rebirth. (Have you seen your soul? Do you remember your previous life? No? Then all this is a nonsense!)

Think about it!

If you met a chArvAka philosopher who told you that what we grasp through our senses is the whole truth about the world, and that the idea that we are anything except the body and mind is ridiculous, what would you say? Would you agree or disagree? Why?

The six Astika schools (also collectively called the Darshanas) – NyAya, Vaisheshika, MimAmsA, VedAnta, SAnkhya a-a-and, here it comes, Yoga – used the Vedas as their source texts, but offered their own different paths to the truth. Each, just like the nAstika schools, was also scientific in its approach – doctrines were based on logic, not on 'you better believe it, because God says so'. Each had a founding sage, who composed a set of sutras containing the doctrines of that school. These pithy sutras were further explained and elaborated on by commentators, who defended the logic of their own school's doctrines while critiquing the logic of the other doctrines.

The top thinkers from different schools often engaged in public debate, usually sponsored by kings. The debates were too complex and intellectual to be understood or appreciated by common folk, but they created a vibrant culture of independent thinking, which filtered down to the masses. More importantly, people were free to follow the doctrines of whichever school of philosophy – Astika or nAstika –

appealed to them. If they felt none of the existing schools had the answers, they simply started their own school, and if they were able to deliver their pitch convincingly and demonstrate that they had the answers, people would sign up.

Take the example of the VedAnta school, which is based on the Upanishads, the philosophical section of the Vedas. Adi Shankara's commentary on the Upanishads, written in the eighth century CE, was the basis of what he called the Advaita VedAnta philosophy. His interpretation was challenged in the eleventh century by Ramanujacharya, who taught a different kind of VedAnta philosophy called VishishTAdvaita. In the thirteenth century, Madhvacharya challenged them both, to come up with a third distinct philosophy under the vedAnta umbrella, called Dvaita. And in the sixteenth century, Vallabhacharya proposed a fourth take on VedAnta, called ShuddhAdvaita. Each of these subsets of the VedAnta school has its own loyal set of followers.

But back to Yoga, which is the Darshana we are interested in at the moment. The Yoga school is essentially built on the doctrines of the SAnkhya school. If SAnkhya is the theory class, Yoga offers the practical lab work through which the theories can be proved, except the lab in this case is our bodies and minds. It is because the two are so closely connected that the great sage Kapila, who composed the definitive text on SAnkhya, the *Sankhya Sutras*, is believed to be not only the father of SAnkhya but of Yoga as well (see page 65 for a story about Sage Kapila).

Our Maharishi P arrived on the scene well after Sage Kapila, but he was the first to formally put down what he saw as the essential doctrines of the ancient practice of yoga. That makes his Yoga Sutras the foundational text of the Yoga school.

Think about it!

Creating one's own school of spiritual philosophy, which draws from everything that went before but is still distinct from all of them, continues as a living tradition in India. For example, Sri Aurobindo called his philosophy 'Integral Yoga', Sadhguru calls his 'Inner Engineering' and Sri Sri Ravi Shankar goes with 'The Art Of Living'.

If you had to create your own philosophy for living a fulfilling life, what would you call it? What would be its main pillars – kindness, fun, food, work-hard-party-hard, respect for all creatures, fairness, family, shopping, giving back to the community, self-love? How would you describe it to others to ensure that they would be intrigued enough and inspired enough to join you on your mission?

However, Maharishi P never claimed the credit for 'inventing' yoga – after all, some version of it had existed in India for millennia before him. Instead, he humbly tacked the word 'anu' – continuing – onto the word 'shAsanam' – teachings. That was his way of acknowledging all the great teachers and practitioners of yoga who came before him, the giants on whose shoulders he had stood to see further than all of us, so that he may bring to us their peerless wisdom in as succinct and comprehensive a manner as possible.

Right. And what of 'atha' – 'now'? Does that have any particular significance as well? What do you think? The word itself – 'Now!' – carries a sense of urgency and readiness, of something that cannot and should not be put off any longer. The Maharishi's call could have meant any number of different things, like:

* **Now** that you have arrived on this earth in human form, with the ability to think and reason, it is time to go beyond your body and your mind, and begin the quest for your higher self.
* **Now** that you have read enough distressing reports about climate change to become severely anxious, binge-watched K-dramas on Netflix till your eyes glazed over, scrolled through so many Instagram posts where everyone seems to be having so much fun that your own life feels utterly pointless...well, set your devices aside – yes, ALL of them – and get started on this new and wonderful adventure. This is where we learn to focus on the greatest storehouse of wisdom, love and strength there is – you!
* **Now** that you have chased after and achieved and acquired so many things that everyone told you would make your life happier and more fulfilling – friends, stuff, popularity, an excellent academic or sports record – and then found that whatever happiness they bring you is soon overtaken by anxiety about the next challenge or fear of losing what you have, maybe it's time to try something different?
* **Now** that, by some random twist of fate, you have picked up this book, why not commit to read it through, and

try out the things – or some of the things – it suggests you do?

Whichever way you look at it, the Maharishi's proposition is intriguing, beguiling, and pretty hard to turn away from, don't you think?

Do it!

Now's a good time.

Maharishi P's 'atha', the first word of the Yoga Sutras, is a clarion call to do something – NOW. Ever thought about how powerful that word is? 'Now' is the opposite of procrastination, laziness, a reluctance to commit to something, the desire to duck what you know you should do, the unwillingness to do something (even though you know that it is the right thing) that is inconvenient, unpleasant or difficult. 'Now' is the first step of a disciplined life. (And guess what an alternative meaning of shAsanam is in Sanskrit? It has the same meaning that 'anushAsan' has in Hindi – discipline!)

Is there something you have been wanting to do for a long time that you just haven't because you haven't said 'Now!' to yourself? Maybe you want to break a bad habit, like putting off school assignments until the day before submission, or develop a good one, like telling yourself nice things about yourself each morning instead of thinking about everything that's wrong with you. Maybe you need to reply to your grandma's WhatsApp message (you haven't done it yet because you have gotten too

used to taking her for granted, even though you often feel a small stab of guilt every time you think about it). Maybe you should have apologized to a friend a week ago for something you did. but your giant-sized ego isn't letting you do that (which means you have been skulking in the school corridors to avoid him, thus putting yourself through all kinds of unnecessary anxiety).

Whatever it is, make a resolution to do it – now. Not tomorrow, not next week, not after your exams, not once you are back from your Goa trip, but now. Obviously, you can't change a bad habit in one day, but you can certainly make a start towards it. Too many good intentions have fallen by the wayside because the intender waited too long to implement them.

If some of it seems too daunting, start with something small and doable – like responding to that message from your grandma. Or even sitting down and making a list of the things you need to do but have been putting off, mainly because your mind is too scattered. But do NOT stop there. Tick off at least two or three items on the list NOW. See how that makes you feel. Mark the tasks you will complete tomorrow, and do them. Give yourself a very strict time limit to finish (or begin, if it is a habit you are trying to cultivate) all the tasks on the list. At the end of the day that you are supposed to complete the tasks, tear up the list. If there are still unfinished tasks on it, too bad. You had your chance, and you didn't take it.

Don't sit around feeling bad about that, though – that's a waste of time. Instead, give yourself another chance. Take a fresh sheet of paper, and make another list, marking some items as things to be done immediately, and do them. Repeat the process as many times as it takes for 'NOW' to become a habit. On the day you tear up a list with ALL the to-do items on it ticked off for the very first time, celebrate. Sit back with your favourite snack, and feel your self-esteem soar.

How Sage Kapila Set the Ball Rolling for the Greatest Deluge the World Never Saw

अश्वत्थः सर्ववृक्षाणां देवर्षीणां च नारदः ।
गन्धर्वाणां चित्ररथः सिद्धानां कपिलो मुनिः ॥ १०.२६॥

ashvatthah sarvavrikshANAm devarshiNAm cha nAradah
gandharvANAm chitrarathah siddhAnAm kapilo munih

Of all the trees, I am the sacred ashvattha; of the divine rishis, I am Narada; of the gandharvas, I am Chitrarathah; among perfected beings, I am Sage Kapila (10.26)
(Krishna to Arjuna, Bhagavat Gita)

Once upon a time, in the ancient kingdom of Kosala, there reigned a great king of the Ikshvaku clan called Sagara. He had been born in exile, in the ashram of Sage Aurva, far away from his father's kingdom, after his poor mother had carried him for no less than *seven years* in her womb. His super-long gestation was the result of his mother being fed a steady diet of poison by her envious fellow queens, who did not have children of their own. When his father died in exile, his mother almost threw herself on his funeral pyre but was restrained by the good sage, who assured her that there were all kinds of good things he could see in her baby's future, and that, more importantly, he would be born soon. As the sage had promised, the queen delivered a bonny boy soon enough – with a h-u-u-uge sigh of relief that her ordeal was at an end. The child was named Sa-gara (in Sanskrit, 'one who is born with poison').

Before we continue with Sagara's story, let's find out a little more about Ikshvaku and his descendants. Ikshvaku was the first king of the Suryavamsha, or the solar dynasty, whose roll call of 'greatest kings' included legendary names like Trishanku, Harishchandra, Dasharatha, Rama and all the kings talked about in this story. Ikshvaku was one of the 10 sons of Manu, who Hindus believe was the first man, progenitor of all humanity. The other great line of kings from Indian mythology was the Chandravamsha, or the lunar dynasty. The Chandravamshis were the descendants of Ilan/Ila, Manu's gender-fluid son. The greatest kings of this line included Yayati, Dushyanta (Shakuntala's husband), Bharata, Shantanu, Bhishma, Pandu, Dhritarashtra, and all the Pandavas and Kauravas. Yayati's son Yadu was the founder of the Yadava clan, to which Krishna belonged.

As an aside, Hindus believe that they are all the sons and daughters of Manu, which is why the Sanskrit word for 'human' is mAnava (just like Pandu's children were Pandavas, and the children of the Kuru clan were Kauravas). Another root of the word 'mAnava' is 'mann', meaning 'to think' – mAnava, therefore, also means 'a being capable of rational (and irrational) thought'.

Right. Back to our main story now. When Sagara came of age and discovered that he was actually heir to a great kingdom, he lost no time in winning it back for himself. One of his two queens, Sumati, had her own adventures with childbearing – she bore him 60,000 sons (mercifully for her, she didn't carry them either serially or parallelly in her womb; their gestation happened, all at the same time, in 60,000 clay pots. As you may have noticed, this is a recurring theme in ancient Indian stories). The other queen, Keshini, who must have felt a bit cheated about it, bore only one son, the regular way – his name was Asamanja.

Asamanja was not, as they say, 'of good character', and consequently, was the bane of his father's life. Unfortunately, he had a certain charisma, and his 60,000 siblings hero-worshipped him, and did as he did. Actually, Sagara had meant to ask for 60,000 daughters as a reward from the gods for his severe penances. Not because he preferred daughters to sons – as if! – but because he had been told that giving a daughter away in marriage would earn him puNya (merit), and he figured, reasonably, that more was definitely merrier. But Indra, lord of the heavens, terrified that the kind of puNya Sagara would earn by giving away 60k daughters in marriage would win him an all-access pass to his own domain, begged Goddess Saraswati to sit on the king's tongue and ensure that his request for 'putri' (daughter) turned into 'putra' (son). Such were the insecurities of the gods, and the perils of having too little differentiation between words.

Be that as it may, the time came when Sagara decided to do the other thing that ancient Indian kings did apart from having many sons – perform an Ashwamedha yagna to expand the extent of his kingdom. Basically, a fine horse was let loose to wander as it may for a year, and was followed everywhere by the king's army. When it wandered into neighbouring kingdoms, the king there had two options – he either let the horse go through unhindered, which indicated that he accepted the overlordship of the yagna-performing king, or he captured the horse, which indicated that he was ready for a fight with the army following it.

Hardly anyone dared to stop the horse, and the boundaries of King Sagara's kingdom expanded steadily through the year. Once again, Indra began to feel threatened. One way to render the yagna null and void was to ensure the horse did not return to the city it had set out from, and Indra decided that was the solution. By hook and by crook, under cover of night, he stole the horse and hid it in the last place anyone would think to look for it – in the ashram of a great sage, located deep inside pAtAla, the netherworld. The name of that great sage was Kapila (yes, that's how long it takes to come to the real hero of the tale when we are talking Indian stories).

The sage, deep in meditation, hadn't the foggiest that there was a stolen horse roaming around in his ashram. The first indication he had that something was amiss was when he heard the roars of 60k + 1 furious, badly behaved princes, accusing him of being a thief and advancing towards him with drawn swords. Indra's hiding place for the horse, as it turned out, was not as brilliant as he had believed – the princes had dug down into the very bowels of the earth in their search for the horse, and found it. When your crew is 60k strong, you can get a lot done.

Incandescent with rage at their lack of respect, Kapila merely glared at the princes, causing a flame to leap eagerly out of his eyes and zoom out like a prince-seeking missile. The next instant, all that was left of the sons of Sagara was a (very large) pile of ashes.

Beside himself with worry about his sons (and, tbh, about the incomplete yagna), Sagara sent his grandson Anshuman to find his dad and uncles, which he did, eventually. Now Anshuman was a sweet and respectful chap – props to his mum for good genes and better upbringing – and Kapila was well pleased with him. He handed the horse to Anshuman, and asked him what he would like more than anything in the world. The boy asked that his dad and uncles be restored to life. Kapila assured him that while this kind of thing took time, it could certainly be arranged. The day the cosmic river Ganga descended from the heavens to the earth and flowed over the ashes of his father and uncles, he promised Anshuman, they would all be resurrected.

A grateful Anshuman bowed and left the ashram with a spring in his step. Little did the young man realize that what Sage Kapila had meant by 'some time' was a few hundred years, maybe a millennium, and that it would take the unstinting efforts of generations of Ikshvakus to make that dream a reality. Eventually, a descendant of Anshuman called Bhagiratha, riding on the collective puNya of all his better ancestors, and adding his own efforts to the mix, succeeded in persuading the goddess to descend.

But there was one last obstacle in the way. The impetuous, feisty goddess was not prepared to rein in her energy even a teensy-weensy bit when she leapt off the heavens. Worried, with good reason, that the force of her descent would knock the earth out of her orbit, Bhagiratha hurriedly began another series of prayers and austerities, this time directed at the great god Shiva. When Shiva responded, Bhagiratha begged him to catch the goddess in his wild, matted locks as she fell. Shiva agreed, and at the appointed moment, stood with his feet firmly planted on the ground, arms akimbo, head turned slightly heavenwards, bracing for impact. Ganga, who had no idea that all this had been plotted, leapt joyfully earthwards... and found herself caught and tied up firmly in Shiva's topknot.

There she swirled, for years and years, miserable and furious by turns until, finally, she mellowed enough to respectfully ask to be allowed to fulfil her promise to Bhagiratha. It was only then that Shiva loosened his locks, ever so slightly, so that Ganga could descend, if only as a mere trickle. She fell gently to earth in the Himalayas, and danced down the mountains and all over the northern plains of India, bringing to the people and the land succour, life and cheer. Guided by an ecstatic

Bhagiratha, she also descended into the vast, deep pit that the sons of Sagara had dug to get to Kapila's ashram in pAtALa, where she flowed over the ashes of his forefathers, restoring them to life. Her promise fulfilled, she began to grow and grow, filling the pit with her waters until she became the ocean, or, as it is called in Sanskrit, sAgara.

That mere trickle, that tiniest fraction of the goddess, continues to sustain millions of Indians (and Bangladeshis, and others) along her 2,525-km course today, as she has over the centuries. At her source, Ganga is known, with much affection and reverence, as BhagIrathi, daughter of Bhagiratha. In memory of that remarkable sage's extraordinary, superhuman exertions to bring the goddess to us, any effort requiring great courage, dedication and tenacity, especially when pitted against seemingly insurmountable odds, is referred to, in many Indian languages, as a 'Bhagiratha prayatna'.

Secret 2

Stay Off the Vritti Train!

योगश्चित्तवृत्ति निरोधः ॥१.२॥

yogashchittavritti nirodhah

Yoga is the stilling of the churning, changing mind (1.2)

The second sutra is Maharishi P's very succinct definition of yoga – simply put, yoga is mind control. Let's begin, as before, by breaking the sutra down to its individual words. There are some BIG words here – in meaning if not in size – so brace yourself.

Yoga – yoga; chitta – mind; vritti – changes, activities, movements; nirodhah – stopping, cessation (the 'sh' in between the yoga and the chitta is just a joining sound, or a 'sandhi', which comes in when two words are joined in Sanskrit. The joining sound is different depending on which two syllables are being joined).

CHITTA

Right. Since it is yoga that is being defined here, we don't have to explain the word itself. Phew. Moving straight away then, to **chitta**. At its simplest, chitta can be translated simply as the mind. But our ancient rishis were deep divers into the psyche –

they figured, very early on, that 'the mind' was not a monolithic entity; it was made up of several subtle, *subtle* layers. In Yoga, the chitta is considered to be made up of three separate layers – manas (data-collecting lower mind), buddhi (decision-making higher mind), and ahamkAra (mind that thinks of itself as 'I,' separate from everyone and everything else, aka 'ego').

Here's how these three are supposed to work together. As long as one is awake, the five 'knowledge-gathering' senses – sight, hearing, smell, taste and touch – continuously feed data from the outer world to manas.* Manas processes this data at an elementary level and presents it to buddhi, which makes a decision and sends manas the order to execute it. Since manas also controls the five 'action-performing'** senses and the body parts associated with each – speaking (tongue), grasping (hands), moving (legs), eliminating (excretory organs) and procreating (reproductive organs) – it is able to ensure that the necessary action is performed.

Let's say there is a red car coming towards you at great speed. Manas takes the input of the eyes and ears (and maybe nose, even, if it can smell burning rubber), processes it and figures that there is a red object advancing at great speed. It passes this information on to buddhi, and then plunges into

★ By the way, your own body is also part of the 'outer world' as far as your senses are concerned, because you can, for instance, see your toes, hear your stomach rumbling and smell your armpits.

★★ In Sanskrit, the knowledge-gathering senses are called the jnAnendriyA, and the action-performing ones, karmendriyA.

its own doubts and insecurities – 'Not sure what I should do at this point, buddy buddhi! Should I pick up something and throw it at the object? That might stop it in its tracks, you know. Or wait, I have a better idea – should I start screaming for help? But will anyone come? Oh, hang on, I could...'

While manas is, erm, losing its mind, buddhi does a super-speedy search through its memory archives and updates the information it got from manas to: 'There is a red car advancing at great speed. It will soon hit this body. When speeding cars hit human bodies, things don't end well'.

Leaping into the driver's seat, buddhi issues manas a terse memo – '*Move!*' Manas, relieved that someone has made a decision, barks out orders at the legs, and they leap out of the way of the oncoming car. Meanwhile, ahamkAra, white as a sheet, begins to yell, 'The car was coming towards ME! It was going to hit MY body! I was terrified! It was MY amazing reflexes that saved ME!'

The relationship between the senses, manas and buddhi is often illustrated in the ancient texts with the cautionary tale of a chariot pulled by five horses. The chariot is the body. The five horses are the five senses, the reins are manas, the charioteer is buddhi. The rider in the chariot is Atman, or Purusha, your true self. If buddhi the charioteer does not have a good grip on the manas-reins, the sense-horses will gallop away in five different directions, either chasing after things that are pleasant to look at, smell, hear, taste and touch, or fleeing from things that aren't. And the chariot? It will veer entirely off track, fall into a ditch or be smashed to smithereens against a rock. The End.

But back to chitta. Manas, buddhi and ahamkAra, then, taken together, is chitta, our subtle, inner body – sense-maker of the world, storehouse of memory, seat of analysis and discrimination, fount of imagination and emotion, generator of 'I-Me-Mine-ness'.

You see now why 'the mind' is so inadequate to describe the chitta?

VRITTI

On to the **vrittis**! All the thoughts, ideas and emotions that are generated in and by the three layers of the chitta are called vrittis. Think of the chitta as a lake and the vrittis as an unending series of waves rising in it. We are so mesmerized by the waves of our thoughts, emotions and desires, all of them arising because of stuff happening in the outside world, that we can't take our eyes off them. We pick our favourite colours and shapes and sizes of waves – 'Omg, my birthday party this year was just the best!' and feel anxious and sad when we realize we can't hold on to them – 'Why can't fun times last longer than they do?' – even though we know that's what waves do: they rise and then they subside.

Now that we think we have identified what a 'happy' wave looks like, we start looking for another one of the exact same colour and shape and size – 'I want my birthday this year to be just as amazing as my last one.' Worse, we classify any wave that doesn't perfectly fit our 'happy wave' specifications as undesirable and begin to hate or fear such waves – 'This year's party wasn't/will not be as much fun, because (pick one or more): my best friend is out of town/the cake was good, but the pizza was meh/I got a couple of seriously lame gifts.'

There's more. Every time it sees a 'non-happy' wave coming, ahamkAra, always self-obsessed, will begin to whine – 'I'm *telling* you, the world has something against me. It *personally* hates me. That's why it never sends me the waves I'm looking for.' Which is rather silly, because the point of waves is that they are each different from the other. Also, even though our ahamkAra may find this hard to believe, the waves really have nothing against any of us personally.

Can you see now how much noise and continuous chaos our thought-waves cause in our chitta lakes? Bet you're tired just reading about it. Oh, also, remember that every time we react to a thought-wave or a desire-wave – with joy, fear, anger, love, hate – that reaction creates its own series of waves! It seems there is no way of escaping the chaos in our heads!

Or is there?

NIRODHAH

Maharishi P assures us there is. Consider this. What if you simply sat on the edge of the chitta lake and observed the waves, without constantly reacting to them? If you did that, *just* that, says the Maharishi, slowly but steadily, you would see something marvellous begin to happen. Suddenly, it will not be the waves controlling you, telling you what to feel in every moment. Instead, it will be you controlling them! The moment you stop reacting to every wave that comes by, you take away the power you yourself have given them over you, and the number of waves will begin to fall dramatically.

Fall, but not entirely cease. A significant number of thought-waves and desire-waves and emotion-waves will continue to rise and fall in chitta, whether you react to them or not. Those waves are the chitta's spontaneous reaction to all the stuff the world outside is throwing at it via the sense organs, so there's nothing you can do about them.

Right? Wrong. Follow my recommendations in the YS, says Maharishi P, and you will see it is possible to reduce even those waves, until they cease entirely.

And why is it important for the number of waves to reduce? Why should there be **nirodhah**, a stilling, of the chitta-vritti? The answer to that lies in the next sutra. Keep going!

Do it!

Looking for a new hobby? Try vritti-watching!

Did you ever get that WhatsApp forward about the significance of the first five emojis that come up in your most-recently-used emojis list? Well, you have now. Open your phone and check which five emojis you used most recently; they will tell you, so the forward says, about your state of mind today. This isn't scientific by any means, but if the angry red face features more in your messages than the rofl one, if you use the heart emoji far more frequently than the facepalm one, if the namaste emoji is your go-to emoji to sign off from conversations and not the 'gimme ten' one, it tells you something about you, the kind of conversations you are part of on a daily basis and the kind of people you have the conversations with.

A better, more scientific, and more honest way (because sometimes we use emojis we don't mean, simply to fulfil someone's expectation or to hide our true feelings) to figure out your state of mind is to sit down somewhere comfortable and quiet, and spend a few minutes observing your chitta-vrittis.

Have you ever tried that before? No? This is actually a very illuminating exercise – and a fun challenge.

What do you have to do? Watch the vrittis rise and fall, but Do. Not. React. to any of them. If you want a metaphor, here you go. The challenge is for you to watch the 'vritti trains' pulling in and out of the chitta station, while resisting the urge to climb into any of them. If you do, you will be whisked away to destinations unknown, and lose the challenge.

Why is this challenge important? Because this is what happens to us all the time! When we are not being mindful, we stumble into every vritti train that arrives on the platform, without pausing to ask where it's headed. We go haring across the emotion-countryside in every direction, hopping in and out of scores of different trains as we try to find our way back to our own station. Then, at the end of the day, we wonder why we feel so disoriented, exhausted and out of control.

Let's say, when you are watching your vrittis, that a thought-wave about a classmate – let's call her K – rises in your chitta lake. She is always giving you these compliments, and she did the same in PE class yesterday, gushing that you were a really good sport because you gave up your turn at basketball for someone who wanted it more. Your friends and you think K is a

complete fake. Your friends tease you about your 'personal exclusive suck-up' and warn you that what K wants in return is to be part of your girl gang. Now, you can watch this thought and let it go, as it most certainly will in a while, but you don't. Instead, you attach yourself to the thought.

An irritation-wave rises in response to the thought of K. Why can't that girl just leave you alone? What was that silly compliment yesterday, about you being a good sport? Doesn't she realize that you only gave up your turn because you hate running and sweating and every other kind of physical activity? You are not a good sport, you are just a lazy bum! From somewhere else, a shame-wave rises, which along the way turns into a self-hate wave. It's true what Maa says, you tell yourself. I have no discipline and no willpower. Now a defiance-wave chugs into the station. Yes, Maa, I am going to be a failure in life. But it's all your fault, really. You are always working, you never have any time for me. A self-pity wave rushes in at full speed. You are suddenly cranky, weepy and very far from the station where you boarded the train. And all because someone gave you a (quite probably well-meaning) compliment!

If, instead, you sat down and examined the vrittis calmly as they came and went, you would end up learning a lot about yourself and the thoughts that pass through your head. You will be able to see which thoughts go away without leaving a trace, and which ones provoke such a strong urge to react that you actually have to restrain yourself physically from climbing into the train. And you will discover some that will surprise you. It's like checking your search history on Google and thinking, 'Oh yaaaa, I did search for that a couple of days ago! How weird, I had forgotten entirely!'

Because thought-waves rise so quickly in succession – the mind, as you know, is as fidgety as a monkey – we often cannot keep track of every single thought that passes through. Sometimes, you find you are in an irritated state of mind even though you had a good day, and you have no idea why. Sitting down calmly and watching your vrittis could help you zero in on the source of your mood.

Going back to our example about your classmate, K. Let's say you were feeling a bit annoyed but couldn't remember why. When the first thought about her rose in your mind, eureka! 'Aaah yes, I am annoyed because she gave me that fake compliment!' Now that you have identified the source of your mood, it is possible to let it go. In other words, it is possible to put that mood on the train and wave goodbye to it, while staying off the train yourself.

The more you observe your vrittis, the better you will get at identifying your chief emotional 'triggers', whether they are behaviours or situations or people or things (it doesn't matter if the emotions they set off are what we think of as 'positive' emotions or 'negative' ones – any strong emotion ends up clouding buddhi). Once you know what those triggers are, your buddhi will learn to spot those particular vrittis well before they chug into the chitta station, and will do what it takes to stop them in their tracks. It works sort of like vaccinating yourself with a weak virus to help your immune system learn its shape and feel, so that when a strong virus enters your body, your antibodies are able to identify and neutralize it before it can do any real harm.

Make this vritti-observation a twice-daily ritual. Do it for just five minutes each time, once soon after you've woken up and freshened up, but before you've eaten or drunk anything, and again, just before you get into bed. You may think the challenge is easy-peasy, because you only have to restrain yourself for five minutes, but it is almost impossible, in the beginning, to NOT get into a vritti train when it comes in. It is almost unconscious, the urge to jump in, but the moment you notice you've done it, jump off, head back to the station, and start over, without letting those other terrible vrittis – 'Never mind, I'm just useless at this kind of thing', or, 'I knew this was a bad idea to begin with', or something else similar – whip up a whole tsunami of waves in your chitta lake and muddy it.

Do this regularly, and you will find that you are able to respond better to your triggers – mindfully rather than impulsively, mildly rather than aggressively. By and by, as you let train after trigger-train come and go, they will lose their power to provoke you. By and by, you will get closer and closer to samatvam, equanimity, the ability to stay calm and composed in every situation. Which, according to the Bhagavat Gita, is what yoga is all about.

योगस्थ: कुरु कर्माणि सङ्गं त्यक्त्वा धनञ्जय ।
सिद्ध्यसिद्ध्यो: समो भूत्वा समत्वं योग उच्यते ॥ २.४८ ॥

yoga-sthah kuru karmANi sangam tyaktvA dhananjaya
siddhy-asiddhyoh samo bhUtvA samatvam yoga uchyate

Be steadfast in the performance of your duty, O Arjuna, and abandon attachment to success and failure. Such equanimity – samatvam – is called yoga (2.48)
(Krishna to Arjuna, Bhagavat Gita)

Secret 3

You Are Not the Storm, You Are Its Calm Centre

तदा द्रष्टुः स्वरूपेऽवस्थानम् ॥१.३॥

tadA drashTu swarUpeYvasthAnam

Then you see yourself as what you truly are (1.3)

Actually, if you do a word-by-word translation of Maharishi P's third sutra, you get a somewhat different translation than the one above, although the sense of it is the same. Let's see where the difference lies, shall we?

tadA – then; drashTuh – the Seer; swarUpeY – in its own form. Which could be translated as: *Then, the Seer is established in its own form.*

Eh, what? Exactly. See why it's just easier to go with the first translation? Still, it's worth spending a paragraph or two on explaining what or who the Seer is. To do this, we need to go back to the fundamental, existential question – 'Who am I, really?'

According to Hindu philosophy, we are neither the gross* physical body

> ★ Not as in 'Ugh, gross!' but as in 'something that is made of matter', something that you can see and touch and feel.

nor the subtle mental body. We are not even our breath, which sustains the life in our bodies. Instead, our true self – whether you call it consciousness or Atman or Purusha – is the spark of cosmic energy that does nothing itself, but *is the reason* that everything else required for us to live in the world happens – our physiological processes, our thoughts and dreams, and our in-out-up-down-and-all-around breaths. That silent, watchful consciousness, the light of the projector bulb by which the movie of our lives plays, is also sometimes referred to as sAkshi, the witness, or, as Maharishi P has done in this sutra, drashTA – the one who sees, or the Seer.

You are probably more familiar with the word drishya, which means 'that which is seen'. The ancient rishis were at pains to teach us how to differentiate drashTA from drishya – the Seer from the seen. Making that distinction is vital. If we don't, we begin to believe we are what we see and feel and think. We forget that we are, in fact, the Seer and Feeler and Thinker. In other words, we start thinking of ourselves as the waves on our chitta lakes, and get carried away by them, instead of thinking of ourselves as the ones *watching* the waves rise and fall in the chitta lake.

When we see ourselves as drashTA, we realize that we are not the storm, but its calm, steady centre. That understanding helps us remain unaffected by the wind and the rain and the roofs and the cars and the cows howling and swirling around us (like in the tornado that carried away Dorothy and Toto in *The Wizard of Oz*). Now we can function, fearlessly, at our highest capacity, for love and compassion and productivity. We can think clearly and calmly about what needs doing, and then go ahead and do it.

Think about it!

When was the last time you kept your head when everyone around you was losing theirs? Perhaps it was a medical crisis at home, or a fight on the playground, or an argument between two of your best friends that was escalating rapidly. Think back to how calm you felt, how easily you were able to see what the real problem was, which everyone else was missing because they were either panicking, or getting mad at each other or the situation. How did that make you feel? Do you wish you could be that way more often?

Maybe it wasn't you, but someone else – a teacher or a parent or a doctor or a classmate – who was able to stay calm and make a good decision in a difficult and unexpected situation. Remember how your own panic disappeared when that person took charge, how you suddenly felt secure, how you and everyone else looked to that person to guide you? How did you feel about that person then? Thinking back, what do you think it was that allowed them to function that way? Was it because they didn't allow their emotions to overwhelm them? Did you wish then, and do you continue to wish now, to have that composure for yourself?

We often feel that emotions are vital, because they are a great spur to action. When you feel anger against an injustice committed, whether to you or someone else, you are able to overcome your usual apathy to try and do something to set it right. When

you feel great love towards another person, place or idea, you willingly make the sacrifices that love demands. But is feeling a strong emotion the only way, or even the right way, to get things done? Are emotions helpful or harmful?
What do you think?

How can you begin to see yourself as drashTA, the Seer? According to Maharishi P, stilling the chitta-vrittis will automatically make this happen. How exactly?

Let's go back to the edge of the chitta lake, where the number of vrittis are somewhat fewer than before, because of our efforts not to react to the vrittis generated by the world. Of course, we are very far away from stilling the world-generated vrittis, but let's say we actually get to that point after, say, two dozen lifetimes of practice (unless, of course, you've been practising for several lifetimes already). Then what? *Then*, when the surface of the chitta lake is absolutely still, when all the mud the thought-waves churned up has settled on the lake bed, you will sec, promises Maharishi P, a marvellous sight. Just like a clear, still lake acts like a mirror, reflecting the reality around it – trees and mountains and birds in flight – while a churning, roiling lake reveals nothing but mud, your chitta lake will finally, now that it is still, reflect the truth of who – or, more accurately, *what* – you really are.

And what are we again, Maharishi P? The Maharishi roars with laughter. Raise your heads, young 'uns, he says, tear your wide-as-saucer eyes away from the still lake now – for however beautiful the image it is reflecting, it is still only an image – and look up! That – that beauty, that light, that wholeness that you are surrounded by – *that* is you. Or as the Upanishads would have it, tat tvam asi – thou art THAT.

Wow. We talk all the time about how relevant the wisdom and lessons of the ancient texts are to the current age, but perhaps one of the most relevant is 'Look up!' As in 'Look up from your phones, your Playstations, even your reading tablets! What you see on your screens – on Insta stories, or on YouTube – or read about in books or newspapers, is only a reflection, and often a DISTORTED one, of the real world. Look up, look around, and see the real thing. Aaaaarrrghhhh!'

Think about it!

Among the many schools of Indian philosophy, the chArvAka was the only one that did not believe in rebirth. All the other schools tell us that the life we are each currently living is not our first one, and certainly not our last. In other words, we will ALL be back. Many, many times. Do you find that a comforting thought or a depressing one?

Fine, fine, Maharishi P, I will take you at your word for now. And yes, it does give me some solace to know that I am more than the swirling storm in my head. But hey, I have very

little hope of stilling my chitta lake enough for it to reflect my true reality. Will just reducing the waves help?

'Of course it will!' replies the good Maharishi. You see, the real problem with thought-waves, emotion-waves and desire-waves is that they muddy up buddhi. When buddhi is clouded, it dithers, and makes the wrong decisions, influenced by emotions of love and hate and 'Mine-ness' rather than 'rightness'. Reduce the number of waves in your chitta lake, and buddhi becomes progressively clearer, lighter, stronger, surer. It is able to command manas with authority, and issue instructions swiftly, before manas gets tangled up in its own doubts and insecurities, and before ahamkAra begins its 'It's all about me, me, me' siren song. As ahamkAra loses its power (because of lack of opportunities to air its pomposities) our sense of I, Me and Mine begins to subside. As we begin to think of Them as Us and Us as Them, our entire chitta expands to embrace all our little separate worlds. Fear disappears – if They are Me, and I am Them, what do I have to fear?

That's something worth aiming for, don't you think?

Do it!

Quit the trash-talk – get with the Seer-talk!

While we work our way to that state of chitta-vritti stillness recommended by Maharishi P, which will reveal ourselves to us as we truly are, it may be useful to trust him, just as we trust our science textbooks and vaccines and Wikipedia, and start behaving as if we were the Seer. One small step towards that is to start talking to ourselves 'right'.

How would you talk to yourself if you truly believed you were not the body or the mind? It would then be silly, or at least somewhat illogical, to say 'I am not good-looking' or 'I am furious', don't you think?

Try this. Instead of saying 'I am not good-looking', practise saying something like, 'The body I am inhabiting does not look like the bodies of actors or models, but it is really great at getting me from place to place, converting what it eats into energy, keeping its heart beating and breath flowing, protecting itself from germs and disease, and oh, *so* many other things.' Follow that up with, 'Note to chitta: Take care of this body, it's the only one you'll inhabit in this lifetime. Be mindful of what you put into it and how you treat it!'

Instead of saying, 'Man, that boy makes me so, SO angry I could punch him in the face right now', try taking a few deep breaths, and then say, 'There is anger rising in the mind because of what that person said, but if the mind waits until the anger-wave subsides, it will be able to make a better decision on how it should deal with that boy's words.' Follow that up with: 'Whatever that person said can only create an anger-wave or a hurt-wave in the mind. It cannot affect me. The real me is blissful, radiant, wise – and beyond the reach of mean words and actions.'

Sure, talking like this to yourself will feel just a wee bit weird and cringey and out-of-comfort-zone in the beginning, but that's because you are trying to change how you see yourself after a lifetime of doing it a particular way. You may be tempted to cast it all aside, but stick with it for a couple of weeks and see how you feel at the end of it. Chances are, simply because you are being mindful about what you say to yourself, simply because you are pausing before you react, your responses will be better than they would have been otherwise.

Of course, even these 'better responses' will create their own waves in the chitta lake, but since these are measured, thoughtful reactions to a situation, the waves they create will be smaller, gentler and less disruptive compared with those created by emotional, impulsive and extreme reactions.

For now, that is plenty.

Baby steps.

Secret 4

Rip Off the Labels – You Can Be Anything, Everything, Nothing

वृत्ति सारूप्यमितरत्र ॥१.४॥

Vritti sArUpyamitaratr

Otherwise, you see yourself as the churnings and changings of your mind (1.4)

This is straightforward enough, especially after our discussion of the previous sutra. Still, let's break it down into the words.

Vritti – vritti (if you need to refresh your memory on what that means, go back to Secret 2); sArUpyam – identification; itaratr – otherwise. In other words, if you are not in yoga, that is, if your chitta lake is not still and you are not able to see your true self reflected in it, you will be trapped in your thoughts so completely that they will become your identity. Once that happens – dire warning alert! – you will live in fear eternally and never be free.

Wow. That escalated quickly.

How did we go from having a thought-churn to being in eternal captivity in two ticks?

Right. Let's take this from the top.

What is the problem with identifying with your thoughts, anyway? Look at it like this. If you say, 'I am a loving person' or 'I am a terrible person' or 'I have no patience' or 'Everyone is always mean to me', you are making loving-ness or terrible-ness or impatience or victimhood part of YOU. Each of these becomes a weight added to your idea of YOU, that you are then forced to lug around – that's probably why it's called 'emotional baggage'.

Second, when you believe something is part of YOU, you get attached to it and develop a certain possessiveness about it, which makes it much harder for you to let it go – whether it is hurt or a desire for revenge or deep love for someone. Third, when you identify with something, you are accepting that it is part of your nature, and we all know that what is natural – like it is natural for a flowering plant to produce flowers, it is natural for bears to hibernate in winter – cannot be changed. When you believe that a habit or a behaviour or an attitude is part of your nature, you will not even bother to try and change it!

Do you see how detrimental it is to think of yourself as your thoughts and feelings? Do you see how, as we give ourselves more and more labels – I am ambitious, ugly, smart, stupid, successful, independent, irresponsible, lazy – we get more and more trapped by them? If we believe we are smart, we get very upset when we don't grasp a science concept in class or do badly in an exam, leading to constant fear and anxiety. If we think of ourselves as stupid, we don't see the point of working hard or trying different ways to understand

SMART
STUPID
UGLY
COOL
WRONG
WINNER
AMBITIOUS
AMAZING

a concept ('I won't get it anyway'), and are consumed by dark self-hate. Either way, we are trapped.

The only way to free ourselves is to think of all our emotions and thoughts as separate from us, happening in a space called the mind. Maharishi P assures us that this is, in fact, true. The best part is, unlike things that happen in the world which we cannot control, our thoughts and emotions all happen in our own minds, which we CAN control. There is even a step-by-step path to get there, and it is called yoga.

What joy to know that we are not condemned to being stupid or irresponsible or lazy forever! What bliss to realize that we are not even condemned to eternally being the independent one or the high-achieving one; that it is perfectly fine to ask someone for help when we need it, or not feel it's the end of the world if we slip up on the achievements once in a while, knowing we can always get back to our self-reliant, class-topping ways when we need to!

It might be a good idea to learn Sutras 2, 3 and 4 by heart, so that you can remind yourself of them as you go through your day. It may also be a good idea to recite these affirmations to yourself as often as you need to.

* I am NOT my thoughts, but I can watch my thoughts as they come and go, and that's a real superpower.

* I am NOT my feelings. But hey, I am the BOSS of them, because I can choose how to react to them.

* I am NOT my body, but I'm so grateful for the gift of this brilliant piece of engineering that allows me to enjoy and cxperience the world.

* I am NOT my mind, but have you ever seen a smarter, quicker, more efficient, data-processing-sense-making-story-spinning-memory-keeping-emotion-generating-decision-taking machine?
* Here's what I AM, though: I am the energy and the awareness that allows all of this, ALL of this, to happen. Pretty cool, huh?

If you prefer to think your thoughts in Sanskrit – yup, not much chance of that, but no harm in checking – or if words set to music speak to you more powerfully, which is more likely – you can say/sing/chant the same sentiments to yourself, in Adi Shankara's own words.

In the eighth century CE, with his mother's blessings, eight-year-old Shankara cast off his worldly attachments and left his home in Kaladi, Kerala, to become a sanyasi and live the hard life of a monk. He began to walk north, seeking a guru for himself, and when he reached the ashram of Guru Govinda Bhagavatpada on the banks of the River Narmada, he knew in his heart that he had come home. But would the guru accept him as a student? There was only one way to find out.

Shankara approached the sage and requested that he be accepted as a student.

'Who are you, child?' asked Bhagavatpada.

Instead of simply stating his name and lineage, the boy genius began to sing. In his sweet, soaring voice, he sang more about what he was NOT than what he was – I am NOT this, I am NOT that – and so profound were his words that the guru, sussing instantly that this was no ordinary child, agreed to teach him.

That résumé that Shankara presented is called the nirvANa shaTkam (in Sanskrit, shaTkam means a six-verse composition) or the Atma shaTkam. Here's the first verse. You can find the other five – all very beautiful – on the internet. The shaTkam has been set to a couple of different tunes by different contemporary composers – pick your favourite off YouTube, and sing! Not any old time, either, but atha – now!

मनोबुद्ध्यहङ्कार चित्तानि नाहं
न च श्रोत्रजिह्वे न च घ्राणनेत्रे ।
न च व्योम भूमिर्न तेजो न वायुः
चिदानन्दरूपः शिवोऽहम् शिवोऽहम् ॥१॥

mano-buddhy-ahamkAra chittAni nAham
na cha shrotra-jihve na cha ghrANa-netre
na cha vyoma bhUmirna tejo na vAyuh
chid-Ananda-rUpah shivOham shivOham

I'm neither manas nor buddhi, nor ahamkAra nor chitta
Neither ear nor tongue am I, nor nose, nor eyes
I'm neither space, nor earth, nor fire, nor air
*My true nature is chidAnanda, pure and blissful consciousness**
*For I am shiva,** I am shiva* (1)

★ In other words, drashTa.
★★ Shiva here is used not to refer to any particular god but to the Sanskrit meaning of the word, which is 'blessed' or 'auspicious'.

CONVERSATION

So, young 'uns, remember we spoke about vrittis, the movements of the mind?

Not much chance of us forgetting, is there, Maharishi? Given the way you went on and on about them?

Haha, glad you've all been listening. Now, ever wondered how vrittis are classified, and how many kinds there are?

Not really, but we know you're dying to tell us, so tell already!

Listen up, then. I've thought about it a long while, and this is my finding – there are FIVE kinds of vrittis. Some kinds are most unhelpful, but there are some that aren't so bad.

Phew, that's good to know. We were beginning to feel distinctly uneasy about having to quieten ALL our vrittis and have NO thoughts at all. But if there are some helpful vrittis, as you say, then yoga is probably a matter of learning how to reduce the unhelpful vrittis, while still letting the helpful ones come and go, right?

*Yes, at least to begin with. But let's take a look at the five kinds of vrittis now. There's **pramANa** (right knowledge), **viparyaya** (wrong knowledge), **vikalpa** (imagination), **smritayah** (memory) and **nidrA** (sleep).*

Ummm, say what? I'm afraid you've lost us, Maharishi.

Secret 5

Know Your Thought-Buckets, and Empty the Unhelpful Ones Regularly

वृत्तयः पञ्चतय्यः क्लिष्टाक्लिष्टाः ॥ १.५ ॥

vrittayah panchatayyah klishTa-aklishTAh

There are five kinds of vrittis, some detrimental, some not (to the yoga practice) (1.5)

प्रमाणविपर्ययविकल्पनिद्रास्मृतयः ॥ १.६ ॥

pramANa-viparyaya-vikalpa-nidrA-smritayah

They are right knowledge, wrong knowledge, imagination, sleep and memory (1.6)

Right. We have now figured out, within just four short sutras, the essence of the entire text of the Yoga Sutras. But this is only the Big Picture. Clearly, it isn't enough to know What (yoga is) and Why (it is important). It is also essential to know How (to get to that state of yoga).

But we're still in the first chapter of the YS, which doesn't concern itself too much with the How – it leaves that to the appropriately named second chapter, sAdhanapAda (sAdhanA is Sanskrit for 'the practice').

On to a few more 'Whats', then!

Right. The Maharishi says that all our thoughts fall into one of five categories – we have either understood something correctly (right knowledge), or we have misunderstood something (wrong knowledge), or we are conjuring up something that isn't real (imagination), or remembering something (memory), or, well, not thinking of anything at all (sleep).

Seriously? Are there only five kinds of thoughts that zip into and out of our minds like quicksilver? Surely not? We have SO many different kinds of thoughts in the space of a single minute, very few of them even related to each other!

Why don't we put Maharishi P's hypothesis to the test? Let's take a typical situation at home: the usual morning rush to get to school on time. What might be the thoughts going through your head? Let's put them down and see if they fit into any one of Patanjali's five categories.

1. *Oh my god, the power's gone!* (Right knowledge)
2. *Now I can't iron my uniform.* (Right knowledge)
3. *I'm going to be punished and PE Ma'am is going to make me run around the field 10 times.* (Imagination)
4. *She hates me anyway, so she will be only too happy for the opportunity to punish me.* (Wrong knowledge/ Imagination)

5. *Why did I not iron my uniform last night as Mum told me to?* (Memory)
6. *Why do I never do things that I know are good for me?* (Memory/ Right knowledge)
7. *I am a completely useless person.* (Wrong knowledge)
8. *I'm such a disappointment to my parents, no wonder they love my brother/sister more.* (Wrong knowledge/ Imagination)
9. *Oh, do be quiet, and hurry up and get readyyyy! Akanksha will be here any minute to pick you up.* (Right knowledge)
10. *I bet her uniform is beautifully ironed and she doesn't have a hair out of place.* (Imagination)
11. *But that's because she has a nanny and a cook and a driver and whatnot, and everything is always done for her.* (Right knowledge)
12. *That's why she does so well at everything in school.* (Wrong knowledge)
13. *I wish my parents were richer and we had a domestic staff of 25 as well.* (Imagination)
14. *It used to be so nice last year when Dad used to iron our uniforms.* (Memory)
15. *Now he says I'm old enough to do it myself and will not do it for me even when I beg. Next, he will be asking me to get a job and support myself before I pass out of 12th grade.* (Imagination)
16. *Omg, Akanksha is here on the dot and I'm not ready yet. Now she's going to be mad.* (Right knowledge!)

NIDRA
EMPTY TRASH
PRAMANA
EMPTY TRASH
SMRITAYAH
LAST YEAR
EMPTY TRASH
VIPARYAYA
EMPTY TRASH
VIKALPA
EMPTY TRASH

Wow! It certainly seems that ALL of our thoughts can and do fit into just five categories! But hey, you are under no obligation to believe this based on just one example. The best way to convince yourself is to try this exercise on your own thoughts. The next time you sit yourself down to watch your vrittis, add another element to the game – see if you can slot each thought that rises, into one of these five categories. If you find that you can do it, well, Maharishi P's hypothesis is validated. Yayyy for him!

Let's assume, for now, that he was right. What do we gain by knowing this? Well, if there were truly an infinite variety of thoughts, the effort involved in identifying each, before controlling and stilling them all, would be overwhelming. On the other hand, knowing that you can toss each of your thoughts into one of just five buckets and then click 'empty trash' on the unhelpful ones, makes the process seem easier, more manageable, don't you think?

But here's Maharishi P again, and this time he is doing a deep dive into each of the five categories, to explain them to us in a little more detail. In his usual, logical fashion, he tells us how to identify whether a thought belongs in the 'right knowledge' bucket or the 'wrong knowledge' one.

Let's say you're thinking about something that happened. Now:

* Did you actually see it (or hear it, or smell it or taste it or feel it) yourself? In other words, did you 'directly perceive' the happening?
* Did you not actually see it happen but conclude that something had happened because you directly perceived *a consequence of it*?

* Did someone or something (a book, a text, a news report) that you trust deeply tell you it happened?

If you can say 'yes' to even one of these questions, says the Maharishi, then it is very likely that what you are thinking about actually happened. In other words, it is right knowledge. It is important to be very sure what right knowledge is, because this is one of the helpful buckets, and we don't want to clutter it with unhelpful stuff that, by rights, belongs in the 'wrong knowledge' bucket.

Let's talk about each of those questions a little more.

The No. 1 source of right knowledge, bar none, according to Maharishi P, is **pratyaksha**, or **direct perception**. Any data you collect using your own sense organs is the one most likely to be right. That automatically means hearsay, gossip, rumour, 'but my friend *swears* that...,' 'but *every*one says that...,' 'but the sky is *really* falling, because Chicken Little felt a piece of it land on its *own* head' – do NOT qualify. Neither do the forwards you receive on WhatsApp. Even news reports can be somewhat suspect – but we didn't need the Maharishi to tell us that!

In the classic children's story 'The Emperor's New Clothes' by Danish author Hans Christian Andersen, two rascally tailors offer to make the emperor a set of royal clothes, the likes of which have never been seen before. Smitten by their descriptions of the softness and lightness of the material they will use, and the kinds of glitter and gold they will embellish it with, the emperor sets aside a room in the palace for the exclusive use of the tailors, and issues orders that they be given all the money and help they need. Months pass, while the tailors work behind closed doors, insisting that their process is patented and top secret. At long last comes the much-awaited announcement – the emperor's new clothes are ready!

A royal procession is planned so that the very special clothes may finally be showcased before the world. The tailors dress the emperor painstakingly and throw open the doors of their studio. When the ministers enter, their jaws drop in astonishment, for as far as they can see, the emperor is not wearing a stitch! But he himself seems so convinced that his robes are fabulous that the ministers, not wishing to attract his ire, fall in line, ooh-ing and aah-ing about the fit, the fabric and the flounces. The emperor walks out into the street, followed by his entire retinue. His people stare, goggle-eyed, at their naked emperor, but being too concerned about their own well-being, join in the general ooh-ing and aah-ing.

Until a little child, not yet well versed in the ways of the world, and trusting only the evidence of his own eyes, says, in a clear, high voice, 'But the emperor has *nothing* on!' A deafening silence descends on the crowd. The very next minute, the emperor, red-faced from both anger and embarrassment, flees for cover, calling for the two blackguards to be rounded up and executed. Needless to say, the rascally duo are nowhere to be found, and despite all the search parties that are sent out, are never heard of again.

If Maharishi P had been around, he might well have leaned over and patted the child proudly, for his innate understanding that pratyaksha was the truest basis of right knowledge.

***

That's not where it ends; there are two other sources of right knowledge. One is **anumAna**, or **inference** (not as good as the first, but still valid). Let's say you have not directly perceived something but can make a calculated guess that something is there, hidden from view, because of something else that you are directly perceiving. For instance, if you see, with your own eyes (direct perception), a column of smoke rising from within a grove of trees, you conclude that there currently is, or recently was, a fire somewhere in the vicinity of the smoke (inference). You can do this because, in your own personal experience, whenever there is smoke, it usually comes from a fire (why, there's even an idiom you have learnt in English – 'no smoke without fire'). The Maharishi accepts this kind of submission as 'right knowledge', but only if the inference works in *every single instance*.

Think about the smoke and fire example. While the Maharishi may have accepted the smoke as evidence of fire in his day, he may be a little chary about accepting it now. Can you think of instances where the presence of smoke, or a smoke-like substance, does not necessarily indicate the presence of a fire? That's right – when a building is being fumigated or when a fog machine is being used on stage! What emerges from both machines looks a lot like smoke but isn't.

The third and final source of right knowledge, according to the YS, is **Agama**, or **testimony**. Literally, Agama means 'that which has come down', and usually refers to scripture. Texts like the Vedas, the Upanishads, the Quran and the Bible – which are all considered revelation by different groups of people, and have been revered for hundreds, or thousands, of years, for their wisdom and guidance, are automatically part of Agama.

We could also look at Agama a little more broadly, as the testimony of someone who has directly perceived something and has passed on that information to you. After all, as humans, our survival depends on learning from other people's experiences and heeding other people's warnings. The question, though, is this: Whose testimony should you take as the truth? It would have to be someone you trust personally, who is not given to lying, exaggerating the truth or embroidering it. It would have to be the word of someone who is himself/herself a calm and composed processor of information, and who has the kind of mental faculties that can reason and analyse a situation clearly. It cannot be someone who is deceitful or dull-witted or lazy or highly emotional, or has their own unsavoury reasons for feeding you certain kinds of information.

Still, good verbal testimony need not always come from someone you know personally. It can come, for instance, from an expert in a particular subject, a book or journal that knowledgeable people whose judgement you trust have given their approval to, or a newspaper, news channel or journal that has had a loyal readership/viewership for years, and is known for checking the facts in every piece of news it puts out – you get the drift.

All of this seems utterly commonsensical. Clearly, anything we perceive directly (pratyaksha), anything that we infer based on our own past experiences (anumAna) and anything conveyed to us by a source we trust (Agama), is likely to be right knowledge, and anything else, likely to be tainted, error-ridden, wrong knowledge. And yet, and yet, we trust our own selves so little that we allow ourselves to be swayed by the opinions and testimonies of random people who have done nothing whatsoever to earn our confidence. We allow advertisements, which are designed to present every product as desirable, to colonize our minds and overwhelm them with greed ('I want it, even though I can't think why I need it') and envy (of everyone else who owns that product). We allow the words of anonymous strangers on the internet to fill our minds with fear, loathing and anger for ourselves and others.

Each of these 'wrong knowledge' thoughts gives rise to an infinite number of vrittis, leading to confusion and delusion.

How wonderful it would be if we could throw out any thought that isn't right knowledge and with it, all the unnecessary fear and anxiety and emotional upheaval that comes in its wake! How calming to have only a fraction of the thoughts we normally do, so that there's tonnes of mind space left over to focus on the things that we consider important – music, physics, reading, sport, cooking a surprise dinner for Mum and Dad, googling fascinating stuff! Thanks to the good Maharishi P, we can now begin the process.

Think about it!

In your estimation, how well does Maharishi P's right-knowledge checklist hold up today? We have SO much, so MUCH information being streamed at us all day and all night, so many experts holding forth on every subject under the sun, so many Instagram influencers telling us where to go on holiday and what to do when we get there. But has all this information made us collectively wiser or collectively more confused? Given that we trust so few authority figures any more, has it become more difficult to figure out what is truly Agama and what isn't? Do we know more truths or fewer? Hey, no pressure to come up with an answer, just let the question marinate awhile in your chitta.

Secret 6

You Can Change Your Nature – Simply Redesign Your Chitta!

विपर्ययः मिथ्याज्ञानमतद्रूपप्रतिष्ठम् ॥ १.८ ॥

viparyayah mithyA-jnAnam-atadrUpa-pratishTham

Viparyaya is false knowledge, which comes from erroneous understanding (1.8)

Now that we've heard Maharishi P hold forth at length about right knowledge, including the three-point test to check for it, do you think he would have put out something similar – a five-point test maybe – to confirm if something is wrong knowledge?

Naah. Remember he was trying the keep the YS as succinct a text as possible! Plus, he expected his readers to be smart enough to realize that anything that wasn't right knowledge was, yup, wrong knowledge. Still, he does take the trouble to define what viparyaya, wrong knowledge, is, but very simply.

Viparyaya, says Maharishi Patanjali, is knowledge that is 'false and has no basis in the true nature of an object (or event or person)'. Then he leaves us to apply our own minds and figure out what that may mean in each instance.

A common example of wrong knowledge given by many commentators on the ancient texts is that of the snake and the rope. Imagine you are walking home at twilight through slushy fields and your eye catches a glistening, sinuous object lying right on your path. Your self-preservation instincts, already soaring because of the near-darkness and the lack of people around, now go into panic mode. The first and loudest thought that pops into your head is – 'Snake!'

Instantly, a series of other thoughts are set into motion – 'I'm too young to die! Bet there is not one dispensary in this godforsaken town that stocks antivenom! I read in the newspaper that 233 people died of snakebite in a village in Sudan last year! How quickly does death come after snakebite? Oh god, I hope it doesn't hurt too much. Wait, there was something we studied in school, about how to suck snake venom out of the body. Needless to say, I cannot remember a word of it. Oh, Maa! Bet you never realized two hours ago that that was the last time you'd ever see me alive...'

As you stand rooted to the ground, paralysed by anxiety but still engaging with what is in front of you, you notice, through your steadily filling eyes, that the snake isn't moving. At all. Your breathing gets a wee bit slower. Maybe the snake is dead. Maybe this isn't your last day on earth after all. As your heartbeat slows to near-normal levels and your mind begins to function again and your tears stop and your vision clears, you realize that the object on the path is not a snake at all but a common rope! Relief comes flooding in. Giving thanks to the universe, you hurry homewards.

But – and this is the scary part – that momentary wrong knowledge has left its mark on your chitta. In the future, you may look for excuses to not go walking in the fields after dark, even if it means ducking your responsibilities. The worst part is that you have no idea that your chitta is scarred. At a conscious level, you feel only relief that the snake turned out to be a rope; the next morning, you might even chuckle as you relate the story to a friend. At a subconscious level, though, the event has made a deep impression, and that impression may play out in unpredictable and distressing ways.

Sometime in your future life, let's say you promise a friend that you will do something for him. You discover, too late, that keeping your promise would require you to walk through the fields at night. For some reason, the thought of doing that is entirely repugnant to you, so you don't keep your promise. When the friend asks you why, you offer a lie, or maybe even whine about how everyone takes you for granted and expects you to do their work for them. The friend is hurt and angry, understandably so. You feel like an awful person but cover it up by telling yourself that it's high time you stood up for yourself. You are upset, defiant and very confused. The vritti storm in your head will take days to settle.

Now, some people – like your parents, who were worried when you decided to take this stroll and cautioned you against it – may think that it is a blessing that you have 'come to your senses' and are no longer traipsing in the fields after dark. But do you see what wrong knowledge has done to you as a person? It has clipped your wings a little, limited your desire and capacity for exploration and discovery, allowed all kinds of unnamed fears to enter your psyche, and, worst of all, made you unsure about yourself. You can't explain your own reactions to people and things, and you are becoming the kind of person you never wanted to be. Woooooo! That's a lot of stuff to deal with, and it all stemmed from one experience!

If this is a taste of the dangers involved in wrong knowledge, *even after you have ascertained that it is wrong knowledge*, imagine what would happen if you *never* discovered that it was wrong knowledge? What if you lived under the impression that it was right knowledge, because 'I saw it with my own eyes'? In the snake example, what if you had turned around and run off screaming, the way you had come, without pausing long enough to check what the glistening object really was? You would have been convinced, forever more, that there had indeed been a snake on the path and that the only reason you escaped with your life was because you fled the scene.

What might this kind of long-term wrong knowledge do to your personality? It might turn you into the kind of person who turns and runs whenever faced with a difficult situation in life, instead of someone who looks it in the eye until, staying with the metaphor, the snake loses its power and becomes a harmless rope. The more you run away from difficult situations, the harder it will become for you to change that behaviour, and the more it will become part of you. That 'habit' will become your instinctive response, part of your 'nature'. And that would be a real pity.

Think about it!

Are all kinds of 'wrong knowledge' harmful? Or could some lead you to a better place? What if you walked into the wrong auditorium in a multiplex and ended up watching a different film from the one you had bought a ticket for? What if, at the end of the 'wrong' film, you found you had not only enjoyed it but were also inspired by it to change the course of your own life, and study law instead of engineering? What if the film awakened some deep-seated empathy within you for others, and you decided to volunteer at an NGO in your summer vacation instead of the cushy internship that was already waiting for you at your aunt's friend's company?

See how fluid all these categories are? The important thing is that while we must strive for right knowledge and keep away from wrong knowledge, we should also remember to keep an open mind, and never be rigid about what is good or bad, right or wrong. Sometimes, the true rightness and wrongness of something are only revealed to us much later.

Can you think of other instances where 'wrong knowledge' turns out to be wonderfully 'right'? Or the opposite – when 'right knowledge' leads to certain misery and despair?

Ancient Indian philosophers have a word for impressions/marks/scars that external events and our own behaviours leave on our chitta. They call these impressions **samskAra** – heard that word before? They believe that it is all the samskAras that we have collected, not just in this life but also from previous lives, that have made each of us who we are today.

You probably know people who are cheerful in the face of great adversity, people who are quick to anger, people who lie habitually, people who are constantly anxious about something, people who stay preternaturally calm amidst chaos, people who simply cannot say no to a friend, people who criticize everyone and everything. According to Indian philosophy, this is because of the samskAras, good and bad, that they have each accumulated in/on their chittas, over several lives. You have also probably heard your adults say about such people, 'Well, he can't help himself. One cannot change one's nature.'

Wait, does that mean we are stuck being the way we are, forever? If I am a lazy person because of my samskAras, and I don't like that, can I never hope to be non-lazy at some point in my life, however hard I try? On the flip side, if I am, by nature, a disciplined person, does that mean I can slack off when I feel like, because my nature will come through for me when I need it? Here's the good – and bad – news: while it is difficult, very difficult, to change your 'nature', Maharishi P assures us that it can most certainly be done. How? By proactively creating different samskAras for yourself in this lifetime!

The thing is, we are creating dozens of samskAras every minute, by our every thought, word and deed. If we can get a little, juuust a little, mindful about these, we can create the samskAras that we want, that we think are valuable to us and to our families and communities. Here's the carrot – if you truly commit to the process, you will begin to see tiny changes in yourself almost immediately. The big changes may take, erm, a few lifetimes, though. (Hey, we're talking Indian philosophers here – and they knew, as we do, that in this land, most big changes come very, very slowly.)

Let's explore this further, this creation of new samskAras. To begin, let's go back to the image of the lake, turbulent with waves, that we first brought up on page 75. Now, the thing about waves, if you think about it, is that they churn up more

than the surface of the lake. They also end up reshaping the lake bed, especially when they proceed in the same direction over and over again. When this has happened enough times, a path, a channel, gets created, through which future waves can move easily. The longer the waves proceed down this channel, the clearer the channel gets; any obstructions – rocks, trees, et al. – are gradually worn down or swept off, making it even easier for future waves to flow through.

Your samskAras are the channels on your own chitta lake bed. If you are habitually lazy, it is because the laziness channels in your chitta are very well established. It is through those channels that your vritti-waves flow each time you are faced with a task, because those are the paths of least resistance.

Now, thinking logically, if this was an actual lake, and you didn't want the waves to proceed 'naturally' down a particular channel, what would you do? Maybe you would dredge the lake bed to create an alternative channel that the waves could use. Maybe you would block the original channel with all kinds of obstacles so that it becomes harder for the wave to move ahead. Maybe you would direct a wave up the offending channel, in the opposite direction from the original wave, so that the latter faces stiff resistance and loses its momentum. There are many ways to do it.

Well, if you want to change your samskAras, you do EXACTLY the same things. Try this for starters: every time an unhelpful thought-wave rises in your mind, counter it with a helpful thought-wave. Every time you feel an unexplained fear or revulsion towards someone or something, raise an opposite wave – compassion, kindness, curiosity. Instead of turning away or hiding from the fears that lurk inside the dark, cobwebby closets of your subconscious, invite them into the sunny living room of your consciousness so that you can look them in the eye and get to know them better.

And yes, do return to walking in the fields again at night – this time with a friend and a powerful torch for company – until you feel confident to do it solo. Go on, you got this!

Do it!

Fancy a career in custom mindscaping?*

100 per cent benefits guaranteed, in this life and the next!

Let's say you are a habitually lazy person. Every time you feel the urge to be lazy about a homework assignment, steer your vritti-waves away from your wide and deep samskAra channels of laziness, and finish it TODAY. Every time you feel hot words rising to your lips when someone annoys you, recognize that it is just your vritti-waves heading for the well-worn anger channel, which you yourself have created by your past behaviour. Then quickly create a vritti-wave coming up the channel in the opposite direction. That opposing wave might take the form of a few deep breaths. Or thinking of the nice things the person you are about to yell

* You know what landscaping is, don't you? Mindscaping is the same kind of thing, except that, instead of contouring land into beautiful lawns and flower beds and water features, you do it to your mind.

at has done for you in the past. Or leaving the room until you have calmed down. Every time a wave of envy and self-pity raises its head – 'It's only because he has that fancy laptop that he is able to get top marks on every assignment and I'm not' – raise a counter-wave – 'He also works really, really hard on his assignments; maybe that counts for something as well?'

See what you did there? You just crafted a range of fresh new samskAras for yourself! The less your vritti-waves use the readymade channels of negative samskAras, the more those channels will fill up with sand. The more you create new channels of positive samskAras by your choices and behaviour, the deeper and wider they will get, until *they* become the channels that your vritti-waves naturally flow through. It's that simple – in theory!

Don't forget to visualize the channels on your chitta lake bed shrug, shift and settle in new ways as you do this. 'See' the awful old ones get narrower and the rush of waves in them dwindle to a trickle as you consciously change your patterns of behaviour. 'See' new channels form, slowly, slowly, but very steadily, as you put your shoulder to the wheel and push, push, push away from the old channels. Visualization is a powerful tool – you will be more reluctant to fall back into lazy, for instance, if it is accompanied by a mental image of the narrowing channel of laziness growing wide again.

Sounds great, right? When should you start? Heed the Maharishi's voice booming down the millennia, young 'uns – atha!

Secret 7

Find Joy in the Present, Inspiration in the Past and Purpose in the Future

शब्दज्ञानानुपाती वस्तुशून्योविकल्पः॥१.९॥

shabda-jnAna-anupAtI vastu-shUnyo-vikalpah

Imagination consists of using words that are not based on any (real) substance or object (1.9)

We have spoken so far about two kinds of vrittis – pramANa, right knowledge, and viparyaya, wrong knowledge. What of the third, fourth and fifth kinds? Do they fall into the helpful category or the unhelpful one? Let's take a closer look at them, shall we?

The third kind of vritti, according to Maharishi P, is vikalpa. He defines it, in his straightforward manner, as 'the use of words that do not correspond to an actual reality'. Now, we could translate that into English as imagination, which is wonderfully positive, for where would we humans be without our rich imagination? But flip the lens, and vikalpa could equally be translated as delusion, a state of utter confusion where we lose sight of the line that separates what is real from what isn't. That is why vikalpa cannot instantly be classified as helpful or unhelpful – it really depends on the context, and the extent of the disconnect between words and object.

Unhelpful/destructive/dangerous kinds of vikalpa could include, or lead to:

* Jumping to conclusions.
* Counting your chickens before they hatch.
* Misunderstanding something someone says, even though you understand the words perfectly (for instance, a friend A describes another friend B as being 'a good sport'; you then proceed to make offensive jokes about B in B's presence, because what you understand by 'a good sport' is someone who can take jokes made at his expense, except A only meant that B is the sort who nurses no grudge if you do better than him at Scrabble or studies).
* Ruining your mental health and equanimity by worrying about things that haven't happened yet, and may never happen.
* Restricting other people's freedoms because you believe they will cause harm to the world, even though they have never done anything criminal, simply because they belong to a particular community or race.
* Restricting the freedoms of people you love and care for because of all the possible harm you imagine could come to them.
* Limiting yourself and your hitherto unexplored strengths, abilities and talents because of your own fears that you will fail.

* Limiting yourself and the vast stores of compassion and generosity you carry within you because of your need to cling to people and things, because you fear that they will abandon you if you share them with others.

* Believing that the world is hostile to you because you look a certain way.

* Believing you don't deserve love or success or happiness because of various shortcomings that you imagine you have.

Helpful/constructive vikalpa could include:

* Imagining a world without hunger, and working towards achieving that in your own neighbourhood.

* Imagining all the possible ways in which a difficult situation may be reasonably resolved and trying hard to make sure that something is done to make that happen.

* Trusting that everyone carries as much good in them as bad, and working towards drawing out the good with open-mindedness and love.

* Believing that you are limitless in your capacity to love people, animals, trees, rivers, mountains, yourself – and then practising it within your own circle of friends, family, neighbourhood and community.

* Believing that you are neither superior nor inferior to anything else in the universe, and treating all beings and non-beings in the same way as you treat yourself – with respect and kindness.

* Trusting that *you* know better than anyone else what actions/decisions are best for you, and working to sharpen your inner voice by spending time with it.
* Trusting that the universe has your back, and that as long as you work hard and unselfishly, you will be guided to wonderful things via all kinds of interesting paths.

These lists only offer a sample of possibilities. Feel free to add to each of them, based on your own experiences.

***

अनुभूतविषयासंप्रमोषः स्मृतिः ॥ १.११ ॥

anubhUta-vishaya-asampramoshah smritih

Memory is the retention of the experience of an object (1.11)

On to a fourth kind of thought-wave, or vritti, called smriti, or memory. Not one of us can deny that this is a powerful, powerful one, taking up most of our mind space on any given day. We are all given to replaying events in our heads over and over again, especially the ones that evoked, when they first occurred, a great deal of emotion in us – fights with friends, praise from Mum or Dad, an enjoyable trip to the beach, an undeserved ticking-off from a favourite teacher, a natural disaster that happened across the world last week, an act of terrorism that occurred too close to home, being invited to your school hero's birthday party, a secret you have sworn with your life to keep, and of course, the loss of someone or something dear.

Maharishi P defines memory, very simply, as once-perceived objects coming back into our consciousness. In that sense, some dreams – like the stress-dreams you have before an exam, in which you find out after reaching the exam hall that you spent the whole of yesterday studying the wrong subject (!!!!) – would also fall into the memory vritti category

Just like vikalpa, memory vrittis cannot, en masse, be bunged into the unhelpful bucket. Memories can fuel our present efforts and give us purpose for the future, but they can also hold us back and keep us paralysed.

Unhelpful/dangerous memory vrittis may include:

* Nursing grudges against someone for real or imagined offences committed in the past; that kind of thing harms you and the people around you far more than the person it is directed towards.

* Hating yourself for some action you have done in the past, and concluding you are an overall loathsome person (while not rousing yourself to do anything to make amends in whatever way possible). For instance, you regret having spoken in anger and destroyed a relationship, and hate yourself for it, but you neither apologize to that person nor work towards controlling your anger against other people in the present.

* Wallowing in and weeping over the memories of a 'glorious past' – past success, past popularity, past relationship, past apartment complex where you had a lot of friends, past school where you were a favourite with the teachers – instead of working hard to make the present equally beautiful, if in a different way.

* Constantly longing for a repeat of a fun time in your life and looking for it in every similar situation in

the present, instead of enjoying the situation for what it is.

Helpful/inspiring memory vrittis may include:

* Going over the memory of an event where you felt hurt and betrayed, and checking if there are other ways of looking at the same event. Instead of making it about you, and how hurt you were, it may be productive to think about the other person's situation and emotions at that point, which could have made them behave the way they did. It may also help to wonder if there was anything in your actions that may have prompted that reaction from the other person. Most importantly, think about what you can learn – about yourself, about your friend, about people in general – from that incident. It can't be – 'I have learnt that you cannot trust anyone', because that kind of thought only traps you in fear and generates most unhelpful delusions. Your takeaway from a situation has to be a thought that helps you grow – 'I have learnt that if someone says something rude to you, it has more to do with them and less to do with you' or 'I have learnt that sarcasm (mine) may not be the best way to respond to an angry person'.
* Using the memory of a beloved grandparent you have recently lost to propel you towards becoming the kind of wonderful human being they always believed you to be.
* Reaching back to the memory of a time when you were winning at everything, to give yourself confidence that you have what it takes within you, and can do it

again; you just have to work hard and be patient until it happens again.

* Looking into the past to see how many people – extended family, friends, teachers, leaders, sportspeople, actors, musicians, scientists, entrepreneurs – have cared for you, helped you, taught you and inspired you, on your journey to become the person you are today, and feeling deep gratitude for all of it; and
* Occasionally revisiting the memories of fun times in your childhood, and using the joy they bring you to work towards creating equally happy memories of your tween or teenage years.

***

अभावप्रत्ययालम्बना तमोवृत्तिर्निद्रा ॥ १.१० ॥

abhAva-pratyaya-Alambana tamo-vritti-nidrA

Deep sleep is that experience based on absence (of content) (1.10)

The fifth, and last type of vritti, is nidrA – deep, dreamless sleep. Actually, Maharishi P lists nidrA fourth on the list of five (the fifth is memory), and there are many theories on why he chose to do this, but that need not concern us. His definition of sleep is interesting, though: Sleep, he says, is not, as we would expect, an absence of thought-waves, but 'a thought-wave about nothingness'.

Um, okay. But seeing as the Maharishi has seen fit to classify deep sleep as a vritti, do you reckon this is a helpful vritti or an unhelpful one? Most people in the world, especially sleep-deprived teenagers, would be unanimous in their opinion: 'Helpful!!!' A few may caution that, just like with anything else, too much sleep or too many thought-waves about nothingness could be as detrimental as too little of them.

Never mind them. Let's go with the teen consensus – and the universal medical consensus – that nidrA is a helpful vritti. Who doesn't like a nice, long chunk of sleep, huh? Unlike the other vrittis, however, which rise unbidden in the chitta, beautiful, restful nidrA has to be worked towards – there's *always* a catch. Maybe it's time to swear off stalking people on social media and binge-watching Netflix until 3 a.m. (guaranteed to create tens of thousands of thought-waves in your chitta lakes and ruin that night's sleep, *and* the next day, completely). Maybe you should get your full quota of shut-eye, which is proven beyond doubt to calm your chitta, infuse you with fresh go-get-it energy each morning, and ensure that you look more human than gargoyle when you wake up.

Worth a try, don't you think?

Think about it!

Most philosophers agree that it is best to live in the present. Of the other two possibilities – living in the past or living in the future – most of us would automatically say the past is far more detrimental, for the future is where hope and possibility lie. Not everyone thinks so, however. In his book *The Screwtape Letters*, a collection of letters from a senior devil to a junior devil, the celebrated author C.S. Lewis, who also wrote the bestselling children's series, The Chronicles of Narnia, was one of the naysayers. In one letter, the senior devil advises the junior one to keep humans away from the Present (because that is a happy place) and from God (also a happy place). Sending them into the Past has some value, continues the senior devil, because they will remain stuck there and never move forward, but trapping them in the Future is the best kind of sport for devils. Because, while humans often look with gratitude to the Past, and with love to the Present, it is their 'fear, avarice, desire and ambition' that looks ahead.

What do you think? Have we romanticized the Future, by making it about possibility, when it is really about fear (of things that could happen) and anxiety (about things we want to make happen), avarice (for more, more, more – bigger car, better job, more money), desire (for things attractive to the senses – clothes, shoes, gadgets) and ambition (the kind that will make you stop at nothing, however unethical or mean, to get to your goal)?

Or does it, as Maharishi P assures us, have both helpful and unhelpful bits – full of hope AND bursting with anxiety, full of wonderful possibility AND riven by ruthless ambition? Is it, as always, the choices WE make that turn the Future into one or the other?

Do it!

Turn bedtime into a celebration of NidrA Devi, dark goddess of no-dream slumber.

There is no debate, whether you look at it from the point of view of science or philosophy, that good sleep is essential for good (physical and mental) health. There is no debate, also, that your sleep will only be deep, dreamless and restorative if your chitta lake is not raging and frothing with a hundred thoughts and emotions at bedtime. But each day is unpredictable, and we cannot always ensure that we are at our calmest when we start readying for bed. However, if calm is what you dearly want to achieve, no matter whether you've had a highly stressful, very busy, or most exciting day, there are ways to do it. Here are some ideas that experts across the board recommend.

* **Turn off the external stimulation**: 30 minutes – okay, 20 minutes – before you get into bed, get off your phone/laptop/tablet/television. Close your textbooks. Close the exciting murder mystery (or self-help book, both count as stimulation) you're reading. Stop feeding your poor, overworked manas with inputs from the outside world. Stop having conversations with people – the easiest way to do that is to either shut yourself in your room or go for a walk by yourself – not a brisk walk but a measured, gentle stroll – on the terrace or within your apartment complex (somewhere safe!). Before they go into unconscious deep-sleep rest, let your senses enjoy some conscious wide-awake rest.
* **Sip a calming brew:** People swear by warm camomile or lavender tea or ayurvedic herbal teas. Whichever you pick, make sure you sip on it at least 60 minutes before bed, or you will be waking up just to use the loo!
* **Listen to some soothing music:** Choose an instrumental piece, where the music is slow-paced and even-toned. Here are some suggestions from Western classical music: 'Moonlight Sonata' by Beethoven; 'Wiegenlied' (German for lullaby) by Johannes Brahms; 'Air on the G String' by Johann Sebastian Bach. Indian classical

instrumental music offers a wide range of instruments and rAgas – sample them off the internet and create a playlist of the pieces you find most soothing. A simple mantra chant, on loop – just a short mantra, not a composition with many verses – also works very well to relax the mind.

* **Meditate briefly, in the dark:** Turn off the lights, close your eyes and lie on your back (or sit up with your back straight). For 10 minutes, watch your mind, seeing the thoughts come and go. If you find it very difficult to watch your thoughts without reacting to them and would prefer to anchor your mind to something else that is steady and repetitive, focus your mind on your breath – in, out, in, out. Or focus it on an affirmation you make to yourself, over and over: 'I am grateful for everything I have been given/Every day, and in every way, I'm getting better and better/ Tomorrow is a blank slate, full of hope and opportunity/ My body is a temple/I am blessed...' Do this sincerely and you will find you are very relaxed at the end of it. If you didn't last until the end and fell asleep after seven minutes, even better!

* **Give your feet a good, s-l-o-w, loving massage:** Using a little warmed-up coconut oil, massage every square inch of your poor feet, which have supported you all day uncomplainingly. A massage stimulates nerve endings and, apparently, stimulating the nerve endings in the feet has the effect of calming the mind. Just make sure you wear absorbent cotton socks over

your oiled feet before you get into bed or you will stain the sheets!

* **Create a pre-sleep routine:** Most importantly, whatever method you pick to help you sleep at night, make an elaborate routine out of it and do the same things, in the same order, around the same time each night. Your body, which is a most eager learner, will figure out soon enough that this routine means that bedtime is nigh and, in a kind of Pavlovian response, will start downing shutters in anticipation, which in turn will cue your mind to get into the 'mood' for sleep.

Honour NidrA Devi this way each night. Impress her by sticking to your sleep routine. When she arrives, don't fight her. Instead, welcome her with gratitude and tumble into her outstretched arms with a sigh of pure relief.

Trust that her blessings will be bountiful. There are few things that a good night's sleep cannot make better. Sweet no-dreams!

Secret 8

Maharishi P's Top Hacks for Success: Long-term Commitment, Steadfast Practice, Great Reverence

अभ्यासवैराग्याभ्यां तन्निरोधः ॥ १.१२ ॥

abhyAsa-vairAgyAbhyAm tannirodhah

Practice and dispassion will still them (the vrittis) (1.12)

स तु दीर्घकालनैरन्तर्यसत्कारादरासेवितो दृढभूमिः ॥ १.१४ ॥

Sa tu dIrgha-kAla-nairantarya-satkAra-adarAsevito driDha-bhUmih

These (practice and dispassion) find themselves on firm ground when they are cultivated over a long period, without interruption, and with reverence (1.14)

CONVERSATION

That was great, Maharishi P, those insights into the helpful and unhelpful vrittis! But the point of yoga, you said, was to still ALL the vrittis.

That's right, but it is by no means easy. That's why we start with identifying and tossing out the unhelpful ones first. That's plenty to begin with.

Good to know! But can we really do it, this tossing out? We've tried for over a week now, but we seem to be getting nowhere. And it's really, really hard to let things like anger and hurt go! It seems not right, somehow, to let people who hurt us off the hook!

A week?! You tried for a week?! HAHAHAHAHAHA!

Ruuude.

Oh, my dear children! (wipes away tears of mirth) One week? To still the mind takes a lifetime – nay, several lifetimes – of discipline, commitment and effort!

Yeah, yeah, yeah. You've said that before.

Here's the good part, though – anyone can do it! And the earlier you begin, the better! Gather closer now, I'm going to let you in on a secret. You only need to do two things to diminish, if not entirely eliminate, the vrittis: abhyAsa – practice, and vairAgya – dispassion. Burn them into your brain.

Only two things? Cool!

'Practice' is the effort involved in focusing the mind. 'Dispassion' is about not constantly craving things, whether it is things that you yourself have experienced or things you have heard others talk about. Both abhyAsa and vairAgya have to be, erm, practised, over a long, long time. AND they have to be practised continuously – every year, every month, every day, every hour, with great reverence. That's the hard part.

No cheat days?

None.

Ugh.

चञ्चलं हि मनः कृष्ण प्रमाथि बलवद्दृढम् |
तस्याहं निग्रहं मन्ये वायोरिव सुदुष्करम् || ६.३४ ||

chanchalam hi manah krishna pramAthi balavadriDham
tasyAham nigraham manye vAyor-iva su-dushkaram

The mind is restless, Krishna, stormy, strong, stubborn
I fear it is harder to control than the wind (6.34)
(Arjuna to Krishna, Bhagavat Gita)

There is no debate about this. Controlling the mind is one of the hardest things on earth. And that is why we are so much in awe of those who can do it to some degree. People who are very disciplined about what and when they eat; people who hit the road for a 10-kiometre run every single day, rain or shine; classmates who always have their assignments done a whole day before they are due; friends who achieve so many different things in the same 24 hours a day that we all have, and on top of that, seem to have time left over for fun things like movies and birthday parties.

How do they do it? Often, it's simply by following a schedule they have drawn up. We are all brilliant at making plans and creating timetables and writing down to-do lists on whiteboards, but how many of us end up sticking to the plans we make?

Sometimes, we default on our plans because they are unreasonable to begin with – for instance, if you have never exercised regularly before, it's silly to plan a mad one-hour workout each day and expect your body to keep up.

More often, though, it is our inability to keep our mind focused on our goal that does us in. All it takes is for an opportunity to present itself – you have decided that you will spend the evening completing your science project, but just as you are getting into it, your phone pings; your best friend wants to watch a film with you on the Discord app. That's it. Your mind, as wretched a foe as can be imagined, hastens to provide you with a dozen 'good' reasons to shelve the science project – you can stay up late and finish it; your friend is going to feel bad if you say no; it is the weekend, so you have all of tomorrow to do it; and the worst one of all – why do you always have to be a wet blanket?

The difference between those who stick to timetables and those who don't boils down to one thing, and one thing only – the former make their minds work for them, the others are slaves to theirs. Think of your mind as your ally in your quest for focus, rather than as an opponent you need to crush, and you will find that there is no friend more steadfast.

Talk to your mind. Observe it closely. Get to know it better. Identify the vritti trains that are most likely to bear it away from its goal. Consciously drill down and stay rooted to your spot when you see those trains approaching. Let your mind know that you're counting on its support to see you through each day's schedule. Make these affirmations out loud: *You and I, mind, we are a team; we can make this happen. Nothing and no one can break us. With you on my side, I have nothing to fear.*

In fact, turn it into a game you two play together. When distractions come along, as they will, challenge your mind to come up with good reasons for why you should NOT follow the distraction. Keep your FOMO (Fear Of Missing Out) strong, but make it about the sense of achievement that you will miss out on by not completing your schedule, instead of making it about the movie-watching experience. See? It's just a matter of flipping the lens!

The best part? The rewards are almost instantaneous. Grit your teeth, hunker down and finish what you meant to, and the kind of joy and pride you will feel can't be swapped for anything. The hard part, the *really* hard part, is sticking to this kind of focus, day after day. We might push ourselves and keep to a schedule for a week, ten days, a fortnight even, but sooner or later, we will slacken our grip on the mind, and sli-i-i-de down that slippery slope that we have clambered up so painstakingly.

The End, then?

Far from it.

It is on the other side of the sliding down that real transformation lies. This is the point at which you make your most important decision, this is where your mind really gets to display its powers. Do you lie there in that cloying swamp of self-pity at the bottom of the slope, turning your back on the summit, reaching into your memory archives to retrieve all the other times you have slipped in the past, and let your mind tell you that you are a loser? Or do you reach into those same archives and recall all the effort you put into clambering up the slope – how coolly you batted away distractions, how unwaveringly you kept your eye on the goal, how gooood you felt each time you got to the next level of the slope? Do you raise your eyes to the shimmering golden pinnacle of this particular slope and urge your mind to imagine what the view must be like from up there? Do you pick yourself up, dust yourself off, and pulling your mind to its feet, begin the climb again, declaring, 'One more time, mind – and this time, I promise, will be our most glorious one yet!'?

This is the part Maharishi P is talking about, when he insists that 'the practice' has to be done over a very long time, and relentlessly, never taking your eyes off the goal no matter what happens along the way. There is no shame in having your focus wander – that is the nature of the beast. What counts is your determination to bring it back on track, because abhyAsa is not about never slipping, it is about getting back on the path each time you fall.

***

And what of vairAgya? It is translated variously as dispassion, desirelessness and non-attachment, but what it essentially means is not clinging on to anything – not people, not emotions, and definitely not the idea of 'I, Me and Mine'. It means not yearning for things that have gone or longing for things yet to come. It also means being detached from the results – the fruits – of your own actions.

Whoaaa! That's a lot to process all at once! Let's break it down a little.

Now, if I'm not supposed to think of anyone or anything as 'mine', because that would come in the way of my own goal of vritti-stilling, doesn't that make me an awful, selfish person? I might as well hang out a sign – 'If anyone needs me, forget it – I'm not available'. If I don't direct my actions towards the specific results that I hope to achieve, won't it make my efforts lazy and slipshod, and turn me into someone who never delivers on time?

It would certainly seem so at first glance, but let's see what happens when we dig a little deeper. What happens when we detach from the idea of 'I, Me, Mine'? Well, it suddenly opens up the possibility of seeing the world as We, Us and Ours!

If you think of the people you are close to as 'My people', you immediately think of everyone else as 'NOT my people'. In a crisis, you will be so intent on protecting those you think of as yours that you will not care what happens to anyone else in the bargain. If you think of your successes as 'I did this', you instantly discount all the sacrifices, the efforts, of dozens of people – some visible, some invisible, some direct, some indirect – from which you have benefitted. Instead of being grateful for and humbled by all that you have received, you will swell with a false sense of pride, seeing anyone who hasn't had the same successes as inferior. If you think of your friend as 'She is MINE', you automatically prevent her from 'belonging' to anyone else. Your mind will turn into a snake pit of anxiety (that she will prefer someone else's company to yours), jealousy (of anyone she is affectionate towards), and rage (when you think she is ignoring you). Instead of surrounding her with love, you will destroy her – and yourself – with your hate.

Do you see how this works? It is when you detach yourself from 'I, Me, Mine' that the magic happens. When you think of every person in the world as your people, you will expand with love and always do the right thing by every human being, regardless of how he looks, where he comes from, or what god he chooses to worship. When you are standing at the summit of your particular mountain and realize that you have so many people to thank for getting you there, you will feel only compassion for everyone else lower down on the slopes and reach out to pass on the blessings you yourself have received. When you think of your friend as a radiant being who makes the world better just by existing, you will never think to stop her from spreading her light.

What about the other part – the part where you don't focus on the results of your efforts but on the effort itself? Remarkably, it is when you focus on the result that your work gets 'sloppy', not when you do not! How does that work?

Let's say you are preparing for an exam. You're wishing so hard for a particular outcome – a 100 per cent score/to beat everyone else/to make your parents proud – that the whole time you are studying, there is an undercurrent of anxiety running through your head. That parallel track will quickly

create hundreds of unnecessary vrittis as you imagine all the consequences of NOT achieving your desired result (which is entirely possible – sadly – even after you've done everything you needed to do) – 'How will Maa feel if I don't make top grade? I'm sure that sneaky Rakesh has got better notes from somewhere. What if there is a question I simply don't know the answer to? How will I top the class then?' With the coming of this vritti-storm, all semblance of calm vanishes from your chitta lake, making it harder for you to absorb information. You see? Now that your single-minded focus is gone, your work, your effort, becomes error-ridden and inefficient.

Instead, if you focused only on your effort, prepping for the exam in the best way you can, giving your work 100 per cent of your attention, wasting not one moment stressing over the outcome, the pressure is immediately off. If your parents and teachers have expectations of you, they will deal with them; your job is only to do your best. If Rakesh got better notes, it's far too late to worry about it now. All you can do is give your very best effort, which you are already doing, and wonderfully well, because there is no outcome-anxiety to distract you. Phewww. What a state of grace!

There's one last bit – the part about practising both focus and dispassion 'with great reverence'. Why is this important? When you revere something – whether it is a god, cricket or science – you give it maximum attention, and A-class priority over other things in your life. It is with that kind of reverent, devotional attitude, says Maharishi P, that you should treat the practice of abhyAsa and vairAgya, if you hope to get any good at either.

He's pretty demanding, our Maharishi, but you see how that's really the only way to be successful in anything, don't you?

Think about it!

In Sanskrit, vairAgya literally means 'devoid of rAga', where rAga means desire or colour. We understand, in some sense, what being without desire means, but what does it mean to be without colour? Could it mean 'to be without bias'? Could it mean that when you practise vairAgya, what you are really doing is casting away the tinted glasses of 'I, Me, Mine' with which you normally view the world? For, is it not true that you see things as they really are only when you view the world through a clear and impartial lens?

Do it!

Step off the love–hate escalators; get on the vairAgya travelator.

Why is it so hard to keep to a regimen, even one that we ourselves have drawn up and which we know is good for us? Because of our attachment to, or desire for, its opposite. How do we let go of that attachment? Here's an exercise you might want to try to practise vairAgya.

* Draw up a daily exercise schedule (or study schedule, or diet schedule – whatever is your need at the moment) for yourself – which isn't too demanding, keeping in mind your own current fitness levels. It will likely involve getting out of bed at a particular time each day, a little earlier than you normally do. How do you ensure you stick with it?

* Make an affirmation to yourself each night before you go to bed that you will wake up on time the next morning and finish the routine you've planned. Make sure there is zero hesitation when you do it. You may not ultimately wake up on time, but at the moment of making the affirmation, be very, very sure that you mean it.

* Finish your prep before you sleep – don't be careless about it. Set your alarm, drape your trackpants and tee over the back of your chair, put your jogging shoes by the front door, and clean socks beside them. Sure, you can do all of this in a minute after you wake up, but doing this the night before shows intent and purpose, which is a great nudge for the mind.

* Make sure you finish dinner by eight and get into bed a little earlier than you usually do, telling yourself that you need to be well rested before you embark on your new project. That will prevent your mind from trotting out its usual excuse the next morning – 'But you slept so late last night! Start exercising from tomorrow instead'.

* When your alarm goes off and you feel like dismissing it and falling back into sleep, pause. Ask yourself

why you want to go back to sleep. Since you've made sure to eliminate the mind's usual excuses, including the one about 'If I open the cupboard now to take out my tracks, the noise will wake my little brother', it will struggle a bit to come up with a convincing excuse. Meanwhile, ask yourself other questions: Do I only want to sleep because I am so 'attached' to the idea of sleep? What actual benefits will I get from staying in bed for another half hour – apart from feeling like a loser for not sticking to my schedule? Is it really that much of a pain to pull on my tracks and shoes and go? Imagine how good it will feel half an hour later!

* Then, go on to the most powerful question: How about I put away thoughts of how good I will feel if I do this and how terrible I will feel if I don't? How about I do this thing simply because it needs to be done? Boom! The mind is entirely stumped – it simply cannot come up with a good counterargument to this one, because it has run headlong into vairAgya, non-attachment – doing something simply because it needs to be done. If you neither desire reward ('How everyone will admire me if I do this!') nor fear punishment ('How everyone will scoff if I don't do this'), you have successfully bested your mind – it can no longer control you.

The more you do this, the better you will get at it. For vairAgya is like a muscle – you have to exercise it regularly to make it strong. Try it and see!

Secret 9

For a Clear, Discerning Mind, Start with Faith

श्रद्धावीर्यस्मृतिसमाधिप्रज्ञापूर्वक इतरेषाम् ॥ १.२० ॥

shraddhA-vIrya-smriti-samAdhi-prajnA-pUrvakah itareshAm

Focus (of the mind) is attained through faith, energy, memory, absorption and discrimination (1.20)

'A journey of a thousand miles begins... under your feet.'
– Lao Tzu

Erm, excuse me, you are saying, that quote actually goes: 'A journey of a thousand miles begins with a single step,' and it was Confucius who said it, not Lao Tzu.

Wrong on both counts! The translation of the original Chinese quote, from the *Tao Te Ching*, which is the foundational text of the ancient Chinese philosophy of Taoism, is actually '... begins under your feet'. What it means is that any journey, however arduous, has to begin somewhere, and if it is you who is making the journey, it stands to reason that that first step has to be made by *your* feet. In that sense, the second version of the quote also works, although it isn't the literal translation. As for who said it, while it is true that both the great Chinese philosophers Lao Tzu and Confucius were contemporaries who lived some 2,500 years ago, it was Lao Tzu who composed the *Tao Te Ching*, and is therefore the author of this line. Always double-check your quote attributions!

Whatever our quibble with who said it, the message the line conveys cannot be argued. Every journey, even one that could end up spanning several lifetimes, has to begin somewhere, and according to Maharishi P, the journey to attaining yoga or stilling the mind, begins with **shraddhA**, faith. ShraddhA is followed by – or generates – **vIrya**, the courage and energy required to undertake the journey and last the course; **smriti**, the art of recollection – never forgetting what the goal is and where it lies; **samAdhi**, deep focus and absorption in the journey; and eventually, **prajnA**, discernment or discrimination – the ability to tell what is real and what isn't, at which point the mind becomes still and clear, and all confusion and delusion disappear, allowing us to make good choices and decisions.

Let's examine each of these 'stages' of the journey one by one, shall we, and see how it may apply to our own lives?

Now, when we hear the word faith, most of us automatically, almost subconsciously, attach the word 'blind' as a prefix. We imagine something that is the very antithesis of logic and reason, based on a set of convictions that cannot be proved. We assume that the people who practise 'faith' are irrational and easily led. We are convinced that they will not only never dream of questioning those beliefs themselves but will also get mad at anyone else who does so.

But Maharishi P isn't talking about that kind of faith. **ShraddhA** is what we may call 'a working faith'. Without having a working faith in things, we could not function in the world.

Everyone has faith in, believes in, *some*thing – friendship, the idea of country, veganism, math guides, the benefits of exercise, animal rights, the benefits of homoeopathy. We go to school every morning not just because we get to hang out with our friends but also because we believe that formal education will serve us well in our later lives, even though we can rattle off the names of several dropouts from the education system who accomplished splendid things. We take part in protests because we believe it is our responsibility to show solidarity for a particular cause, even though we know that many protests do not achieve what they set out to. Not particularly rational behaviour, is it? But this kind of faith is vital if we are to live reasonably hopeful, meaningful, happy lives.

ShraddhA is also a questioning faith. You start out on the journey believing in its benefits, but you do not get so attached to it that you become blind to its faults or neglect to question the bits that you don't understand or agree with. You enrol for a particular coaching class because it comes highly recommended by your peers, but if you find it isn't working for you – after you've given it a proper, sincere chance – you opt out (if they haven't already made you pay the entire year's fees in advance, that is!) and try another. You buy a book because a friend whose reading choices usually match yours told you she loved it, but you feel no guilt at putting it aside if you're bored stiff 50 pages in.

No matter how a journey ends, however, there is no doubt about how it begins – with a good measure of faith.

It's the same with every journey, says Maharishi P, and especially so with the hardest, most demanding, most frustrating ones, like the long, lonely one to mind control. If it has to work for you at all, if you have to even take the very first step, you must implicitly trust the process, the goal and the teacher.

Where will that faith come from, when you are on your journey to mind control? Perhaps you have recently become aware that you are spending far more time on your phone than is good for you. You have tried to regulate it, but it hasn't worked. You are disgusted that you have such a Pavlovian response to the ping-ping-ping of your notifications, and are wondering how to discipline your wayward mind. Then, by some random chance (or not-so-random chance, because the universe is even better at listening to your thoughts than Alexa is), you happen upon this book. Hmmm. It is based on something written at least 2,000 years ago, but you are intrigued and are willing to give its techniques a shot. If it has worked for seers and sages, and if it is still around and being studied so many centuries after it was written, there must be something to it. Right? Right! *Ta-daaa!* ShraddhA – even if it is nascent as of now – has arrived!

Naturally, every journey you embark on will make some demands on you, but some will ask for a lot more than others. A journey towards a better performance in the interschool sports tournament will demand that you wake up earlier than you normally do, put your body through a punishing schedule several times a week and also find the time to finish schoolwork, when you'd much, much rather take a two-hour nap. A journey towards knocking off a few kilos will mean staying away from your favourite junk foods, committing to some kind of exercise and resisting the temptation to step on the scales three times a day (because there is nothing more frustrating than discovering you haven't lost a single gram between 1 p.m. and 7 p.m., even though you skipped your teatime snack). A journey towards buying your mum a birthday gift will mean pinching your pennies and denying yourself after-school treats (or – hot tip! – you could just badger Dad for the money).

The journey towards mind control, yoga, is way more difficult, particularly because, unlike in the three examples we have just discussed, there is no predictable end in sight. There are also few concrete ways to measure how far you have come – unlike in our examples, where the scoreboard, the scales, and the width of your mum's smile, respectively, serve as excellent metrics. There are no tangible rewards, either, to keep you motivated along the way. All of it is enough to make you so dispirited that you abandon the whole enterprise.

Come, come, says the Maharishi, chin up! All you need to do is keep the faith! For, if you truly believe in the 'rightness' of the journey and the goal, **vIrya**, the energy and courage to make the sacrifices required, will emerge from some deep well of strength you don't even know you carry inside you. It will walk beside you, a steadfast and loyal companion, and serve as both staff (when you're making big strides) and crutch (when you are limping along).

Yet, we are only human, and our faith will, at one point or another, begin to waver. When you are a young human born in the twenty-first century, one who is used to her efforts instantly getting results, whether they are voice directions on maps, likes on your posts, responses to your WhatsApp messages, information on movie show times, cricket scores, and what that headache possibly means (brain tumour, of course, never mind that you haven't been able to see the blackboard clearly for weeks and you are probably just short-sighted!), the slow, slow process of getting results on the mind-control journey, together with the 'long-term commitment, steadfast practice and great reverence' that we talked about in Secret 8, can be particularly aggravating.

When faith wavers, energy goes into a slump, making it even more difficult to keep going.

Don't lose heart, says the Maharishi, what can help you at this stage is **smriti**, the recollection of why you set out on this journey in the first place.

Think about the person you were a couple of weeks ago, a complete slave to your phone, with seemingly no agency to even think for yourself. Do you really want to go back to being that person?

Remember that you undertook this journey voluntarily, and that the Maharishi had been upfront with you about the effort and time this was going to take.

Pause and take stock of the small, small triumphs you have had over the last fortnight, and recall how those triumphs made you feel at the time. Would you really trade in all similar future triumphs simply because your faith is a little shaky at this point, or is it a better idea to keep pushing, head down, until another small win brings the faith roaring back?

Be brutally honest with yourself – are you thinking about quitting the journey simply because you're missing your old life, where you did what was easy and lazy, and you were the centre of the social scene, always on top of everyone's posts and reels, or because the process itself doesn't work? In other words, has the process failed you, or have you failed the process?

Once you've been through this exercise of recollection and introspection, you will be able to make an informed decision on your future course of action. You may decide that it is worth your while to persevere through the current crisis of faith, or you may decide that this particular path to mind control isn't for you. Either way, you would have undertaken the Maharishi-recommended 'due diligence' before you made your decision. Bully for you!

If you decide to stick with it, what do you suppose will happen? That's right – that little reassessment you have just done of your journey so far and the benefits it has already given you will only strengthen your faith, which will help you stay more committed to the course henceforth.

As this process goes on – (1) doing the work; (2) pausing to question, assess and reflect; and (3) deciding to continue – you will become more and more focused on the journey, reaching the state that the Maharishi refers to as **samAdhi**, complete

absorption; the journey, and not the getting to the goal, will become your joy. Doing the little, incremental things you need to do every day, in every moment, to control your mind, will become part of muscle memory, a habit. Side by side, with no further effort on your part, discernment – **prajnA** – the ability to tell what is important and what isn't, will emerge, and you will 'see' with greater clarity.

No longer will you need to put your notifications on mute or bury your phone in a sack of rice so that you aren't distracted by it. That invisible chain that tethers you to the phone will itself rust, break and fall away, and you will only reach for your phone (now where in heck did I keep it?!) after your homework assignments are all done, to check on whatever has been going on in your world. You will enjoy the reels and catch up on the gossip and then, almost subconsciously, you will put it away and go out to catch a game of football with your apartment building friends. It may seem an impossible scenario from where you're standing now, but rest assured it will happen.

As Maharishi P promises, it's that formidable trio – shraddhA-vIrya-smriti, faith-vigour-recollection – that will help you stay on the path. Burn the words into your brain.

Think about it!

Why is it that some people are able to decide to do something – change their lifestyle for the better, break a bad habit, read 36 books a year, give up sugar for six months – and then see it through with what seems like very little effort, while others, even when they understand that something is good for them and truly want to do it, are unable to summon up the discipline and the willpower to actually follow up on their decisions?

According to Indian philosophy, some of it has to do with each person's samskAras, the subconscious patterns of behaviour that we have brought into this life from previous lives. Another part has to do with the three forces, or guNas, that are believed to shape the visible world – Prakriti – and everything in it. Each of us, like everything else in the world, contain all three guNas within us, but in different proportions. How these three combine in us also shapes our behaviour.

What are these three forces, or guNas, of Prakriti? One is sattva, a calm, tranquil state, marked by clarity and lightness. Think of a beautiful, balmy day, with white clouds, shot through with sunlight, scudding across a blue sky. The second is tamas, a force of inertia and resistance, marked by heaviness. Think of large granite boulders. The last is rajas, which is about movement, vitality and action, marked by vigour and energy. Think of a river rushing down a mountain, in full flow, heading for a steep drop into a gorge.

With respect to your own self, you can think of sattva as a phase in which you understand what you need to do, and are ready to begin the journey to where you want to go. You feel a sense of well-being, you are full of sunlight. But there is an obstacle, or several obstacles – large and seemingly immovable – to overcome before you can get to your destination. Those obstacles are your tamas, in the shape of laziness, negative thoughts, a lack of self-belief. The only way to overcome tamas is through rajas – vigorous activity that, when it is deployed over and over, cuts through even severe resistance, just like a river wears down solid rock.

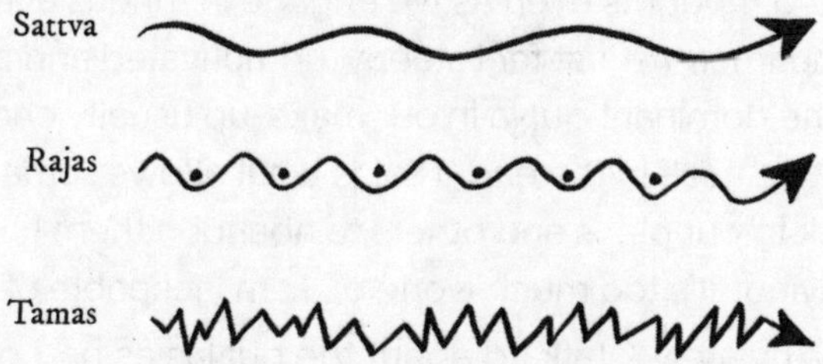

(Speaking of rivers, remember Ganga in the story of Sage Kapila, on page 65? Hers is a cautionary tale about unrestrained rajas. In that case, does immovable, invincible Shiva represent a necessary tamas?)

Now, each of us is born with certain proportions of these three guNas already hardwired into our systems, because of the patterns of thinking – samskAras – we have cultivated in our previous lives. Some people are naturally sAttvik – introspective, clear-headed and content, most of the time, even with their own company; some naturally rAjasik – always active, sometimes to the point of hyperactivity, and happiest when they are among people and doing something; and others naturally tAmasik – indecisive, sluggish in thought and action, and unable to move forward in any direction because of both.

Although each of us starts life with the guNas combined in a certain proportion, the three change their configuration within our minds (and our bodies) uncountable times *every single day*. Sometimes we feel serene and calm and in control. Sometimes we are full of passion and energy, tossed about by our roller-coaster emotions and never-ending thoughts even as we engage in furious activity. Sometimes we just feel sleepy, unmotivated and blah. But the dominant guNa in our make-up usually ends up asserting itself in the end. That is what allows some of us to stick to our plans and others to abandon them halfway, saying, 'it's too much work', or 'I am incapable of it'.

Why are we talking about the guNas as part of Secret 9? Because we can connect them to shraddhA, vIrya and smriti!

Let's say you have decided you want to wake up at 6 a.m. each morning, a full half hour earlier than you usually do, so that you can put in some work before school on the sci-fi fantasy novel you have started writing. You have come to this decision after realizing that you cannot work on it after school because homework takes up such a lot of your time. At this point, you know why you have made this decision and are full of faith, shraddhA, in the process. Which guNa do you think is dominant in this moment?

A week later, after you haven't been able to write a word for two successive days, you are frustrated and cranky. Smriti, your memory, reminds you of the days when you slept peacefully until 6:30 a.m., and taunts you with other projects you took up and did not complete, telling you that you don't have it in you to finish this novel. Which guNa is taking over your mind at this point?

Before you go to sleep that night, you force yourself to sit quietly, breathe deep, hush your thoughts, and think about your novel. Is it so bad that it is best to abandon it and move on to some other activity? Or is it just a phase that will pass? Which guNa(s) are you wilfully denying oxygen to here? Which guNa(s) are you inviting in?

You reread the first few pages. A smile curves the corners of your mouth. Your writing isn't so bad, after all! In that moment, because of that thought, a different side of your memory wakes up, reminding you of the time your Class 5 English teacher gave you five stars on your essay, and the second prize you won for creative writing at the interschool cultural festival. Of course, you have it in you to write a halfway decent novel! What guNa is in the ascendant in this moment?

As faith returns, it brings in its wake vIrya, renewed energy. You not only want to get back to writing, you are willing to experiment with a 5:45 a.m. start! For the next few days, you write like a demon, plot twists and sparkling dialogue spilling out of your head onto the pages. You are so charged that you find it difficult even to have a good night's sleep, waking up several times to check if your alarm has gone off yet. Which guNa is front and centre in that week?

You finish a big chunk of the book. You want to go on, but exhaustion overtakes you. Through the weekend and half of the next week, you are only able to wake up at 6:45 a.m., and that too with some difficulty. What guNa is dominant at this point?

Strangely, that period of passiveness and inactivity does not demotivate you as you had feared it would. A few days later, refreshed and recharged, you are able to take up the thread of the writing again.

Do you see how this continuous and never-ending dance of the guNas works, and how it influences your 'mood'

and sense of purpose? Do you understand why everyone does not have the same level of energy or calm or lethargy, and why, therefore, you should be compassionate towards people who 'fail' – including yourself – instead of judging them, and be inspired by those who are able to overcome tamas, instead of hating on them?

Here are two important takeaways, though:

* By simply being aware of the guNa dance, you can regain some control of your mind, nudging the unhelpful guNas out so that the helpful ones can take up more space more often.
* Every guNa has its purpose and too much of any one guNa is dangerous – without rajas, for example, the glorious ideas that sattva dreams up would remain just that, ideas. Without tamas to slow you down, rajas would wring you out with its ambition and greed. You see why it's a bad idea to, say, detest tamas or yearn for sattva?

Think about it.

(1) What kind of positive role may tamas play in your day?
(2) When may it become important to wilfully rouse yourself from the comfort zone of sattva and move to rajas?
(3) When does rajas become an unfavourable state to be in?

Secret 10

A Four-Ingredient Recipe for Calmness (Garnished with a Most Vital Fifth Ingredient)

मैत्रीकरुणामुदितोपेक्षाणांसुखदुःखपुण्यापुण्यविषयाणांभावनातःचित्त-प्रसादनम् ॥ १.३३ ॥

maitrI-karunA-muditA-upekshANAm-sukha-duhkha-puNya-apuNya-vishayANAm-bhAvanAtah-chitta-prasAdanam

For a clear, calm mind, cultivate friendliness, compassion, joy (in the joys of others) and equanimity, whether in the midst of happiness or suffering, virtue or vice (1.33)

It can't get simpler or more straightforward than that. In one of the longer sutras (which, by the way, is only ONE word long!) of the YS, Maharishi P lays out four must-do's that anyone, repeat *anyone*, can put into practice, starting today. While anyone can see why following this recipe would lead to a better life, how exactly does it lead to a calm mind? Let's take the ingredients one by one and see, shall we?

Ingredient 1 – MaitrI, or Friendship

Build friendships with happy people

A Sanskrit word that many of us in India are familiar with is 'satsang'. In popular usage, it refers to an afternoon or evening gathering that happens in someone's home or an ashram or temple, with bhajan singing, a discourse, or both, as the main agenda. (The side agenda – which participants look forward to almost as eagerly – is the prasad, the food that is served at the end of the session. Just saying.) The literal meaning of satsang in Sanskrit, however, is simply 'the company of good people'. And that is what the Maharishi is referring to when he talks of making friends with the joyous (you could also sing with them if you wished, but it isn't mandatory).

How does the company of happy people lead to a calm mind? To understand this better, think of its opposite – what does being in the company of unhappy people do to your mind? We have all had the experience of being around people who are constantly complaining about something or someone. They bemoan their lot, blame others for their problems, lash out in anger at the smallest provocation and believe that the world is out to gyp them, harm them and ruin them. They are suspicious of the government, of doctors, school managements, corporate organizations, strangers, people of a different religion, their relatives, and the vendor they have been buying their vegetables from for the last 20 years. They do not see – and will refuse to consider it even if you suggest it to them – that most of their unhappiness is of their own making.

The problem is that unhappiness is infectious. Hanging around with unhappy people disturbs your chitta lake like few other things can. All kinds of thought-waves that were entirely absent an hour before show up in strength – annoyance (with the unhappy person), anger (with yourself for getting into this situation of being closeted with them), a re-evaluation of your own life (I have the same problems as he does – is my life also sucky, then? Have people been taking me for a ride as well? How stupid of me not to have seen it before!). When you finally take your leave, you carry that negativity within you (even though, apart from this interaction, you've had a perfectly lovely day) and snap at your parents for no reason when you get home, hurting them and ruining their evening.

Exactly the opposite happens when you spend time with people who have a cheerful, positive outlook on life. For happiness is infectious too. Thought-waves will arise in your mind as a result of this interaction as well, and these will also cause you to re-evaluate your life, but in the opposite direction. Imagined problems retreat into the distance, any crankiness you were feeling before you met this happy person dissipates, you begin to see your glass as half full instead of half empty. You enter your home humming a happy tune and your parents, suffused in the warm glow of your cheerfulness, suspend the argument they were having and return to their tasks.

Of course, a Patanjali-style calm mind requires the absence of even positive thought-waves or vrittis, but the Maharishi, being a reasonable sort of man, realizes that *that* will only be achieved in stages. In the first stage, he seems to suggest, replacing dark, turbulent vritti storms with gentle, frothy vritti surf is serious progress.

Ingredient 2 – KaruNA, or Compassion

Be kind to the unhappy

It's true that unhappy people spread negativity. But that, cautions the Maharishi, is no reason to despise them. Our natures, as we discussed in Secret 9, are a product of patterns of behaviour and ways of thinking that we have not only carried over from previous lives but developed in this one. And since we haven't really lived the other person's life, we have no right to sit in judgement on them.

Even while you limit the amount of time you spend with them, send only kind and compassionate thoughts and words their way. Show them through your body language that you care. Give their rant your heartfelt attention and react appropriately, without feeling an instant need to give them unsolicited advice ('Yeah, yeah, you told me the same thing last week – here's what you should do to handle this situation') or hold yourself up as a wonderful example of positive thinking ('Yeah, yeah, the same thing happens to me all the time, but I just do x and y, and the problem goes away'). Sometimes, all people need to feel less unhappy is to know they are being heard. Sometimes, a warm hug or a kind gesture ('I was at the mall yesterday and remembered you love this brand of candy, so I brought you some') will do the trick.

How does this kind of behaviour on your part calm your mind? Let's say you chose to feel contempt rather than compassion for your whiny friend. Contempt will allow you to feel superior, bringing in its wake arrogance, leading to an inflated sense of 'I', which isn't in the least conducive to calming your mind (because what increases in direct proportion to your sense of 'I, Me, Mine' is the sense of everyone else being the 'other', to be hated, crushed and

lived in fear of). Compassion, on the other hand, springs from or leads to empathy, a gut-level understanding of what it might be like to walk in the other person's shoes. Empathy dissolves the boundaries between people, expanding your sense of 'I' to include the other person. Fear and hate reduce proportionately, calming the mind, making room for love and understanding.

Ingredient 3 – MuditA, or Vicarious Joy
Take joy in the well-being of others

This is a no-brainer – feeling joy at other people's joys, whether those joys are a result of their achieving success, wealth, fame or something else, is bound to keep you perennially joyful yourself, because the world is full of people getting rich(er), (more) successful and (more) famous. And yet, how few of us can generate this most important emotion of vicarious joy! Instead, the moment we have news of someone else's joy, even someone we know and love – your friend topped an exam, reached 10k followers on social media, found love, got a great job, was picked for an award – we find ourselves caught up in a toxic vritti maelstrom, gripped by insecurity, envy and hate – both for ourselves (for being inadequate in some way) and for the other person (for no real reason at all).

We don't like feeling the way we do, because it shows us up as bad losers, petty-minded and small-hearted, so we furiously ascribe reasons to make our behaviour sound legit. She doesn't deserve it/I'm not upset at him winning, I'm just thinking of what a giant loser I am/Who said it was about me? I'm just feeling bad for XYZ. She worked much harder and deserved the success more/The judges are unfair/The judges are idiots/The teacher is partial/He is already rich and good-looking, surely he doesn't need one more thing working for him?/It's easy when your parents support you so much/I could have done the same if I lived in a larger house and had a room of my own/Why are the silly reels she puts out even a thing? People are morons to like them so much/What I don't like about him is his ambition – thank God I'm not like that/ The universe is unfair.

If it's someone we don't know who achieves success, at the cost of someone else that we prefer – a rival team beats our favourite team, a film we did not care for wins an Oscar, a political party/person we did not vote for triumphs in the elections – we get equally agitated, seeing their loss as ours. If we pause to think about it for just a moment, we will see how insanely irrational this is – after all, there are so many, many factors that determine these kinds of results. How we feel about a particular team or film or election candidate doesn't matter a whit to anyone except ourselves, and definitely doesn't count very much towards the ultimate result.

In such cases at least, it should be easier to be detached from the result. But our sense of Me and Mine is so large that we feel our side's failure like it is our own, and absolutely hate the other team/political party for winning (apart from loathing our own for 'letting us down'). The kind of collective negative energy this generates spills over into the streets, leading to violence of the worst kind – verbal, emotional, physical. Imagine the kind of turbulence that accompanies this kind of violence in the rioters' own chitta lakes! That is violence we inflict voluntarily and unnecessarily upon ourselves.

Forget success, we find it hard even to find joy in other people's virtuousness. If someone we know is unusually forbearing, cheerful in the face of adversity, comfortable in their own skin, resolute about always speaking the truth (even when it comes to excuses about not submitting homework on time) and practises a high level of discipline, we are immediately suspicious, and are determined to pull them down to our level. Goody two shoes, we will say, a regular suck-up. Hypocrite. Wet blanket. Sissy. Opinionated. Drama queen. Stuck up. Bore.

If each of us strove instead to find happiness in other people's joys, what a wonderful world it would be! If we chose to be inspired by good people, instead of trying to pull them down, our minds would be in a constant state of muditA, leaving no room or opportunity for the damaging vrittis of hate, fear, love and anger to rise in them. Practise this the next time you hear about someone's achievements – and feel your mind and heart expand.

Ingredient 4 – UpekshA, or Equanimity

Be even-minded about the non-virtuous

If Ingredient 3 of the calmness recipe seemed like a struggle to procure, Ingredient 4 is infinitely harder.

Think about it. With some practice and willpower, we can definitely learn to take more joy in the successes of our friends and strangers who haven't done us any harm, like rival sporting teams. This is because we ourselves feel small when we resent our friends' achievements, and feel a natural urge to reach for our nobler selves so that we may change that situation. But upekshA demands that we feel at least equanimity, if not joy, at the actions (or achievements) of even those who are non-virtuous, people who have given us ample reason to dislike them! We are taught from childhood to scorn and distance ourselves from the mean, cruel, arrogant, selfish and greedy, and most of us feel a natural revulsion towards such people. And here is Maharishi P, asking us to be equanimous towards them (at least he doesn't ask us to love them, yet, unlike Jesus in the Bible)!*

Equanimity does not mean that we do not protest or work against the actions of the non-virtuous. It means that we do it with no anger or hate in our hearts but simply because it needs to be done. It means realizing that someone's bad behaviour does not give us the licence to behave badly

> ✪ In the Gospel according to Matthew, verses 5:43 to 5:48, Jesus gives some difficult-to-follow advice to his apostles, accompanied by some sound logic: 'You have heard that it was said, "Love your neighbour and hate your enemy." But I tell you, love your enemies and pray for those who persecute you, that you may be children of your Father in heaven. He causes His sun to rise on the evil and the good, and sends rain on the righteous and the unrighteous. If you love those who love you, what reward will you get? Are not even the tax collectors doing that? And if you greet only your own people, what are you doing more than others? Do not even pagans do that? Be perfect, therefore, as your heavenly Father is perfect.'

KEEP
CALM

towards them in return. That would solve nothing, and in fact, would pull us down to the same level of non-virtuousness. As Mahatma Gandhi echoed in his writings, millennia after Maharishi Patanjali, 'An eye for an eye would only succeed in making the whole world blind'.

The Maharishi asks this difficult thing – upekshA – of us, with good reason. We all know, through personal and collective experience, how anger and hate are far more harmful to the one feeling those emotions than they are to the person they are feeling it against. Also, when our mind is clouded by negative emotions (or any emotions at all), chances are that our action will be ill-advised, and almost certainly not 'right action'. Far better to clear our minds of (destructive) emotions before we do what needs to be done, don't you think? Needless to say, that clearing out will automatically lead to a calmer mind.

Ingredient 5 – Ishvara praNidhAna, or Devotion to the Supreme
Meditate on the syllable 'Aum' – it is the name of the Infinite

ईश्वरप्रणिधानाद्वा ॥ १.२३ ॥

Ishvara-praNidhAnAd-vA

(Concentration may also be attained) from devotion to Ishvara (1.23)

तस्य वाचकः प्रणवः ॥ १.२७ ॥

tasya vAchakah praNavah

...who is expressed as 'Aum' (1.27)

The Yoga Sutras make up a very practical text, packed with well-organized practices and tips to help you get to the state of yoga. Maharishi P himself is a hard-nosed teacher, who usually keeps a Supreme Being entirely out of the equation, asking you instead to put your faith in yourself. But even he cannot resist dedicating a few sutras to the power of devotion. That, he seems to be telling us, is a real game changer.

Devotion to what or whom? Maharishi Patanjali recommends that anyone who wants to be master of his mind should be devoted to an entity he calls 'Ishvara'. Being his usual thorough self, the meticulous teacher goes on to provide a definition of Ishvara: a Very Special Being, the divine spark in all of Nature, who presides over the natural world, but is not Itself affected by its rules or laws.

What kinds of laws? We, as mere mortals, are told to be mindful of our actions because each of those actions generates a set of consequences; Ishvara's actions, says the Maharishi, do not. We are all born and have to die some day; Ishvara is eternal, unbound by time and space. Everything we do creates samskAras – mental pathways, habits, ways of being that are unique to us – that cling to us like leeches and follow us from one lifetime to the next; Ishvara is unchanging, faultless, free of such burdens. In short, Ishvara is someone or something that we can revere because It represents the utter freedom that we all yearn for so much.

Now, that idea of bowing before a Supreme Being – whom most people simply call God – may not sit well with some of us, because we live in what we think of as the Scientific Age. After all, you may argue, haven't we proved several times over that we are entirely capable of fashioning a better life for ourselves, by ourselves? We have created information superhighways and dredged the oceans and gone to the moon and penetrated the icy wastes of Antarctica, all by ourselves, using our own brilliant minds and hands, with no help from aliens or superbeings. This idea of God is, you may conclude, meant only for some fuddy-duddy ancients who didn't know any better.

Guess what, though? The idea of a superbeing didn't sit well with many people in India even in the Maharishi's time! Our ancient rishis were nothing if not rational – they questioned *every*thing and only came to their conclusions based on relentless experimentation, often on their own minds and bodies. And yet, many brilliant ones finally came around, in one way or another, to Maharishi Patanjali's view – that when you believe in and submit to the idea of a universal, cosmic energy that is greater, nobler, more powerful than you, your own journey to be a better, more compassionate person, or to achieve the kind of clear, still mind that the Maharishi recommends, becomes easier and less burdensome.

According to Maharishi P, the easiest and most foolproof way of accessing this supreme energy is by repeating Its name. And Ishvara's name, he says, the syllable or sound that represents it, is 'Om'.

Why that syllable particularly? The rishis believed that Om – or, more correctly, Aum – was the OG sound, the one that accompanied the birth of the universe. Why? Think about how the sounds Aaa, Uuu and Mmm are produced. When you say a full-throated Aaa, you do not use your lips or teeth or tongue, you only ensure that you keep your mouth open, and the sound seemingly emerges from the very pit of your abdomen. Uuu also does not involve teeth or tongue, but it does involve some moulding of the lips, and the sound itself seems to reside in the chest region. With Mmm, the lips are brought together, signifying a natural end to the process – and this time it is the head region that vibrates with the sound.

In other words, just producing the sound 'Om' engages the entire extent of your body's breathing and sound-producing apparatus without the props of teeth and tongue, and represents, in your individual body, the repeating cycle of life – engaging with the world (at Aaa) to withdrawal into yourself (at Mmm), wakefulness to sleep, birth to death, spring to fall, day to night, kinetic energy to potential energy, expanding universe to shrinking universe. Pretty cool, huh?

Therefore, young 'uns, the Maharishi seems to be saying, repeat the word Om, which is the name of the Very Special Being, the Purusha Vishesha, and meditate on it any old time you like – when you feel an emotional thought-storm rising, when you are tempted to do or say something that you know will not end well for you, when you are scared, when you are happily engaged in some task, when you are sitting in the school bus, just before you go to bed, as soon as you wake up. Be devoted to the chanting of Ishvara's name, says Maharishi P; do it with the kind of passion you reserve for other things you are devoted to – K-drama, cricket, celebrity gossip. Chanting Om/Aum mindfully will remind you that everything – happiness and grief, success and failure, fame and notoriety, anger and calm – are temporary states, none of them to be taken seriously, for Aaa *will* turn to Uuuu and then Mmm, only to come back to Aaa again.

Each time the cycle begins again – a new day, a new class, a new school project – know that you have been granted an amazing privilege, yet another chance to do things better – grab it! Each time, focus harder on building friendships with positive, cheerful people (maitrI), be kinder to negative, miserable, whiny people (karuNA), take a greater pleasure in other people's successes and joys (muditA), hate less on those who do wrong, whether to you or others (upekshA), and you will find that the emotional storms in your chitta lake will begin to happen less often, be less intense, and eventually lose their power over you.

See how being devoted to Ishvara, or repeating – insert your own preferred possessive gender-pronoun here – name, can help you live a better, calmer, happier, less fearful life?

Think about it!

What does it mean, really, to submit to the idea of God? Look at it this way. Think about someone you trust implicitly, who you believe will always do their best by you – a parent, maybe an older sibling, a favourite aunt or grandparent, a dear friend, or someone else entirely.

Now think about how your life would be if that person were not part of it. You would almost certainly find each day harder to negotiate. You would be less happy, because there is no one planning nice birthday surprises or cooking you something because they know it is your favourite. You will feel less safe and secure, because there is no one you can run to when you've done something stupid, knowing that theywill support you through your dark days, even though they may be angry for a while. You will feel the weight of the world on your shoulders constantly, because there is no one who will willingly lift it from your shoulders onto their own, even briefly.

Would you still be able to survive in the world, becoming steadily more self-reliant? Of course! Maybe it will just be a little harder, a little scarier and a little lonelier, though. Getting to self-reliance without a loving guide to show you the way or a dear companion by your side, will also take longer – without a trusted sounding board to bounce our dilemmas off, we often make wrong turns on the journey and then have to work our way slowly back to the right one.

That, according to Maharishi P, is exactly how it works for a would-be yogi who does not submit to Ishvara, the lord of the laws of nature. The yogi-in-waiting can most certainly get to his destination – an understanding of his true self – by himself, but the journey will be more riddled with doubt, anxiety, loneliness and fear than otherwise. If, instead, he believes that it is Ishvara and not he who is driving the bus taking him to his destination, he will be able to stop stressing and enjoy the Journey and the scenery. Even when the bus takes a 'wrong' turn – 'but the Google Maps lady is saying to turn left, Ishvara, not right!' – this passenger will believe that Ishvara took the turn for a reason, to show him a view that he may have otherwise missed, and be grateful for the 'exclusive' detour experience as well!

But not everyone is able to practise Ishvara praNidhAna, or devotion to Ishvara, that Maharishi P recommends so highly; some of us simply cannot trust anyone but ourselves to drive our bus. Too many of us believe that we are excellent drivers ourselves, and great planners to boot – given that we've made our bookings at hotels along the route way ahead of time, spent enough time and effort studying our maps to find the most scenic route, AND put a Plan B and a Plan C in place as well, how could we NOT get to where we are headed?

Well, good for you if you are one of them, the Maharishi seems to be saying, for self-belief is also a wonderful virtue! But, he goes on, if you've been on the fence about God and devotion, if you've wished that you could just transfer your burdens to another pair of shoulders and go to sleep for three months (metaphorically speaking!), if you think you may benefit from yoking your own hard work, good planning and self-belief to the power of the universe, it may be worth your while to try out this particular recommendation of mine and see where it takes you!

Well, that's fair enough, don't you think?

PS: What image does 'God driving your bus' bring to mind? Yes! The battlefield of Kurukshetra from the Mahabharata, where Krishna was driving Arjuna's chariot!

On to Sadhana!

Right. So according to Maharishi P, meditating upon the primal syllable Om, and cultivating the qualities of maitrI, karuNA, muditA and upekshA, are good ways to fight the challenges that stand in the way of a calm mind, like 'disease, apathy, indecision, doubt, carelessness, laziness, confusion, attachment and delusion' (yup, it was Maharishi Patanjali himself who drew up this very comprehensive list of mental 'distractions').

Once you've done that, and got to a somewhat calm state in your mind, you can begin to go deeper into meditation, which will help you get closer to the yoga ideal – the state of absolute mind-stillness or samAdhi. Maharishi Patanjali spends the rest of the samAdhipAda, the first 'foot' of the YS, talking about this, defining the different levels of samAdhi, from lowest to highest, and then suggesting various ways and means to get there.

But those definitions and methods are for those who have known about the 10 secrets we have discussed in this section for a long, long time, and have been practising them for several years already. Wannabe yogis like us can safely skip those and head to the next 'foot' of the YS, the sAdhanapAda, or the 'Practice Foot', where Maharishi P helps us with some baby-step processes and basic prep to get us started.

Are you ready, willing and able to take on whatever challenges those processes may pose in your glorious quest for an enlightened mind?

Ummm.

You don't sound so sure. What about *superpowers*, then? Would you like some of those? Oooh! There, *that*'s got your attention! Like we mentioned earlier in the book (but maybe you were not listening keenly enough then), superpowers are part of the yogi package deal as well! Ready for sAdhanA now? Come on, then!

Think about it!

Why did the Maharishi speak about how to get to samAdhi in the first chapter of the YS, and the basic practices in the second? That seems a bit cart-before-the-horse, doesn't it? A logical mind would have started with the practices and then proceeded to the ultimate goal, surely! That's what some scholars think. They argue that, given that our Maharishi was perfectly logical, it couldn't have been he who designed it this way. Someone along the centuries must have, while shuffling the pages around, put them back together the wrong way.

Others declare that the Maharishi was not only logical but smart as heck. He holds out the shining carrot of samAdhi in the first chapter, they explain, precisely so that yogi aspirants will urge their steeds through all the practices recommended in the second, keeping the faith because of the incentive they have already been provided. What do you think? Which method would you pick if you had to lay out, to someone who didn't know a thing about it, a many-step journey to a difficult goal?

Readying for Ascent

NINE POWERFUL PRACTICES FROM THE SADHANAPADA

PRACTICE 1: Base-camp drill: The three-step essential prep

PRACTICE 2: Before starting the journey, study the map

PRACTICE 3: As the first step towards a calm mind, banish these five fatal flaws

PRACTICE 4: When you begin a practice, make it non-negotiable – no excuses allowed!

PRACTICE 5: Put cleanliness and contentment on top of the must-do checklist

PRACTICE 6: Feeling demotivated? Think of what's waiting at the end of this particular rainbow!

PRACTICE 7: Still the body so that you can focus on the mind

PRACTICE 8: To invigorate your life force, regulate your breath

PRACTICE 9: Hold firm the reins, and the horses will fall in line

CONVERSATION

How art thee, Maharishi P? *Now* what are you going to help us see?

Well, a ladder, for one – an eight-rung ladder that I've assembled especially for you to climb!

A ladder? Errmm, oh-kay. We assume the view from the top is stunning?

Oh it is, it is, never doubt it. The stunning-est view you have (n)ever seen.

Hehe, funneeee (not!). And, Maharishi P, we hear there are superpowers in the mix as well?

Oh yes, tonnes of 'em, scattered like diamonds along the way up – easy pickings once you get to the higher rungs.

No worries! We've come equipped. Ropes, check. Crampons, check. Ice picks, check. Oxygen tanks, check. We're all set.

Hehehehehe.

What?

Leave it be for now, your climbing equipment. No need to burden yourself with such ambition. Let's see you get past the first two rungs of the ladder to the third and fourth, and then we'll take stock.

The first two rungs? Pssh. Try us, Maharishi. We are not total amateurs. We *know* stuff now – chitta, vritti, abhyAsa, vairAgya, samskAra, maitrI, karuNA...see?

There's a great difference, young 'uns, between words and action.

Of course. Still, the first two rungs can't be *that* hard to scale!

That's what they ALL say.

Practice I

Base-camp Drill: The Three-Step Essential Prep

तपः स्वाध्यायेश्वरप्रणिधानानि क्रियायोगः ॥ २.१ ॥

tapah svAdhyAya-Ishvara-praNidhAnAni kriyA-yogah

KriyA yoga comprises self-discipline, study and dedication to Ishvara (2.1)

In a nice segue from the samAdhipAda section, which we ended by talking about Ishvara praNidhAna, devotion to Ishvara, here we are at the first sutra of the second 'foot' of the YS, talking about – yes, Ishvara, again! For someone who insists that we contain the universe within ourselves, you are thinking, the Maharishi does mention a superbeing *outside* of us a lot! What gives?

Actually, that is not strictly true. Only six of the YS's 195 sutras are Ishvara related. Plus, even though he himself believed implicitly in every human's intrinsic ability to control the mind, the Maharishi was also a practical teacher who really wanted to help his students. Through years of thinking, teaching, learning and living the philosophy of yoga, he had probably seen how faith in a greater power seemed to help people, himself included, through their doubts, difficulties and despair on the long, hard journey of self-discovery. As a good teacher, he would never have withheld that particular 'hot tip' from his students.

In this sutra, the Maharishi defines kriyA yoga – which can be translated as the 'work towards yoga' – and indicates that this is Very Essential Prep towards ascending the eight-rung 'ladder to freedom' – ashTAnga – that he has so thoughtfully designed for us.

And what is kriyA yoga exactly? A process involving three elements – tapah or austerity (scary word – let's call it discipline instead, which isn't very much more cheerful but at least has the benefit of being familiar, given how many times it comes up when teachers and principals are around), svAdhyAya or self-study (this is beginning to sound more and more like school now) and devotion to Ishvara.

Tapah, or Discipline

Make a plan. Then stick to it.

First things first – discipline. Ugh. Easily one of the dourest words in the English language. But words are magical, changeable, subjective things – the word summer, for instance, can evoke dread or joy depending on whether you live in Delhi or Dublin. It's the same with discipline. Discipline is a plodding bore of a word if you're thinking walking in school corridors with your oiled hair neatly brushed down, your shirt tucked in and your hands clasped behind your back, but it is a dazzling, chest-thumper of a word if you're thinking about how good it felt when, with tremendous effort, you managed to stick to your New Year's resolution for a whole month.

Is that because we resent someone *else* imposing discipline on us? That may be part of it, but here's the

kicker – discipline isn't fun, and is in fact much harder to practise when we impose it on ourselves. It only becomes worth it *after* the fact; it is only when we have gritted our teeth and pushed ourselves and completed the challenge we took on, which would not have happened if we hadn't been disciplined, that we truly begin to appreciate it.

Let's pause for a moment there and think about the Sanskrit word the Maharishi uses to denote austerity – tapah,* which literally means 'heat'. (In mythological comics, rishis engaged in deep austerities – or tapas – are shown with smoke rising from the tops of their heads, because of all the 'heat' or energy their meditation has produced. You know what happens next, of course – the thick fumes enter svarga (heaven), asphyxiating the gods, and Indra has to go running to Shiva or Vishnu and beg them to grant the rishi the boon he is seeking and put the gods out of their misery. You may not want to go that far with your austerities, but see how you can even nudge the gods if you are disciplined!)

Now, what does heat have to do with discipline? Well, one way to transform your life and make it better by, say, changing your (unhelpful) habits, your (unhealthy) diet and

* Its derivative, tAp or tApa, is the word for heat in many Indian languages. Which English word related to heat also has the same root sound? That's right – temperature!

your (unfavourable) lifestyle, is through self-discipline. And as science has proven to us, for any kind of transformation to happen in the world of matter – for baingan to turn into bharta, mountain snows into summer rivers, bauxite to aluminium, flower to fruit – the most essential 'raw material' is... heat! Taking that analogy further, heat, as we all know, is a form of energy. Discipline – sticking to a plan – requires a LOT of energy. No wonder Maharishi P used that particular word for discipline!

SvAdhyAya, or Self-study
Give yourself some me-time
What about the next element of kriyA yoga, svAdhyAya? Maharishi P likely meant the regular reading and reflecting on the wise lessons to be found in books of scripture, or the repeated chanting of a mantra to absorb its power. But the core idea of svAdhyAya – which could also be translated as 'study of the self' – is to find the time and space to reconnect with yourself. A good way to do this is to just spend some quiet time by yourself each day, decoupling from the world, away from devices and conversations and breaking news and opinions, and examining the thoughts and emotions that the events of the day have created in your head.

What might you gain from such an exercise? A better understanding of yourself and your patterns of behaviour, both helpful ones and unhelpful ones, so that you can teach yourself to avoid the unhelpful ones in the future. An opportunity to sort through your thoughts, consign them to their respective buckets (see page 101)) and then let them ALL go, so that you can start the next day with a clean slate. A chance to forgive yourself for things you could have done better, so that your headspace becomes lighter and clearer. And, finally, a blessed pause in which you resolve to be a better version of yourself the next day. See how important svAdhyAya is as a daily mind detox?

Most importantly, svAdhyAya helps you get comfortable with living inside your own head. Too many of us are fleeing from ourselves, looking for entertainments and distractions outside and finding ways to keep 'busy' so that we don't have to spend time with our thoughts, because who knows what slimy memory-thing might come crawling out of our mental sewers? Being able to spend time inside your head without fear or loathing is the first step to figuring out all the things that are cluttering and stinking up your mind-palace – the too-large couch of ego, the broken picture frames of old hurts you haven't been able to let go of, the spoilt milk of envy sitting in the fridge. Only when you have identified those problems can you sling that apron on, pick up a broom, grab a giant trash bag (biodegradable, of course!), and begin the joyful process of decluttering and redecoration. KonMari, anyone?

Ishvara PraNidhAna, or Devotion

Make your work an offering to the universe

The word 'kriyA' in kriyA yoga has the same root as karma, which makes kriyA an action word, a technique that involves 'doing' something. How can we turn Ishvara praNidhAna, or devotion, which is more a 'feeling' thing, into a 'doing' thing? Easy-peasy, says Maharishi P. Offer up anything and everything you 'do' in the course of your day to the universe, with reverence and devotion. Instead of studying because you want to achieve something for yourself – a better rank in the exam, admission into a better college, the respect of your peers, all of which lead to stress, which churns up emotion-waves and muddies the chitta lake – do your studies simply because that is your duty as a student, not because you want a prize at the end of it.

What does that mean in practice though – 'offer my work to the universe'? Here are some ideas for what you may say to yourself as you go through your day.

* Today's study session I offer to the sun, for showing up every morning and never calling in sick.
* This annoying economics project I offer to the wind, for bringing rain-laden monsoon clouds to us each year, even though we have done nothing but pollute its space the past couple of hundred years.
* All these chores my dad makes me do each weekend when I'd rather be lying on the couch, scrolling on my phone, I offer to the goddess who makes water gush out of my bathroom tap, lovely and hot/cool, whenever I feel like a bath, never sulking that we are vomiting our poisonous effluents into her riverine body.
* These two hours I'm spending babysitting my little sister (because Maa says I must, uff!) and not being out with my friends, I offer to the tree, which has just

burst into bloom at the end of my street, and gives me so much joy every time I look at it, even though I have done nothing for it in return.

* Everything I do or say or think is my small way of 'giving back' to the universe for all the blessings I have received from it.

See what you did there? When you take the time to remember and acknowledge someone's or something's contribution to your happiness, your heart fills with gratitude, and that person or thing takes centre stage – your work is no longer selfish, no longer about you. When you perform a task as a way of giving back, the work becomes light, something you *want* to do (because it is the right thing) instead of something you *have* to do. Plus, you expect nothing in return for it because it is you, in fact, who is doing the returning, for favours already received! When you do something as an 'offering', a word that has something of a sacred ring to it, your effort will automatically become better, for you wouldn't want your offering to be slipshod, half-hearted or distasteful. What a great technique to keep ugly thoughts, words and actions in check, don't you think?

To reiterate, what you offer to the universe, be it thought, word or deed, has to be the best you can summon up – the cleanest, freshest, good-est, right-est, that you are capable of. You cannot, must not, offer any thought, word or deed that is small or mean or arrogant – that would just pollute the universe and bring terrible consequences for not just you but for everyone else. What that means is that even while you are offering your 'work', you are constantly mindful of the quality of that work – is it good enough to match the flawless radiance of the sun, the undiscriminating benevolence of the wind, the crystal clarity of water? That is a BIG ask, and we may never get there, but at least we are consistently striving for it. And that's already a win.

Do it!

Turbocharge your vital energy, then get out of the way.

How does one summon up the kind of energy, the will, for kriyA yoga, aka unwavering discipline, introspection and devotion? Try these techniques and see if they work for you. But watch out for the pitfalls!

1. Conserve your energy – then focus it. Each of us is a pulsating ball of unimaginable amounts of vital life energy, or prANa, and we can achieve amazing things with it if we channel it properly.

But most of us fritter away our prANa in unhelpful, energy-guzzling pursuits – worrying about the future, regretting the past, playing mind games with other people, hating on ourselves, talking too much, giving negative thoughts an all-access pass into our heads, imagining everyone else is out to get us. Our energy flows this way and that, dissipates and drains away; we have very little left over to do the things that we had resolved to do. Think about it. If you're up late chatting with a friend, you will have very little energy left over to wake up early enough to finish your revision for the chemistry test tomorrow. If you fret about how many revisions the class topper has finished, you will not have enough energy left in your tank to even complete one revision yourself.

Be very mindful, therefore, of your thoughts, which will indicate very clearly where and how you are using up your energy. As you raise dams to prevent your energy from flowing away, and gather it all into a giant reservoir, so that you may then channel it into one – or three – important activities, you will notice the quality of your energy itself begin to change – it will become lighter, clearer, stronger, bigger. You will finish your assignments quicker and they will be better crafted, because of the attention and focus you have given them, and you will still have time left over for chatting with your friends. Once you experience the power of this focused energy for yourself, you will be smitten. You will begin to stick to the plans you made, with very little effort. Discipline, tapah, will become a way of life. Hurray!

2. Take time to pause, revisit, recalibrate. It's wonderful that you have figured out how to ride your turbocharged prANa by cutting out unhelpful distractions. It's even more admirable that you have learnt not to be affected by your friends' and family's reactions to the new you – 'Oh, come on! Nothing earth-shattering will happen if you don't exercise for one day!' 'So how long is THIS new fad going to last?' 'You're not fun any more! Live a little!' But make sure to pause every once in a while and think about why you're doing what you're doing. Is your new routine really working for you as you had hoped it would? Are you being inflexible about your routine simply because it makes you feel powerful and admired, or because it is doing good things for you?

One thing most ancient sages agreed upon is the need for balance – in everything you do. Torturing the body through too-rigorous exercise or too-extreme diets, for instance, whatever your goal may be, is deeply frowned upon, whether we're talking Krishna in the Gita, or the Buddha. Make sure to give whatever routine you pick a gooooood test drive – because you will never know its benefits, or the lack of them, if you abandon it too soon – but don't hesitate to change it around, try something else or drop it – yes, really! – if it doesn't seem right when you sit down to re-evaluate it honestly.

3. Harness the power of a good story for yourself. Maharishi P recommends japa – the repeating of a mantra over and over to harness its power and centre yourself – as a method of svAdhyAya. You could do the same. If ancient Sanskrit chants aren't your thing, repeat positive affirmations. In other words, tell yourself empowering stories about yourself each day, in any language: 'I am whole; I am complete; I carry the power of the universe within me; today, I will be the absolute best version of myself; for the next six hours, I will not think a single critical thought about my body.'

As part of your self-study routine, apart from spending time with yourself, make time to read a few pages from an inspirational book each day, whether it is a book of scripture, a biography of a sportsperson or scientist or social activist or YouTuber you admire, an uplifting story about courage and love in the face of adversity, or anything else that puts a smile on your face, lifts your heart and gives you the impetus to be better yourself.

4. Mind that ego! So yes, you have cut out many, many distractions from your life, gathered your energy, learnt to walk the middle path and not go off at the deep end, and are spending quiet time with yourself – that's wonderful! Congratulations! Now, be careful, be very, very careful, that you don't get too self-congratulatory about it all. Be wary of feeling superior to everyone else who is unable to have the same discipline and commitment as you do. It is great to feel good about yourself but not at the cost of looking down on everyone else. Don't get judgy about your friends who still enjoy going to parties and hanging out, just because you have stopped doing it for your own reasons. Don't get so attached to your own new lifestyle that you become a conversation hog, yakking about its brilliance at every forum – it is attention-seeking, smacks of insecurity and puts everyone else off.

Instead, understand you are doing something that, at this point in time, is something YOU want to try in your quest to be a better, calmer, more centred person. If and when, and ONLY if and when, anyone asks you what your routine is, because they are considering trying it themselves, share it with them generously, talking not only about the triumphs but also about the challenges along the way. Volunteer your time and/or talents to a community service activity, or to a charity of some kind – when you take time out for others, for no reward or payback, your self-absorption, the obsession with me, me, me, disappears, at least briefly, and you are able to see things as they are, and not through the coloured lens of how they affect you personally. Be grateful each day for the power inside you that allows you to be this determined, focused person, and give thanks to the universe for guiding you here. Et voila! You are practising Ishvara praNidhAna without even breaking a sweat!

Think about it!

What are the possible obstacles one may encounter in the journey to self-awareness and a still, clear mind? According to our precise Maharishi P, who is so brilliant at reducing every seemingly ginormous problem to a few bullet points, the five obstacles, or kleshas, are ignorance (avidyA), egotism (asmitA), love (rAga), hate (dvesha) and the desire to cling to life (abhinivesha, or the fear of death), and it is the first, ignorance, that creates all the others.

Now, let's take a minute to examine the five kleshas, one by one. We have spoken of most of them earlier, but using different words, like 'emotions' and 'ahamkAra'. There is no harm in going over them again, however, if only to fix it better in our heads.

Ignorance, or **avidyA**, the primary and greatest obstacle to our progress, is not being able to see that we are, in fact, complete, whole, eternal beings that nothing or no one can hurt or destroy. Because we can't see this, we feel incomplete and fearful, and look desperately for things to make us feel powerful and secure. We fight others for things and people that we believe will fulfil us, putting ourselves and our needs first (egotism or **asmitA**), get attached to or feel love for (**rAga**) everything and everyone we think of as helpful in our quest for security, feel loathing or hate (**dvesha**) for everything and everyone who we are certain will impede our progress, and live our lives in the paralysing fear that we will not find what we are looking for before the Grim Reaper comes to get us (**abhinivesha**).

We spin round and round on this carousel at breakneck speed, unable to make it stop, unable to get off, always dreading what lies ahead. Ugh. What a miserable, pathetic life that sounds like, and all because of our ignorance of our true nature!

avidyA

asmitA

rAga

dvesha

abhinivesha

Are we condemned to this kind of existence forever, then? Not according to Maharishi P! In fact, the greatest reassurance he gives us lies in his use of the word klesha, or obstacle, to describe the impediments to a clear mind, instead of something far more dire, like 'evil'. An obstacle, the way most of us understand it, is something that can be removed, not something that is fundamentally part of the path or of ourselves. And since an obstacle on a path is something outside of us, not inside, we can get rid of it with complete detachment, like a gardener would pull out weeds and throw them aside, with little guilt or pain. Phew.

Can you think of examples from your own life where one or more of these kleshas have caused or are causing you emotional distress? Now that you have identified and tagged the offending klesha, do you think it will be easier for you to think about how to roll it off your path, or at least diminish it?

Practice 2

Before Starting the Journey, Study the Map

यम नियमासन प्राणायाम प्रत्याहार धारणा ध्यान समाधयोऽष्टावङ्गानि ॥२.२९॥

yama niyama-asana prANAyAma pratyAhAra dhAraNA dhyAna samAdhayO-ashTau-angAni

The eight limbs of yoga are: yama (abstention), niyama (observance), Asana (posture), prANAyAma (control of the breath), pratyAhAra (withdrawal from sense objects), dhAraNA (concentration), dhyAna (meditation) and, finally, samAdhi (complete absorption in the Atman or self) (2.29)

Even if you had never heard of terms like chitta and vritti before starting to read this book, you would have almost certainly heard the phrase ashTAnga yoga. That phrase today is used to describe a particular set of Asanas or postures in haTha yoga, or physical yoga, that 'flow' from one to the other (a technique called vinyAsa), and essentially involve the body and the breath. You may have heard someone in the family talk about ashTAnga yoga as the routine they did in yoga class that morning, you may have seen a sign advertising it outside a yoga school, and you may even have tried it yourself (if you have ever done a suryanamaskAr, you have practised part of what is called the 'primary series' of the ashTAnga yoga routine). Remarkably, ashTAnga yoga has only been around for about a hundred years.

Maharishi P's Yoga Sutras, and his concept of ashTAnga (he never himself refers to it as ashTAnga 'yoga'), on the other hand, were first conceived some 2,000 years ago. And in the twenty-ninth sutra of the sAdhanapAda, the Maharishi neatly sets forth the eight limbs – or ashTa anga – of his brand of holistic yoga, which comprises a LOT more than just breath, body and flow. Far from being mainly about posture, Patanjali's ashTAnga has posture or Asana as only ONE of its eight limbs – or rungs, if you think of it as a ladder. What are the others, then? We shall see in a bit.

As always, whenever one is beginning a long and arduous journey, it is best to study the map first, for the unexpected is always harder to handle than something you have already braced for. Let's say you are headed to a friend's place and Google Maps shows you that you will hit a one-kilometre-long traffic-choked stretch of road around five kilometres from where you are now. You may groan initially, even beat yourself up for not setting out 15 minutes earlier, like you meant to, but your mind begins to accept the possibility of a long wait at that point, and adjusts its expectations of when you will get to your destination accordingly. That knowledge will even allow you to phone and warn your friend about the delay, and get that tension off your plate as well. When you do get to the bottleneck, you settle back into the music playing on your headphones, with a resigned sigh, but are not unduly hassled.

Now imagine the situation if you didn't know there was a jam on the way. Every minute in the jam increases your frustration, until you eventually succumb to your favourite self-created story where you are always the victim and the universe has something personally against you. Which, in turn, will end up ruining the evening ahead not just for you but for your friend as well, apart from strengthening your victim story, because of all the dark samskAras or impressions that your thoughts are bound to leave on your psyche. Wooooooo!

That is why it makes sense to familiarize yourself with the ashTAnga map as well. Understanding, even at a fundamental level, what is involved in each of the eight steps the Maharishi lists in this sutra will help you get an idea of the kind of terrain, and the peculiar challenges involved, on this particular journey. Remember, however, that there is no universal formula or fail-safe hack that will work for everyone here – *you alone* can identify the bits that are tough and steep for you, and will probably take you more time to negotiate. *You alone* know which bits, at least in a zoomed-out view, seem more within the scope of your abilities and talents, and will therefore be easier for you to handle.

Because the journey to the shining pinnacle of a still, clear enlightened mind is far, far more you-dependent than most others, your innate nature, the specific emotional baggage you're carrying and the strength of your own will to stay the course will all determine how difficult this journey will be for you and how long you will take to get from one rung to the next.

Right. With that disclaimer, let's get to Maharishi P's eight rungs.

1. Yama, or things one must NOT do.
2. niyama, or things one MUST do.

3. Asana or posture, i.e., finding a comfortable position in which to do the meditation and breath practices.
4. PrANAyAma or breath control, without which there is no possibility of bringing the mind to a calm enough state to even begin the process of meditation.
5. PratyAhAra, or decoupling from the relentless activity of the senses as they consume the world and feed its delights and horrors to you on the flickering screen of your mind, in a never-ending Breaking News cycle.
6. dhAraNA or concentration, the most basic kind, where you practise observing something, either a physical object outside of you, or your own breath.
7. dhyAna or meditation, where you focus so intently on something that it becomes your whole world and everything else fades into nothingness around you.
8. And finally, samAdhi, where the line that separates you from the object you are focusing intently on blurs and then fades entirely, and you *become* that thing yourself. What?! Wow. Yeah. Which is why, at the highest levels of meditation practice, it may be a good idea to focus on something wholesome and admirable that you *want* to become, not, say, on the kitchen sink or a dead cockroach in the middle of the floor.

Be that as it may, you have now read through the list and have some faint idea of what the journey involves. What are your thoughts?

Ugh, you're probably thinking as you read the first and second item on the list. I thought the Yoga Sutras were about high-level, super-sophisticated stuff like meditation

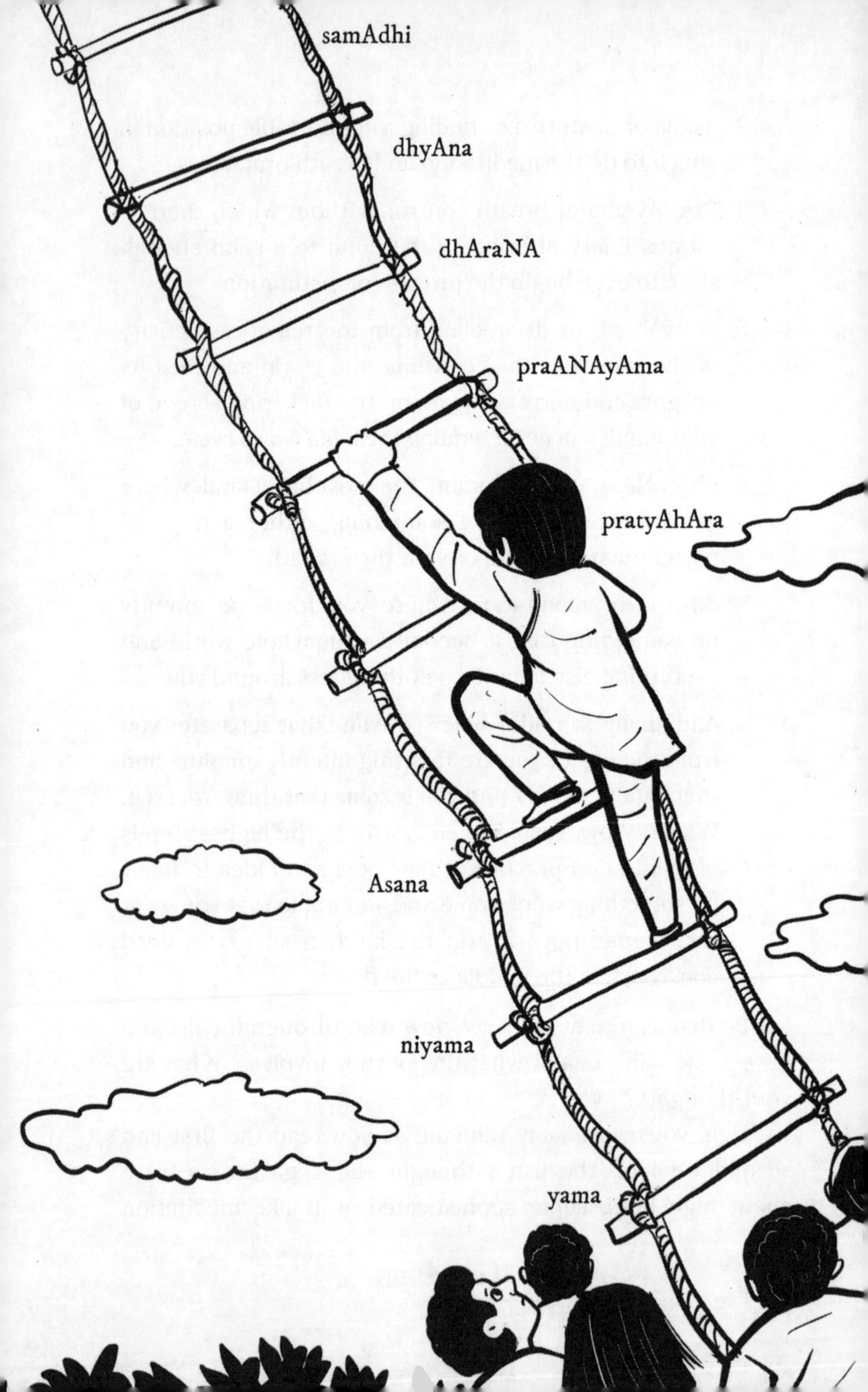
samAdhi
dhyAna
dhAraNA
praANAyAma
pratyAhAra
Asana
niyama
yama

(which would lead to that round, shining halo that saint-type people have around their heads in calendar pictures and mythological comics – imagine how cool that would look in a selfie!). But hey, Maharishi P, the first and second steps sound more like the rules in my school prospectus: homework HAS to be submitted on time, uniform skirts are NOT to end above the knees, boys HAVE to keep their hair short...

Ah well, sorry to burst your bubble, young 'uns, chuckles Maharishi P, but maybe, just maybe, your schools have the right idea. It's only once you've got the unglamorous stuff in place that you can even attempt the higher, cooler stuff. The bitter truth is that the road to greatness is lined with the boring paving stones of hard work, discipline and regular visits to the barber. Sigh.

Do it!

Intimidated by a mega-task? Divide and conquer!

If there is one thing we can all learn from Maharishi P, even without getting into any of the practices he recommends for the formidable journey to self-awareness and liberation, it is that things always seem a little bit easier, a little more manageable, a little less daunting, when we break them down into bite-sized chunks, like he does. How can we apply this in our lives?

Let's say you have to prepare for a tough exam that is coming up in four weeks. You have no idea how large the portions are or how familiar (or unfamiliar) you are with some of the topics, but you have decided to go ahead and have a panic attack anyway because 'everyone' has said the subject is really, really hard. Well, let's see if we can come up with our own eight-rung ladder to conquering this particular monster.

1. STOP. HYPERVENTILATING. NOW. It is a COMPLETE waste of time and energy, and accomplishes NOTHING useful. Okay? Okay. Right, that's a good start.

2. Identify and assemble all the 'raw material' in one place – the textbooks, the notes, the lab records, the guides, the sample question papers, the YouTube videos from your tried-and-tested online coaching channels that explain the concepts you are supposed to know, in a different, sometimes better, way from your textbook. Stack the books up on your desk in one or two neat piles. In your textbooks and notebooks, bookmark the chapters you are going to be tested on so that you have a sense of how many pages of study are involved. Now take in all of it at a glance. This is your new universe. This is ALL you have to study to be prepared. The amorphous, fearsome monster in your head now has shape and form. You can decide how to handle it.

3. Get in deeper. Take the time to explore each chapter in some detail, and make a master list of all the different topics you have to cover. Include information like which topics involve solving mathematical problems or balancing chemical equations, which involve learning to draw and label diagrams or maps, which ones involve learning things by heart, and so on.

4. Take time to plan. With all this information at hand, make a timetable for the next four weeks, leaving enough time for a couple of revisions towards the end. Don't be unrealistic about your capabilities – you have lived with yourself long enough to know you cannot do a four-hour-long study session at one stretch, don't you? So break up the study sessions in your timetable into two-hour chunks, with a 20-minute downtime in between. If that also seems like a lot, break the two-hour chunks into 25-minute bits, with a 5-minute break in between to stretch, walk around, get a drink of water, sit quietly with your eyes closed and breathe.

Sure, this step, and all the ones before it, will take time and effort. Yes, you will feel many times during the process that it is a waste of time and that you would rather be studying instead of preparing to study. Do not heed those voices. Being prepared takes a large part of the fear out of the task – now that you know, clearly and absolutely, what the extent of the task is, now that you have slotted bits of the task into neat time bubbles until you run out of time or study topics, your mind knows it can be done. (PS: Needless to say, do not spend more than 1.5 days over these steps.)

5. Set up your study space. This is a fairly relaxed, even enjoyable, task. Clean your desk thoroughly. Adjust the height of your work chair (if it's that kind of chair) or make it more comfortable with a cushion or two. Get some music going while you sharpen your pencils, break out a new set of gel pens, get your notebooks together, fill your water bottle. If you use a laptop, place it at the kind of height and angle on your desk where it is comfortable for your eyes and your hands to use. Maybe even spend 15–20 minutes putting up some inspirational quotes or pictures of your role models (NOT your crushes!), and your timetable on the wall you will be facing. This step will give you the much-needed and most helpful pause between planning for what is to be done and actually beginning to do it.

6. Gather and ground. The day and the time of the first slot on your study timetable is almost here! But there's one last thing left to do. Settle into your study space 10–15 minutes before your first study slot, to gather and ground yourself before you begin. Some deep breathing, with your eyes closed, may be a good idea. You may also want to repeat some affirmations to yourself or ask for strength from the universe for the task that lies ahead. Tell yourself that you have done your best so far in terms of preparation and you are now ready to plunge in. Also tell yourself that your job is only to give your 100 per cent to the task, not to worry about the outcome. Hark, the clock has struck the hour – open your books and begin!

Remember to do this gathering and grounding at the start of each day of study, never mind whether you have or have not achieved what you set out to do the day before. Use the time to let go of all the baggage of the previous day, and ready

CALM DOWN
ASSEMBLE
ASSESS
PLAN
SET UP
GET-SET-GO
RE-EVALUATE
CALM DOWN

yourself for a fresh start. This day is a brand-new one, offering a brand-new opportunity. Seize it!

7. Re-evaluate and rejig. Every three days, say – NOT every three hours! – spend some time checking how closely you have been sticking to your original timetable. It is likely that you have miscalculated how much time a particular topic would take you to understand and/or feel confident about. It is now time to make some decisions – do you want to only spend enough time henceforth 'sort of' understanding a concept or a problem-solving method, so that you can cover more concepts in a 'sort of' way? Or would you rather understand something well, never mind if it takes a bit longer, and never mind if it means you know nothing about a couple of other concepts?

There is no right answer to this question – you have to pick one that you feel is best for you. Do you want to add more study hours for the next couple of days so that you are back on track with your timetable on Day 5? Do you want to rejig your timetable so that you push out topics you are more comfortable with to the last week before revision, and tackle the difficult ones now? Now that you are looking at your timetable with a better understanding of the challenges involved, you will be able to make a better plan for yourself.

Do not waste time beating yourself up for taking so much longer than you had intended over a particular topic. Remember what the Maharishi said – it is a pointless exercise to regret the past or worry about the future? You have the present, and the present is full of possibility. Don't fritter it away.

8. Make peace with what you have achieved. The day of the exam is finally here. You may not have completed everything you meant to – the two revisions, all 289 problems, the three sample papers – but you have done your very best and that's the most you can do. Whatever marks you score in this exam, you have learnt a lot more about the topics of your study in these past four weeks. You have also learnt about yourself – how you respond to pressure, how much you can achieve when you put in effort, how much easier it is to tackle something big when you have spent time preparing yourself mentally for it. You have discovered what your specific challenges are, and you can, in the future, take steps to tackle them so that your effort is better. If that isn't a win, what is?

Now give yourself a nice pat on the back, spend 10 minutes gathering and grounding yourself in silence, and go rock that exam!

All the best!

Practice 3

For a Calm Mind, Banish These Five Fatal Flaws

अहिंसासत्यास्तेय ब्रह्मचर्यापरिग्रहाः यमाः ॥ २.३० ॥

ahimsA-satya-asteya brahmacharya-aparigrahAh yamAh

Non-violence, truthfulness, not stealing, being loyal, letting go of unnecessary possessions – these are the yamas (2.30)

Hang on a minute, Maharishi P, you say, we thought the yamas were things one must NOT do. And yet you list the 'good' stuff here – ahimsA, or non-violence, satya, or truthfulness, and so on. Wouldn't it have made more sense if you had listed their opposites – himsA (violence) and asatya (untruthfulness) – as the yamas?

Well, says the Maharishi, technically speaking, what I am listing here under the yamas are the 'abstentions', or the restraints you must put on your behaviour – you must abstain from being violent, which means, if you flip it around, that you must practise non-violence. Or you must restrain yourself from lying, which means, if you flip it around, that you must practise truthfulness. In each of the five yamas, there is something that you must actively stop yourself from doing so that you may practise its opposite. Which is why this sutra is worded this way. Makes sense?

Umm, sort of. But phew, glad to know that we were on the right track about what must not be done.

Now, let's dig deeper into each of the five yamas.

The First Yama: ahimsA, or Non-violence

This is an old, old idea in India, one that comes up over and over again in the ancient texts, whether in the Upanishads, the Jain and Buddhist texts or Emperor Ashoka's injunctions to his people through his rock edicts. More recently, it was one of the ideas (the other was 'satya', the second yama) around which Mahatma Gandhi built India's freedom struggle, contending that if a country was birthed in violence, it would be burdened with the wrong kind of baggage, the kind that would hamper its spiritual growth and development. The fact that his idea found favour with ordinary Indians and they rose as one to follow him is testimony to the high esteem in which most people of this land hold non-violence (although it may not always seem that way, especially when you catch the prime-time news).

What does it really mean, though, ahimsA? In a very literal sense, it means not causing physical harm to anyone or anything. Orthodox Jains, for one, take physical ahimsA more seriously than many other cultures or communities do. They not only do not eat meat but also avoid all root vegetables, because (1) the plant has to be destroyed to get to the vegetable, and (2) the process of pulling out the plant may harm organisms in the soil. They walk barefoot to reduce the possibility of hurting creatures on the ground unknowingly, sweep the ground before them as they walk to ensure that as many creatures as possible are taken out of harm's way, and wear a mask to avoid inadvertently breathing in airborne organisms. That may still not be enough to not cause any injury at all, and they realize that, but no one can fault them for not trying.

Maharishi P, however, does not define or put down the 'rules' of ahimsA – that was just not the way of the ancient rishis, who believed that it was up to each individual to decide how and to what extent they wanted to put an idea, an eternal truth, into practice. According to the general wisdom of the time, and according to the commentators of the Yoga Sutras, however, a fairly universal and practical understanding of the idea of ahimsA was that animals were not to be part of a yogi's diet. Another understood 'rule' was that one should never resort to physical violence against another human being, even under serious provocation.

Yet, reflect on it a moment, and you will see that the idea of ahimsA goes far deeper than that. While physical violence is the most visible form of violence, many of us are fortunate enough to not face too much of that in our daily lives. What about mental violence, though, and emotional violence, and violence done to our spirit? Those forms of violence are far more common, and they are inflicted so casually and unthinkingly that we don't even realize it is being done until it is too late. What's more, we are just as guilty of inflicting them on others.

Time and time again, the ancient texts remind us that it isn't just wrong 'action' that is harmful. A wrong word or a wrong thought is just as bad and more dangerous, because we aren't half as mindful about it. We get annoyed, and hot, angry words leave our tongues before a millisecond has passed.

Someone says something, perhaps without even meaning to be hurtful, but we don't pause even a moment to consider before allowing a series of violent thoughts to bubble up in our chitta lakes. What very few of us realize is that these kinds of thoughts have very little impact on the person we are hating on – for they are not even aware of it! They do have a huge impact on our own minds, however. Practising ahimsA, therefore, is as much about not causing harm to *yourself* as it is about not causing harm to others.

If this kind of self-harm is unintentional (we think we are causing harm to others, while in fact we are hurting ourselves), there is the other kind of himsA, where we intentionally, voluntarily, cause harm to ourselves. We tell ourselves stories about ourselves and our families and our countries in which we are not good enough, smart enough, rich enough, strong enough, beautiful enough, successful enough, or deserving enough of love and respect from ourselves and others. We convince ourselves that everything we are and have is somehow inferior, and feel a deep sense of shame and self-hate. We are angry, self-critical and full of hate for the world, which we see as somehow responsible for putting us in this position. And we get so consumed in this hate of everyone else, we get so, so good at it with practice, that we just cannot see that it is not the world but we ourselves who are responsible for making us feel the way we do.

How can we get out of this vicious cycle of violent thoughts? By becoming aware of them. Really, it's that simple.

Maharishi P makes that process simpler. First of all, he lets you pass the buck for your violent reactions to something deep and subconscious that you really cannot control – your samskAras. (As a quick refresher, our samskAras are deeply buried scars or impressions that we carry in our psyche because of something that has happened to us in the past. We 'instinctively' dislike a particular vegetable or colour, we 'instinctively' react in a certain way – with fear, distaste or joy – to a person or situation, because of these subconscious impressions.) If you don't even know those triggers are there, how can you possibly stop those reactions from bubbling up to the surface, right? Right. Great, so that means you are off the hook on that one.

Almost as soon as these reactions rise to the conscious level, you think or say or do something violent. Now, since this violence is a snap reaction to a subconscious samskAra, there is once again nothing you can do to control it, right?

Wrong this time! – says Maharishi P, rubbing his hands with glee. Did you think I'd let you get away so easily? Between your subconscious response and your conscious one is a middle stage, a moment of conscious choice, an if-then-else decision box that lies entirely within your control. When you practise watching your thoughts, and become aware of them even as they rise from your subconscious, you have the opportunity to nip the unhelpful ones in the bud, to steer them away before they turn into thought, word, action, to neutralize each with a non-violent response of equal strength. It is that briefest of gaps that you must focus all your energies on – *that* is where you truly practise ahimsA.

Do you see how the very process of consciously taking positive action to deflect a negative reaction can end up making you feel good about yourself? Do you see how this could slowly lead to a sense of accomplishment, a feeling of being in control of your life and, eventually, to a calmer mind? Apart from the fact that by actively choosing in every moment not to be violent, you are creating a healthier, more peaceful atmosphere around you, which will embrace everyone in your orbit, inspiring them to make better choices too.

Yup, Maharishi P certainly knew what he was doing when he picked ahimsA as the No. 1 yama, the one that in fact leads to every other. How? Let's see.

The Second Yama: satya, or Truthfulness

If you tell the truth, you don't have to remember anything.

– Mark Twain

If you needed onc simple argument for why it's always better to tell the truth, it's this one by the irrepressible American humorist and writer Mark Twain. From the calm mind perspective, this is a no-brainer: not having to remember, keep track of, or worry about getting caught in the lies you have told will most certainly ensure a more peaceful chitta lake than otherwise. As an old German saying cautions, '*Lügen haben kurze Beine*' (Lies have short legs, i.e., they will be easily caught)!

However, the ancient Indic texts are never willing to let it go at a simple 'Thou Shalt Not Lie'. While one must, of course, always aim to tell the truth, *how* you tell the truth is equally important. Take a moment to study this popular shloka from thc *Manusmriti*, a text on duties, rights, laws and virtues, which dates to around 2,000 years ago.

सत्यं ब्रूयात् प्रियं ब्रूयान्न ब्रूयात् सत्यमप्रियम्
प्रियं च नानृतं ब्रूयादेष धर्मः सनातनः ॥ ४.१३८ ॥

satyam brUyAt priyam brUyAt na brUyAt satyam apriyam
priyam cha nAnrtam brUyAt-esha dharmah sanAtanah (4.138)

Essentially, the shloka presents three 'rules' of speaking the truth:

1. Speak the truth, but speak it sweetly.
2. Avoid speaking truths that are harsh.
3. Do not speak an untruth, even if it is a sweet one.

Right. Let's take these rules one by one. What could it mean, to speak the truth sweetly? Let's say you want to tell your friend that he is deluding himself about winning a particular sprint at the interschool sports championship. You have very good reasons for your belief – you are a stats guy, and you have studied the finishing time of the other competitors in the field. You have timed your friend and you know that his personal best is at least two whole seconds behind three of the others running the race. You want to make sure that your friend doesn't go into the race with unrealistic expectations, so that he doesn't end up being too disappointed later. How would you convey this information to him? One way is to say, 'Bro, your best timing is about two seconds behind the top runners of the other schools. There's no way you can win. Just saying.' You are certainly speaking the truth, but is there some other, *sweeter* way you could say the same thing?

Maybe you could say, 'You're up against three or four serious challengers this time, but hey, anything could happen on the day. Just focus on giving your best, and we'll see.' Or, 'So there are all these stats I've compiled and it looks like it's going to be a tough race. But listen, the others are faster "on paper", so they are bound to be under a lot of pressure to win. You have none... So just go out there and run like a crazy man – what have you got to lose?'

You see? You're giving your friend the same information but you are breaking the truth to him gently. If you were on the receiving end, which kind of truth would you prefer to hear?

On to the next 'rule'. If a truth is a harsh one, there is perhaps no need to say it. At all. Eh? This one is bound to get many of us indignant – there is always a need to tell the truth, isn't there? Isn't that what we have always been taught?

Really? Think about it. Sure, you have been taught not to lie, you have been taught to tell the truth, and if you are very, very lucky, you have grown up among adults who have walked the talk; adults who haven't simply instructed you to be truthful, but have also demonstrated truthfulness themselves in their dealings with you and others. But has anyone ever told you that you must speak the truth indiscriminately, whether it is required or not? Probably not. That is what this rule is about. Imagine if we spoke all the thoughts that crossed our minds when we looked at or interacted with others, just because they were true! It would probably go something like this: 'Ugh, does he *actually* think that weird hair suits him? Omg, that is such an ugly shade of nail polish! Oh, quit the flattery – I know what you really want is to copy my homework! Whoa! A full-on British accent, just because you went to London over the summer – seriously?'

Now these, in your opinion, may be the 'truth', but these kinds of unkind truths need not be spoken. One good way to decide whether to speak a truth or not is to put it through what is called the hitam-(beneficial)–mitam (measured)–priyam (sweet)–satyam (truth) test. In other words, ask yourself these questions before you speak:

1. **Hitam** – Will this truth benefit my listener? (Will it help my friend to know that I do not approve of her choice of nail polish? Not really, given that nail polish is a matter of individual taste. *Then keep your opinion to yourself.*)
2. **Mitam** – Is it really necessary to say it? If yes, how do I say it in the briefest and most measured way? (I would like to tease him about his freshly acquired accent, but instead of being sarcastic about it, maybe I could just respond to him in a very exaggerated accent myself. Then I have had my fun, we both can laugh and it's over. *Fine, keep it light, and short.*)
3. **Priyam** – I definitely need to tell her this for her own good, but how can I do it in the nicest possible, least unkind way? (*Spend a moment, or many moments, thinking about it.*)
4. **Satyam** – And the fourth, most important of all – Is what I am about to say actually true? Is it based on hearsay and rumour or have I verified it properly? In other words, does it pass the pratyaksha–anumAna–Agama tests that qualify any piece of information as 'right knowledge' (see page 104)? (Umm, I suppose I'm not one hundred per cent sure. *Hold back until you are.* This has become really important in the current age – especially on WhatsApp, where people unthinkingly forward messages and news reports that are entirely unconfirmed.)

On to Rule 3, which is the most straightforward one of all. Don't say an untruth, however sweet it may be. Do not, in other words, flatter to deceive. If your friend asks you how she looks in a particular outfit, do not gush that she looks fantastic if you don't think so. But instead of saying the truth harshly – 'I hate it' – apply Rules 1 and 2, say very little, and cushion the blow. 'It's nice, but...' or 'This is just my opinion, but I like you better in blue...' or 'Not what I would have picked, but you should always wear what YOU feel confident in...'

Now, if you aren't just *saying* these things, but actually *mean* them as well, that is, if you really feel, say, in your heart, that one should wear what makes one feel confident, your statement will ring that much truer, and you will be sticking closer to the second yama of truthfulness. Now, how can you truly feel kindly towards your friend's choices and not just fake it for the sake of being kind? By practising ahimsA, the first yama, assiduously! If you can stop mean and petty thoughts about other people – their clothes, their manner, their looks – from rising in your mind in the first place, you will never need to lie about your feelings. See how ahimsA, the first yama, is the foundation of the second?

And of the third, and fourth, and fifth, as we shall discover.

The Third Yama: asteya, or Non-stealing

Once again, this seems like a no-brainer. Clearly, taking what belongs to someone else is wrong and must not be done. But can we dig a little deeper into this as well?

Stealing someone's material possessions is one thing, but what about taking away from people other things that are less tangible and usually far more valuable? Their dignity, for instance. Their rights and freedoms. What about ruining their peace of mind, with your negative attitude and your anger and unreasonableness? What about stealing their best ideas and passing them off as your own, without giving them credit?

What about – here it comes, the nuance within the nuance – *wishing* you could take something away from someone? Or wishing you had what they have, even if you aren't actually able to steal it from them? Their popularity, their success, their wealth, their position in society (or in school), their circle of friends? According to Maharishi P, even *entertaining* the thought of stealing or grabbing from someone what is theirs is just as bad as actually doing it.

The thing is, using someone as a role model and being inspired by them is very, very different from envying them what they have. Envy, the green-eyed monster, pollutes your mind lake and does not allow you to feel muditA (see page 167), joy in others' happiness, turning you into a mean-spirited creature. Maybe you haven't thought about it this way before, but feeling envy is the same as taking away or stealing the achievements of another person. It is reducing them to people who somehow, even if only in your own mind, do not deserve what they have.

Once again, how do you stop this kind of stealing? By cultivating ahimsA, what else! If you practise blocking envy every time it rises in your mind and flip it into inspiration, you will automatically not indulge in this kind of 'stealing' .The other way, of course, is practising contentment – instead of dwelling on what you do NOT have, count your blessings and give thanks for what you DO. When you fill yourself with gratitude, there is no room left for envy – it's as simple as that.

The Fourth Yama – Brahmacharya, or Restraint

Brahmacharya means restraint of all kinds, but let us explore one particular kind in some detail – restraint of the senses, or *sensual* restraint. What's that? Let's see.

Anything attractive to the senses – delicious food and drink, great clothes, beautiful people, fine smells, exciting music, rich, luxurious spaces, fancy cars, titillating content, both online and offline – brings us what is called sensual pleasure. And while we must enjoy and be grateful for beautiful things, for they are all part of the spectacular world that we have the privilege of living in, we must always guard against the danger of overdoing any of it, of getting so attached to sensual pleasures that we become their slaves and they turn into something we cannot do without, an addiction we cannot break.

What are some examples in our daily lives where we exhibit dangerously addictive behaviour where sensual pleasures are concerned? Watching Instagram reels for two straight hours, without even realizing how much time has passed. Binge-watching an entire series on an OTT platform the day it releases, even though we know we should be doing something more important. Stuffing our faces with junk food *while* binge-watching a series, with no awareness of how much we have consumed. Going on dangerous crash diets because we hate the shape of our bodies, instead of working towards losing weight in a disciplined way, with regular exercise and moderate eating over months. Exercising like crazy, going from nothing to a 30-minute HIIT workout that cannot be good for us, for the same reason as above.

Watching inappropriate content on loop. Listening to the 'unclean' versions of the songs of your favourite band or singer ad nauseam – and letting the explicit lyrics and foul language burrow into your brain until you lose your sense of discrimination, and begin to believe that all the anger and negativity and obscenity the songs contain is entirely justified. Staying up late into the night playing online games endlessly, unable to break away. Making a fake ID so that you can sneak into a bar that you are legally, um, *barred* from because of your age, and then quaffing a pint or two as well, all of which could get you into very real trouble with very real authorities. Hanging out with people who do things that you know are wrong but telling yourself it is fine since you are not doing those things yourself. Spending far too much time with people who have a very different lifestyle from what you can afford, and spending money you know you shouldn't be, because you so desperately want to be 'one of the gang'. Driving a friend's bike or car (because your parents have not bought you your own yet, because you are too young to have a licence) at dangerous speeds for the rush it gives you. You see? The list is endless.

Can you imagine what a tsunami this kind of addictive behaviour can create in your chitta lake? Do you see how it would lead to a feeling of being entirely out of control of your life, not being able to stick to any plan you make, as you yo-yo between the high of your addiction and the low of not being able to do more of it, because real life and school and exams come in the way? Can you imagine the conflict that will rage between that side of your mind which knows what you are doing is wrong, or at least, not sensible, and the side that urges you to do it anyway? How can you even aspire to a calm mind and the higher rewards it brings if you are constantly being swayed this way and that by the pulls of your senses?

Here's the short answer: You can't.

Now, how is ahimsA connected to the fourth yama? Very intimately! What we are really doing when we obsessively chase sensual pleasures is harming ourselves very deeply, inflicting himsA or violence on our own psyches. By cultivating kind, non-hurtful behaviour towards ourselves, we automatically press the brakes on this kind of unrestrained passion, which leads us towards brahmacharya. *Ta-daa!*

The Fifth Yama: aparigraha, or Letting Go of (inessential) Possessions

The earth has enough to satisfy every man's need, but not every man's greed. – Mahatma Gandhi

Again, something you have heard several times before – minimalism, i.e., buying and owning just what you need, is good for you, good for your home and good for the planet. And yet, even as our homes and closets overflow with 'stuff', we are constantly looking outward, for the next 'thing' to add to our possessions. The fifth and last yama, aparigraha, is about snapping out of this vicious cycle, of preparing ourselves for letting go. Not of *everything* – the Maharishi is not cruel enough to suggest that – but of the 'inessentials'. That is a fair ask, don't you think?

The thing is, as Maharishi P might have said, what is outside reflects what is inside. A cluttered desk is usually evidence of a cluttered mind – although there are any number of people who will swear that they do their best work in the midst of clutter. Plus, possessing something – whether it is a car or shoes or a house plant or a pet – means becoming responsible for it. When you are responsible for something, you have to devote a significant part of your effort and attention towards making sure that it is in its best possible, most functional, healthiest shape at all times. That takes up a lot of mind space. Given that we have limited mind space, it makes sense to list out, every once in a while, the possessions

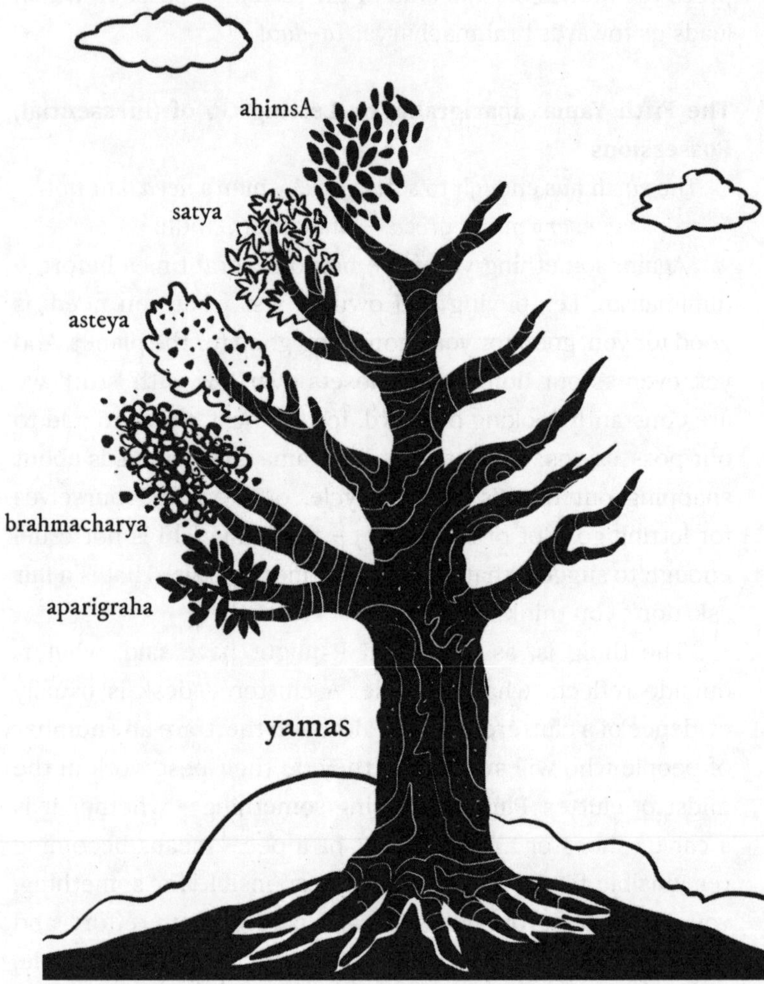
ahimsA
satya
asteya
brahmacharya
aparigraha
yamas

that are consuming it. Then we can review them, one by one, ruthlessly divide them into essential and non-essential (mind you, do this thoughtfully: just because a pet – or a sibling – is behaving badly doesn't make them suddenly inessential!), and let go of the things we can do without, so that we free up space for calm. More importantly, be very, very mindful when you add possessions to your life – think thrice about whether you really, really *need* that thing – as opposed to *wanting* that thing – before you add it. Simple!

While we're at it, why not also examine the stuff inside our heads, and let go of the inessentials there? Past anger, old grudges and hurts, longing for things that are beyond our reach, regret for things we could have done better, fear for everything that lies in our future – all these live rent-free in our minds, cluttering it up. Undertake a weekly, or even daily, spring-cleaning of your chitta lake – dive in, check out all the junk that has been deposited there that day, and throw it out. You will instantly feel lighter, happier, calmer, freer – do it!

Practice 4

When You Begin a Practice, Make It Non-negotiable – No Excuses Allowed!

जातिदेशकालसमयानवच्छिन्नाः सार्वभौमा महाव्रतम् ॥ २.३१ ॥

jAti-desha-kAla-samaya-anavachcHinnAh sArva-bhaumAh mahA-vratam

These (yamas) are sArvabhaumAh (universal) and should be treated as mahAvratam (great vows). Their practice is independent of class, place, time or circumstance. (2.31)

Sutra 31 of the sAdhanapAda, the corollary to the previous one, which lists the yamas (page 214), is probably the harshest and most rigid of Maharishi P's injunctions for yogis in pursuit of a calm mind. It effectively cuts off any excuses one may offer up to explain why one is abandoning the practice of the yamas, even for a teeny-weeny bit of time or in a very specific situation.

'I shall be vegetarian through the week but will eat meat on the weekend', will not wash with the Maharishi. You are still committing himsA on weekends, he will allege, wagging his finger at us. If that sounds unreasonable, think about this statement: 'I will not get into fistfights through the week, but come the weekend and all bets are off!' Ah, you will say instantly, it doesn't work like that – if you are going to stop getting into fights, you have to *stop* getting into fights, never mind what day of the week it is. You see? If an excuse is lame in one situation, it is lame in every situation.

The trouble is, the moment we start offering excuses, we will offer them repeatedly, to ourselves and to others, whenever things begin to get difficult or inconvenient.

* Yes, I know I said I would only take the metro instead of cabs to save money, but I don't feel like getting out of bed early today and I was up studying really late last night, so *just for today*, I'm going to call a cab.
* Yes, I know I said I made a rule that I would donate a garment I own every time I bought a new one, so that the pieces of clothing I have will never exceed a particular number, but *just this once*, I won't, because I love everything I already have, and I will never get this new one at this price ever again.
* Yes, I know I said I would not lie, but Maa is being really annoying and she doesn't understand why I just have to go to this party and it's really not fair of her at all, so *just this one time*, I'm going to tell a lie – actually, it isn't even a lie, I just won't tell her the whole truth, and that doesn't count as a lie, does it?
* Yes, I know I said I would never yell and scream in anger, but I have just moved to this new school where shouting over everyone else seems to be the only way

to be heard, so *just as long as* I am within the school premises I will drop that promise I made to myself. One must adapt to one's circumstances, right?

And so on.

So yes, Maharishi P is very demanding, and VERY clear on this rule – but he never said becoming a yogi was an easy task or that everyone could do it. But that's no reason to toss the Yoga Sutras aside and abandon their lessons entirely. Maybe we cannot all be yogis – soldiers and butchers, for instance, *have* to do what we might consider himsA as part of their job description or dharma – but we can all try, in most circumstances (samaya), in most places (desha) and at most times (kAla), whatever our jobs or life situations may be (jAti), to integrate the yamas – ahimsA, satya, asteya, brahmacharya, aparigraha – into our lives and stick to them. When we choose

to abandon them momentarily, we can strive to be as honest with ourselves as possible about the reason for abandoning them. When we spot a lame excuse, we can actively choose not to use it, doing instead what is difficult but right.

That, in itself, would be a great contribution towards ahimsA, towards ourselves and others, and help us grow into fine people with uncluttered minds that can distinguish clearly between right and wrong, which in turn, will help us make better decisions. In Maharishi P's book, it may not count as an unqualified win, but he will certainly be there on the sidelines, looking on encouragingly, cheering us on. Give it a few more lifetimes, young 'uns, he will be saying, and maybe even YOU could become a yogi – imagine that!

Think about it!

Some interpreters of the Yoga Sutras, including Swami Vivekananda, interpret aparigraha, the fifth yama, as not just restraining ourselves from hoarding things we do not need but also as 'refusing gifts from other people'. According to Swami V, receiving gifts from someone transfers to us the intent (which may not always be the best) that is in the mind of the giver, and makes us slavish, incapable of thinking freely and independently.

Ouch. That's harsh. And mayyybe a little bit 'extra'? Surely receiving a gift cannot have such a terrible effect on our minds?

Now, of course a friend may bring you a thoughtfully chosen gift with genuine affection, but there is also a chance that the gift-giver may be thinking these thoughts below, while picking a gift for you. Or maybe you've had one or more of these thoughts yourself while picking a gift for someone else.

* I can't possibly go to his birthday party with no gift at all, so I must step out and buy something now, when I'd rather be chilling at home – what a pain!
* I don't know why she always brings me such expensive gifts. Now I will have to give her something of a similar price even though I cannot really afford it and don't even want to get her a gift. Sigh.
* Ah man, I can't be bothered to step out in 40 degree C heat to look for a gift for my cousin now; lemme just go through gifts people gave me for my birthday three months ago, which I won't use, and rewrap one for him. What he doesn't know can't hurt him.
* I don't even like her very much and we've hardly ever had a heart-to-heart conversation, but because we're part of the same gang, I'll have to pool in with the others for her gift. Ugh.
* She did such a sweet, elaborate surprise for my sixteenth birthday, and got so many other friends involved in it – I will feel like an absolute worm if I don't do something in return that's at least half as good. But I'm just useless at things like these! What do I dooooo? Stressssssss!!!

Even if you never reveal your pre-gift thoughts to the recipient, do you think it is possible that those thoughts and emotions may have infected the gift somehow? More importantly, do you see how receiving something – especially a material something – from someone, places a sort of burden of debt on the recipient? Of course, the debt may be something that you can easily resolve, by gifting the giver something of equal value on a different occasion. Until then, however, can you truly speak your mind to the giver of the gift, especially when you do not agree with his opinions or attitude or behaviour, or will you feel a little delicate about it? Isn't that equivalent to being slavish, of being 'incapable of thinking freely or independently'? There is no easy solution to this, given the culture of the societies we live in. One thing each of us could start doing to make it better for the recipients of our gifts, however, is to think only warm and generous thoughts of them while picking the gift (if you can't, forget about the gift – that is more honest, at least, and will keep your interaction 'cleaner'). When you do give the gift, hand it over with love, while harbouring no expectations of any service, favour or material object in return. Whether or not this kind of effort on your part makes any difference to the recipient, it will certainly make you feel lighter, happier and freer. Always a win!

Practice 5

Put Cleanliness and Contentment on Top of the Must-do Checklist

शौच संतोष तपः स्वाध्यायेश्वरप्रणिधानानि नियमाः ॥ २.३२॥

shaucha santosha tapah svAdhyAya-Ishvara-pranidhAnAni niyamAh

Cleanliness, contentment, self-discipline, self-study and devotion to the Lord are the niyamas (2.32)

If the yamas or restraints – the Must-Nots – are more concerned with our behaviour towards other people, the niyamas or observances – the Musts – are more inward-looking, concerned with our own selves. If you have been paying very close attention, you would have noticed that the third, fourth and fifth niyamas in the sutra above are a reiteration of the three principles of kriyA yoga, which we have already discussed in some detail in Practice 1 (see page 187). Clearly, these are very important Musts in Maharishi P's opinion.

But there are also two new Musts – attributes we haven't encountered earlier. Let's see what they are.

The First Niyama: Shaucha, or Cleanliness

Cleanliness? Really?? Yes. Really. We all know that Indians place an enormous value on bathing daily, apart from cleaning out our ears, nose, teeth, throat, navel and butt, and washing our feet and hands. Now you know why: it is an imperative, even according to scripture, to maintain strict and thorough personal hygiene. There is probably a bit of science and public health involved in such a stricture as well – these texts, after all, were composed millennia ago by some of the wisest, most curious and most rational people, in a tropical land, where germs have always flourished as luxuriantly as the flora and as abundantly as the fauna. Plus, even in the centuries before showerheads and flushing toilets, water, in liquid form, has always been plentiful and accessible in these parts. Realizing that their injunctions on washing up would be taken more seriously if they made it a prerequisite to religious ritual and/or spiritual practice, the clever ancients linked up the two.*

There is another practical reason as well. You cannot really focus on the mind, which is the stated goal of most of the ancient texts and practices, if you are itchy and sweaty and smelly. Just as cleaning up your workspace declutters your mind, cleaning your body makes it possible to 'forget' about the body for a while and channel your energies towards the mind. If it isn't a habit already, you might consider including a

★ Nor is the emphasis on cleanliness limited to Hinduism. Judaism, Christianity and Islam, even though they were founded in far more arid lands with much less access to water, have strict rules on washing up before prayer and other rituals.

bath in your daily morning regimen rather than, or in addition to, your evening one, even if it means you have to wake up even earlier than usual to catch the school bus.

As always, however, external cleanliness of the body is only one part of shaucha. There is also an internal cleanliness, which can be most easily achieved by thinking of your body as a sacred place, a temple if you will, or a mosque or a church or a gurdwara. Just as you would not litter a sacred place, do not 'litter' your body with food that is unsuitable, inappropriate or unhealthy. No longer can any of us use ignorance as an excuse – most of the messaging aimed at us today is about what and what not to eat and drink. Unfortunately, however, these messages are inextricably linked with a more toxic one – eat and drink such and such, and do *this* kind of high-intensity exercise, so that your body *looks* a particular way.

It is important to note that the ancient texts that concerned themselves with spiritual development never talked about how a body should look. There seems to have been an intrinsic understanding that bodies come in all shapes and sizes, and what was important was that you took care of them so that they worked well, not so that they looked good. If they also happened to look good – and the understanding of what is 'good-looking' changes from age to age and culture to culture – because you took care of them, well, that was a bonus. If you were focused on connecting with your higher self, you wouldn't care about your nice-looking body, or even notice it, because Maharishi P and other yoga practitioners believed that the body was only a vehicle for the mind, not something to obsess about.

Right. Are we done with shaucha, then? Not quite. For there is also the small (not!) matter of mental and emotional cleanliness. How do you keep your mind clean? By realizing that we are not only what we eat, but also what we consume. On a moment-to-moment basis. So be very, very mindful of the junk you are throwing into your mind – whether it is the books you are reading, the movies you are watching, the content you are consuming, or, most importantly, the conversations you are part of. Make an excuse and walk away from toxic, gossipy or pointless conversations, even those you are not directly participating in; put your phone away when you have spent a regulated amount of time on it; actively choose to read or watch inspirational and/or calming or life-affirming content over mindless comedy, violence, obscenity or dystopian narratives, especially if you have spent too much time on that kind of thing recently.

Make it a daily practice to scrub the inside of your mind just as hard and just as well as you scrub the outside of your body, and enjoy the fresh, clean, happy glow that results!

Do it!

When no one's noticing, quietly turn the tide of a toxic conversation.

Sure, you can, and should, walk away from a 'contaminated' conversation with an excuse whenever possible, but that's just it – it's not always possible, especially when that conversation is happening within a family setting or when you're in the middle of a sleepover with a close group of friends. What do you do then? Needless to say, Maharishi P has a simple but effective solution.

वितर्कबाधने प्रतिपक्षभावनम् ॥ २.३३ ॥

vitarka-bAdhane pratipaksha-bhAvanam (2.33)

Which simply translates to – when harassed by negative thoughts, cultivate thoughts that counteract them. Simple! Now, Maharishi Patanjali may have meant the negative thoughts that arise in our own minds, but we can apply this suggestion just as well to a situation where the negativity is arising from the conversations around us. Instead of just cultivating thoughts to counter that negativity, turn the thoughts into words and say them out loud.

How does that work? Let's see.

If a grumpy uncle says, 'This country will never amount to anything. Our people are just the worst – corrupt, incompetent, self-serving', one or both of the following responses will usually follow from others in the group: 'You're so right – we have no hope of progress', or 'Nonsense. We have always been ahead of every other country...our 5,000-year-old culture, our ancient heritage, our visionary knowledge systems...it's people like you, who always think the West is better, that are the problem'.

At this point, you can step in quietly, saying, 'Well, you know, there is no debate that we have always been pretty amazing in some ways, but we also do get things wrong on many occasions. If each of us just tried each day to be a better version of ourselves and contributed in some way to making this country better, things would begin to change, at least in our neighbourhoods.' The adults may laugh at what they would see as your youthful idealism, but they cannot really counter what you are saying, and becoming aware that young people like you are listening into their cynical conversation, may choose to tone it down. Your intervention will also give the pacifist adults in the group the opening to chip in with, 'That's right. We can sit here and pontificate all we want, but that serves no purpose. Come on now, dinner's served!' You see?

If a friend, X, starts talking badly about another friend, Y, in her absence, saying, 'I thought she was my friend, but man, she was so rude to me yesterday! Who does she think she is?' and Z chimes in with, 'I have no idea why you are so close to her – I've never liked her much myself. She's sweet as honey when she wants something, but otherwise she looks through you', say 'Really? Maybe she was going through something that day, X, that none of us knows about. And hey, Z, I'm genuinely surprised to hear you say that about Y. She really likes you – remember how she always brings you an extra-large slice of cake whenever her mum bakes, because she knows you love it?'

See what you did there? By introducing doubt into X's assertion – maybe Y was going through something – and reminding Z of something nice Y has done for her in the past, you are forcing X and Z to reconsider what they said and preventing the conversation from turning into a full-blown 'Let's slam Y' slugfest. And because you have chosen your words well and refrained from guilting X or Z, or sounding like an annoying goody two shoes yourself, which would have happened had you said – 'I think you two are very mean to talk about Y like that. I would never do such a thing myself', you have actually steered the conversation into calmer waters.

Try this technique the next time you find yourself in such a situation and see what happens!

The Second Niyama: Santosha, or Contentment

Oh, come on, Maharishi P, it isn't fair of you to put contentment on the Must list! How can I, after all, force myself to be content when everyone else seems to have more than I do, when the world is less fair to me than it is to others, when everything that I do seems to go wrong? How's this, instead – I promise to be content in a few days/months/years – when I have a few more things to call my own, when I have moved out of this dead-end town to my dream college, when my luck turns?

Nope, says the Maharishi. Nahin, nyet, nada. The future is only an illusion, young 'uns, and there is no guarantee that when you get there and have all the things you are dreaming of today, you will not want something more, just a little more, to be content. The trick is to find contentment in the here and now. Try these easy hacks to get there.

* Instead of thinking about those who have more than you, think about those who have less, and somehow still seem far more content.
* Instead of thinking about your dream college, make the most of your last year at school, and think about the

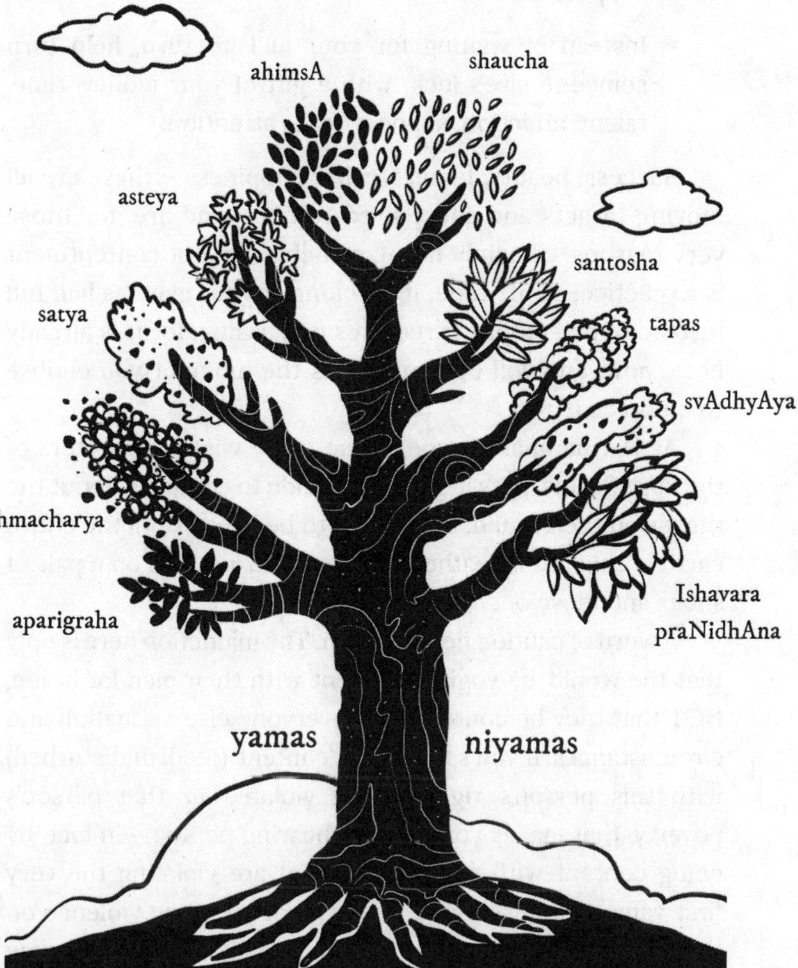

ahimsA
shaucha
asteya
santosha
satya
tapas
svAdhyAya
brahmacharya
Ishavara
praNidhAna
aparigraha
yamas
niyamas

millions of unfortunates who probably didn't even get this far in their education because they had to work to support their families.

* Instead of waiting for your luck to turn, help turn someone else's luck, with a gift of your money, time, talent, affection, support, food, attention.

Success, beauty, fame, wealth, happiness – these are all moving targets and short-lived to boot, and are, for those very reasons, certainly not worth chasing. But contentment is a practice, an attitude; it's looking at your glass as half full instead of half empty. It requires no chasing, for it is already here, now, and will become yours the moment you choose to embrace it.

As Hariharananda, one of the many wise interpreters of the Yoga Sutras, puts it, you can decide to complain about the thorns on the ground, and refuse to be happy until the entire earth is covered in leather, or you could just pull on a pair of shoes and move on.

A word of caution here, though. The injunction here is only that the would-be yogi be content with their *own* lot in life, NOT that they be content with everyone else's situation and circumstances. If you say you are 'content' (read: undisturbed) with this person's rights being violated or that person's poverty, that makes you a cold, uncaring person – in fact, by being content with such things, you are violating the very first yama – ahimsA. Sure, you are not inflicting violence on the vulnerable person, but by not stepping in to help in some way, you are allowing violence to be done on your watch, and that is only a shade less terrible than being violent to them yourself. That's just how these things roll.

Practice 6

Feeling Demotivated? Think of What's Waiting at the End of This Particular Rainbow!

Like anyone who has immersed himself in the study of the human mind, Maharishi P understood human failings intimately. And he knew for certain that the biggest stumbling block to anyone on a quest for a calm mind would be staying the tough course, day after challenging day. So, while he compressed all the five yamas into a single sutra and the five niyamas into another one, and spent another couple of sutras issuing dire cautions on how you *had* to practise them, *whatever* the time, place or circumstance, he spelled out the rewards of practising yoga in – hold your breath – ELEVEN sutras of the 195! Clearly, Maharishi P believed that the carrot was far more effective than the stick where human nature was concerned.

Eleven sutras would take up too much room in this book, so let's explore just eight of them, and only in their English versions.

In the presence of a non-violent person, all enmity is forgotten (2.35)

Could this be true? Sometimes, in pictorial depictions of saints and in stories told about them, not just in Hinduism but also in Christianity (specifically St. Francis of Assisi) and the Sufi tradition in Islam, you will find that the saint, either while walking or dancing through a forest or a field, or sitting in deep meditation, is surrounded by animals, both predators and prey. The predators have lost their aggression and the prey their fear, simply because of the deep calm radiating from the saint, who commits no violence himself.*

Imagine being able to stop a fight, calm down frayed tempers or subvert people's natural violent behaviour, simply by being entirely non-violent in thought, word and deed yourself! You probably have seen this in action around you, in small ways – when a person that everyone respects for their fairness and lack of bias enters an argument, both warring sides immediately begin to behave a little better, presenting their arguments in a more rational fashion, or toning down their voices and words, in some embarrassment. Even if you think it is too much of a stretch to believe that someone who has spent a lifetime (or several!) mindfully avoiding violence

★ Does this image trigger a memory of a tiny artefact that we discussed earlier in this very book? That's right, the Pashupati seal from Mohenjo-daro (page 19)! The animals that surround the yogi in that seal include a tiger, antelope and bull, but the herbivores are standing, perfectly calm, in the presence of the apex predator of the Indian jungle.

would be able to have such an effect on the natural behaviour of animals, this kind of thing – people minding themselves around you – is something to aim for, don't you think? Start practising ahimsA today and see what happens!

***

When one is invariably truthful, all of one's actions bear (good) fruit

(2.36)

Once again, we have seen this play out around us, day after day. Journalists who are perceived to be more 'truthful', i.e., unbiased, are trusted, and garner a lot of followers. Such followers are themselves thinking, questioning people who do not have an agenda and do not automatically support a political party or an ideology, but simply want to know the facts of a situation so that they can make up their own minds. Teachers who are more transparent about how they award marks are respected more, and a friend who will not lie to make you feel better is the one you go to when you need good, solid advice. You see how a truthful person's actions always 'bear good fruit'?

At times when people do not obey, respect, trust or listen to a truthful person (because most people like to blame others and not themselves for their shortcomings), telling the truth allows the truthful person herself to be at peace, which is the best fruit of all. Satya is where it's at!

***

When one restrains himself from stealing from others, all the jewels of the world appear

(2.37)

This one is straightforward enough. A person who displays no intention of taking away anything that is someone else's, so content is he with what he himself has, will instantly invite trust, because everyone in his orbit will feel safe around him. They can let their guard down and be themselves, confident that nothing sneaky will happen when they aren't paying attention. When people are not fearful, they will respond more reasonably, rationally, respectfully and compassionately to others around them, and everyone in that circle experiences calm and contentment.

Such a person, should he ever want to raise funds for a good cause or a new enterprise, will find no shortage of donors and investors. People will press their money and resources upon him because they feel confident that it will be used in the 'right' way. Even if he himself is not looking to raise money, others will want to hire him and put him in a position of responsibility. And if his family or he himself needed any other kind of help, friends and strangers would come forward willingly to offer it. Maybe that was what Maharishi P meant when he said that those who restrain themselves from stealing would receive 'all jewels'. For what can be a greater treasure than the love and trust of people, and knowing that you made it happen simply by not casting a greedy eye on their possessions? Who can feel wealthier than a man who truly believes he already has everything he wants and needs? A great carrot for practising asteya, what?

***

When one is established in restraint, power and vigour are attained

(2.38)

Remember we talked about the importance of brahmacharya or sensual restraint, earlier in this section (page 224)? In this sutra, Maharishi P provides a great incentive for practising it, an incentive that human beings love – power!

In the samAdhipAda section, if you recall, we spoke about the chariot pulled by five horses, where the chariot is the body, the horses are our senses, the reins are our lower mind, and the charioteer is our higher mind. In this situation, what kind of charioteer do you think would feel more powerful? The one whose grip on the reins is so weak that each horse pulls in a different direction and drags the chariot off the path, or the one who is able to maintain just the right tension on the reins, ensuring that neither are the horses hurt nor are they able to exercise their will over his? The latter, of course! Right there, you can see how restraint results in power.

Imagine how good you will feel, how *powerful*, if you are able to control the horses of your senses! NO, you will say to your eyes as they stray towards some inappropriate content, and they will obediently slink away from it, because you sound like you mean business. NO, you will admonish your ears as they tune in to some malicious gossip about a friend, and they will instantly switch channels back to what your teacher is saying. NO, you will frown at your treacherous nose and tongue, one inhaling, the other salivating, as the aroma of something that you are trying to avoid eating wafts through the air towards you, and they will shut down, so that you are no longer tempted. Woahhhhhh!

And that power will transmit itself to people around you, who will look up to you as a role model and an inspiration. From you they will draw strength in believing that achieving such restraint is possible, and try it for themselves. Win-win all around!

***

When one is free of covetousness, he gains knowledge of the whys and wherefores of births

(2.39)

Wait, what? 'Knowledge of the whys and wherefores of births' is gained simply by not coveting things and letting go of inessentials, otherwise known as aparigraha? That escalated quickly, from jewels and power! Hey, Maharishi P, what are you actually trying to say in this sutra?

Our cryptic Maharishi is probably chuckling at our confusion, but the commentators of the YS did not have that luxury. They had to ruminate on it and give us an interpretation, and so they did. One way to think of the message of this sutra is this: when your attention isn't on holding on to your possessions and your people (whom you consider your possessions!) tightly, you are able to focus on other things. When your attention isn't consumed by what is outside, you can direct it inwards to see what secrets your deepest consciousness holds.

Think about it this way. When we are on a trek, climbing a hill with friends or family, so many of us are focused on getting to the top or to the final point *first*, that we never stop to enjoy the views at every stage, breathe deeply of the pure air scented with wildflowers or help someone else along. If we had, maybe we would have had things revealed to us that we had never suspected existed – a dazzling butterfly or miniature frog, for instance, or a great kindness from a stranger. In the trek of our lives, we are so burdened by the things we are holding on so tightly to, stuffed into a giant backpack on our backs and a similarly large one strapped to our chests, that even our view of the path ahead becomes obscured, and we go down trails that someone who went before us has helpfully marked as dangerous. Worse, we lose sight of the path behind us and cannot therefore enjoy how far we've already come.

Now imagine setting those backpacks down and actually, um, tossing them off the edge of a convenient cliff. How different the journey will be from then on, how light, how free, how revealing of the beauty that surrounds you in every moment! You will suddenly remember why you undertook this trek in the first place (to enjoy every step, every high and every low on the path, to hopefully discover new things about yourself, to draw courage and hope from the stories of others along the same path), and all the events that led to you making

the decision to do it. With that clarity, you are able to go ahead with renewed vigour, free of fear, full of joy, unburdened by the weighty backpacks of inessentials.

For a yogi at the highest level of aparigraha – non-attachment – that clarity may well reveal the answer to those most existential of all questions – Who am I? and Where did I come from? In other words, the 'whys and wherefores of births.' Since most of us aren't going to get to that level of aparigraha in this lifetime, let's just trust Maharishi P on this and focus on chucking our personal backpacks, shall we?

***

Through cleanliness, one develops distaste for one's body and a lessening of contact with others

(2.40)

In addition, one achieves a pure heart, a cheerful mind, focus, control of the senses, and more

(2.41)

Sutra 40, at first glance, seems counter-intuitive. Didn't Maharishi P indicate earlier in Practise 5 that shaucha, at the first level, meant the external and internal cleanliness of the body? That we should treat our bodies as sacred spaces, as temples? Now he wants us to develop an active distaste for them? What gives, Maharishi?

Here's what. The point of yoga is to see the truth as it is, unobscured by all the veils that cover it. And the truth is that we are not our bodies or our minds but the spark of consciousness within and beyond the body-mind 'covering'.

So, say the YS's commentators, while it is vital that we keep our bodies clean from the outside and the inside, for they are the containers of our consciousness and we cannot function without their support, we should never become so attached to our bodies that we would spend time, effort, money and mind space in decorating them (or torturing them!) to make them superficially beautiful, whether to ourselves or to others. And that is what the Maharishi meant when he advocated cultivating a 'distaste' for the body.

In other words, the yogis recommended cultivating a healthy 'detachment' from the body, to treat it like you would, say, a car. You ensure that the car is in tip-top shape so that it can get you from place to place safely and efficiently, and doesn't break down on the highway right in the middle of a long journey, but apart from that, you have very little emotional attachment to it. Also, if you *have* to get somewhere by a particular time, a car of any colour, shape or make will do.

Unfortunately, we are so quick to develop deep attachments to even inanimate things, thinking of them not just as ours but as 'us' – 'Ruin my new sneakers and I'll ruin your day!' or 'I would go crazy if I lost my phone, it is an extension of my hand, my life, my identity!' – that even 'sneaker detachment' or 'phone detachment' may not be possible for many of us. More than a bit silly, this attachment to things that we have ourselves created to make our lives easier (not harder!), if you pause to think about it.

And what of the 'lessening of contact with others' bit? Well, what the good Maharishi is talking about here is merely at the physical level. When you realize that what is beyond the body is what is important, you will treat everyone you meet with the same level of respect and courtesy, no matter how their bodies look; you will stop judging people by the colour of their skin, the whiteness of their teeth, their height, weight, shape. You will stop being attracted to people's bodies – this kind of attraction, as we all know, is the cause of so much emotional turmoil and so much crime in the world – and will instead be drawn to their souls, their true, radiant selves.

Yup, it isn't body love you need, young 'uns, says Maharishi P, hopping up and down in his excitement, not even body positivity, but body *neutrality* – that's the ticket!

Sigh. If you say so, Maharishi P.

***

As a result of contentment, the highest happiness is attained

(2.42)

The days that make us happy make us wise.

– John Masefield

Most of us live so much in the future or the past, roiled by emotional roller coasters and constant anxiety, that we barely pause for even a moment to recall the times in our lives when we were at our most content, whatever that means to each of us. If we only did that, we would know that we are at our most content when we live deeply in the present, experiencing, if only briefly, a complete absence of anxiety and desire.

Once we know this, we can break down that past moment of contentment further, to figure out what it was about it that made us pause and dwell in the moment. That kind of reflection brings wisdom – when we know what makes us content, we can work towards achieving that state more often.

Hang on a minute, you are saying. A complete absence of anxiety sounds alluring enough, but a complete absence of desire? Wouldn't that make us apathetic, robot-like and, ugh, boring? Most people certainly seem to think so. What's the fun, they will demand, where is the *purpose* of your life, if you aren't chasing after something? Where is your ambition, buddy? It's discontent that drives the world to progress, my friend! And so on. But if you have sincerely reflected on your past moments of deep happiness, you will know that you were at your most content when you felt complete and whole, when you did not want or need anything from the world. It is that kind of absence of desire that, according to the good Maharishi, leads to contentment.

Not only is your contentment good for you, it is good for everyone around you as well. Swami Vivekananda takes it a bit further – he declares that it is your *responsibility* to be content (in other words, it is your responsibility to become free of

desire) because it is simply what you owe the world, given all the blessings you have received from it. 'What business have you with clouded faces?' he once raged. 'If you have a clouded face, do not go out that day, shut yourself up in your room. What right have you to carry this disease out into the world?'

Ouch.

***

Just for completeness, here are the last three sutras in this section.

Through austerity and self-discipline, impurities are removed, and the perfection of the body and the sense organs result

(2.43)

Through the study of scripture, a connection is established with the deity of one's choice

(2.44)

From submission and devotion to God, one achieves (the ultimate goal of) samAdhi

(2.45)

And that's a wrap of the rewards and incentives section of the sAdhanapAda, young 'uns! All fired up and ready to dig your heels in and stay the course?

You're welcome.

Practice 7

Still the Body so that You Can Focus on the Mind

स्थिरसुखमासनम् ॥ २.४६ ॥

sthira-sukham-Asanam

(Good) posture is one that is steady and comfortable (2.46)

How many times has a parent or teacher or another well-meaning (or interfering) adult punched you between the shoulder blades (aaaarghhhhhh!) and pulled you up for slouching over your books, your phone, your computer? Keep sitting like that, they may have added helpfully, and your spine will stay that way! Or an equally popular variant: Keep sitting like that, and nothing of what you read will remain in your head!

Well, what do you know, if Maharishi P and his commentators are to be believed, those well-meaning adults may be right, at least about the second part! But before we get into the whys and wherefores of that, let us look a little closer at one of the shortest, pithiest sutras in the YS, which simply states that a posture, any posture, that is sthira or steady, and sukham or comfortable, qualifies as Asana.

That's it? (Yes.) Then why do yoga classes teach so many different Asanas? *(We'll come to that.)* Why do students get so competitive and beat themselves up (metaphorically) when they can't twist themselves into a particular one? *(Only those students who do this know the answer to that. YogAsana was never meant to be competitive, and a discipline that is based on the understanding that each body is different would never insist that everyone hold every Asana in exactly the same way.)* If the idea was simply to choose a position that was sthira and sukham, I would choose shavAsana, the corpse pose – why bother torturing my body with any other? *(Umm, unfortunately, that pose would not work for the yogi – or you. You'll see why. Read on.)*

To understand why shavAsana would not be the ideal posture for you, you have to know a little bit about the physiology of the human body according to Maharishi P, as well as the Yoga philosophy. Brace yourself for a bunch of new words and concepts!

***

So, according to ancient Indian medical and spiritual theory, prANa is a catch-all term for the energy present in the universe, whether it is natural forces like heat, light, energy and magnetism, or the vital energy, the life force, present in living things. Breathing in and out activates and nurtures the prANa, so prANa is often used in the sense of 'breath', although the word actually means something deeper, more subtle, and more intangible – it isn't something you can feel on your skin, like your breath. Also, unlike the breath, which only nourishes the physical body with oxygen and evacuates it of carbon dioxide, prANa also nourishes our mental, intellectual, emotional and spiritual bodies.

Now, just like your respiratory system is the main conduit for the breath entering and leaving your body, there is believed to be another, parallel system of nADIs or channels running through your body, which generates and distributes prANa – don't look for these nADIs in a book of anatomy, though; they are not physical channels. The three principal nADIs are located in the spinal column – the iDA, on the left, the pingalA, on the right, and the sushumNA, in the centre. The iDA carries a gentle, cooling, feminine energy, associated with the moon, and nourishes the right side of the brain – the creative, arty, visual, intuitive side. The pingalA carries a warm, active, masculine energy, associated with the sun, and nourishes the left side of the brain – the analytical, logical, fact-loving side. And yes, whether we identify as male, female or anything else in between or beyond, we all contain both masculine and feminine energies within us – woohoo!

The sushumNA, the central channel, is the most important. At its base, which is the base of the spine, lies a coiled-up 'serpent' of explosive spiritual energy, called the kunDalini. Along the length of the sushumNA nADI are six centres of consciousness called chakras. The seventh and highest chakra lies in the centre of the brain.

Now, the point of yoga is to 'awaken' the kunDalini serpent so that it uncoils and rises through the chakras along the sushumNA nADI. As it passes each chakra, different levels of consciousness are reached. The way to awaken the serpent is to ensure that it is supplied with lots of prANa, i.e., by having both the cool feminine and warm masculine prANA from the iDA and pingalA flow uninterruptedly through the kunDalini.

That seems easy enough, and you would think that it would happen naturally enough, without your having to do anything about it. And it would, EXCEPT. Except what? Except that we ourselves unthinkingly create blocks in our nADIs with our negative thoughts, our fears, our desires, our anger and our laziness, and obstruct the flow of our prANa, in the same way that fatty diets block the arteries of our hearts and don't allow that brilliant, efficient muscle to do its thing. According to Maharishi P, by following the practices he has outlined in the sAdhanapAda – kriyA yoga, the yamas and the niyamas, all of which lead to the calming of our chitta lakes – we will slowly but surely unblock our nADIs, sending prANa gushing joyously into the sushumNA, and forcing our innate 'serpent power' to awake, arise and not stop till the goal of rising all the way up to the seventh chakra and liberating us from fear is reached.

***

Do you see now why shavAsana would not help in this grand endeavour? How would the serpent of your spiritual power 'rise' if you are yourself supine? It is for the same reason that studying while lying down on your stomach or your back is simply not as effective as studying at a desk. Maharishi P and his bunch therefore recommend that you pick an Asana that is not only sthira and sukham but also straight-backed, with the head, chest and hips aligned along one line.

What is the first Asana that comes to mind when you think about a straight-backed, seated posture? That's right, padmAsana or the lotus position, the very same that the ancient yogi on the Mohenjo-daro seal chose for his (or her) meditation.

By the way, the cross-legged pose is the chosen one for a reason; it has three points of contact with the floor – the two knees, and the tail bone. Why is that a good thing? Because, as anyone who designs furniture knows, a three-legged table or stool (where the three points of contact with the floor are the vertices of a triangle) is the most stable piece of furniture, even more so than a four-legged one! If you are looking for sthira, no Asana could be better than a 'three-legged triangle' one like padmAsana.

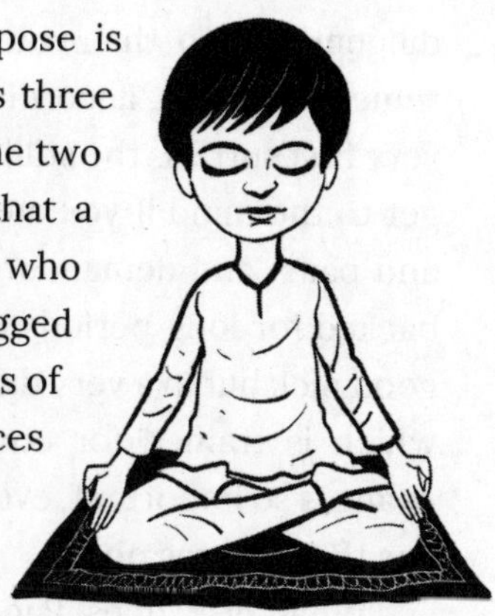

Oh-kay, if it is so evident that this is the best Asana, why do yoga teachers teach SO many others?

For a very good reason. While padmAsana scores high on sthira, there is a second condition Maharishi P needs fulfilled before he considers it a good Asana – it should also be sukham, comfortable. Sitting straight-backed and cross-legged on the floor for lengths of time is definitely not sukham for most of us slouchers and chair-sitters. To get to sukham in any posture, your body has to be regularly stretched, twisted and bent to get all the kinks out of your spine, its different muscle groups have to be strengthened so that they can hold weight without wobbling, it has to learn to be limber and fluid so that it can move seamlessly between positions, and most importantly, it has to be trained to stay still and not fidget. All these are achieved by the practice of haTha yoga, or the yoga of postures.

But here's the plot twist: while haTha yoga practice seemingly focuses on the body, the real point of doing it diligently is so that you can *forget* about the body! If you remember, yoga, according to Maharishi P's definition in the very first sutra, is the stilling of the mind, but how can you even get to the mind if you are distracted by your body's twitches and pains and demands? To be able to sit still and straight-backed for long periods of time, your body has to be in very good nick but in a very different way from a sportsman's body, which is trained for constant movement. And that is why Asana is so important, even though the Maharishi himself only has three sutras on it.

What else does Patanjali have to say about Asana? In Sutra 47, he tells us that a posture can be considered perfected when holding it becomes effortless, in such a way that the body *relaxes* into the pose completely, leaving the mind free to immerse itself in non-worldly, transcendental thoughts. To find that kind of comfort in a posture, any posture, in our waking state – just think of how many times we change our position even in deep sleep, trying to find one that is comfortable – requires a lot of mindful practice. In other words, you will never get there if you skip your yoga classes!

In the next sutra, and the last one to do with Asana, Maharishi P makes a big and rather cryptic claim. When you do manage to perfect your Asana, he says, you will no longer be 'afflicted by dualities and opposites'. What could that possibly mean? Think about the illustrations you have seen of rishis and asuras engaged in deep penance. There they stand for years and years, on top of a mountain or deep inside a jungle, usually in vrikshAsana, the tree pose, balancing on one foot (imagine finding sthira and sukham in *this* pose!), their arms raised to the sky in a namaste, so still and unmoving that termites build anthills around them and creepers entwine themselves around their limbs. Do you think these meditators felt the pouring rain or the blazing sun as the seasons changed, knew the onset of night or day, felt joy or sorrow? Not a bit! So comfortable and stable were their bodies in the Asana, so immersed their minds in thoughts of the Infinite, that opposite sensations like heat and cold were all the same to them. And that was what the good Maharishi meant – the one who perfects Asana loses awareness of the body so completely that all dualities simply dissolve in the face of their meditative fire.

If that's the physical aspect of being unaware of dualities, what about the spiritual aspect? When you are so unaware of dualities at a physical level, and no longer feel that you have to physically 'protect' yourself against any aspect of Nature, you will truly understand, at a deep, deep level, that you are part of Nature, not separate from it. You will see that every other creature on the planet is also like you, part of Nature, and therefore, no different from you at all. *Ta-daa!* That's another duality – one which makes you see yourself as different from everyone else – outta the window!

Now you know what to aim for in your next yoga class!

The Seven Lotuses of Your Consciousness

Oooh, that sounds all exotic and intriguing, doesn't it? It actually is! So, these seven centres of consciousness, each represented as a lotus (because that is how they apparently appear to those who have been fortunate enough to reach a level of consciousness where they can actually 'see' these energy centres) are called your chakras. Six of them, as we discussed earlier, are believed to be present at various levels along your spine, in the sushumNA nADI, and the seventh and highest is in the centre of the top of your head. Our minds are wont to dwell in one or more of these chakras, and which chakra(s) they choose to spend their time in determines our level of consciousness.

Unfortunately for us, our minds usually get stuck in one of the three lower chakras. The effort – through reining in the horses of our senses, eating right, keeping our bodies in good shape, blocking our negative thoughts and words with positive ones, and, here it comes, prANAyAma or breath control (which we will talk about in more detail in the next section) – is to push the mind out of the lower chakras and towards the higher ones by strapping on to the mind the booster rockets of kunDalini power, the spiritual energy that lies coiled and passive at the base of our spine.

Where exactly are the seven chakras supposed to be located? Let's see.

1. The **moolAdhAra or root chakra** is located at the base of the spine. As its name suggests, it keeps us rooted to the earth, the element it is associated with, and stabilizes us. This is where the kunDalini, or the vast reserve of spiritual energy we all carry, lies coiled,

waiting to be awakened. If our minds only dwell in the root chakra, which lies in the neighbourhood of our organs of evacuation, we will only be concerned with matters of survival – food, water, shelter, safety, and whatever else makes us feel secure – and not be able to look beyond them. But if we are able to feel stable, comfortable and content with what we have, we will arouse the coiled energy that lies in the moolAdhAra, and will be able to get our thoughts flowing in the right direction – upwards.

2. The **svAdhishThAna or sacral chakra** is located a little below the navel in the region of the sacrum (the triangular bone composed of five fused vertebrae at the bottom of the spine). This chakra is associated with pleasure and creative energy when the kunDalini is flowing upwards, and sensuality, desire, I–Me–Myself-ness and fear (of death) when it is flowing in the wrong direction. If our mind spends most of its time here – as it often does – we will only chase after sensual pleasures, our fear of impending death propelling us onward to collect more and more of them before our time runs out. There will be no mind space left for pure joy, contentment or the expanded sense of 'I' that makes us embrace the whole world as our own. Getting our spiritual energies to flow – flow is rather appropriate here, since this chakra is associated with the water element – to higher realms past this particular chakra can be a real challenge.
3. The **maNipura or solar plexus chakra** is the third, and is located just behind the navel. It is the fire chakra, associated with the fire of digestion and metabolism,

and the emotions of greed and jealousy* (when spiritual energy is flowing downwards), and joy and generosity (when it is flowing upwards). Once again, not a great chakra for the mind to get stuck at, since the need and greed to feed yourself, both literally and metaphorically, can be a huge stumbling block to going any further. If you eat just enough, and the right foods, to keep your digestive fire burning bright and strong, however, your metabolism will be brisk instead of sluggish and your mind will be able to move past that and go higher. (To realize the truth of this, just think back to the last time you had an upset stomach. Could you think about anything else at all until that was resolved?)

4. On to the **anAhata or heart chakra** (you can guess where it is located in the body), the first of the 'higher' chakras, associated with the lightness and all-pervasiveness of the air element! When our mind dwells in the region of the anAhata, we feel serene, balanced and calm. We are able to see opposing points of view and different ways of being as having every right to exist, we are able to feel what Maharishi P refers to as muditA, joy in other people's joy, karuNA or compassion for those who are grieving, and upekshA or detachment (instead of hate) towards those who do wrong. We are able to see our

★ In many Indian languages, the word for jealousy has something to do with fire or burning, and often with the stomach as well. Do you see why that is the emotion associated with the maNipura chakra? The next time you start feeling jealous of someone, observe where in your body you feel it and you will realize that you feel it in your gut!

way forward with clarity since we are not being roiled by our fears and loves and hates, and experience love (maybe that's why losing one's love brings physical pain in the region of the heart) – and bliss. All this, of course, when the kunDalini energy has not done a U-turn and is spiralling downwards – when that happens, love turns sour, the heart shrinks into itself and jealousy goes into the ascendant.

5. Next, the **vishuddha or throat chakra**, located in the region of the thyroid gland, associated with gratitude (when energy is static or proceeding upwards) and grief (when energy is flowing in the opposite direction).* As we have discussed on several different occasions in this book, an attitude of gratitude can make you feel expansive (no wonder the element this chakra is associated with is 'space'); cultivating it consciously will help in pulling the energy up into your vishuddha chakra.

   What causes a block in this chakra, and prevents energy from flowing further upwards? Experts say it is feelings of guilt that we carry within us, or the fear of speaking up. Now that you know, you can work on those and get rid of them. If you are feeling guilty about something, see what you can do about it. Maybe you confess or apologize to the person you feel you have wronged, maybe you let the guilt go when you realize you have nothing to feel guilty about. If you are fearful about speaking out

★ Ever noticed how both being overwhelmed with gratitude and being overwhelmed with grief make you feel a 'lump in the throat'? Now you know why.

against someone but feel guilty about not doing it (a double whammy there), maybe you can think of some other way to express your opinion – through a note or an email instead of a face-to-face confrontation.

6. The sixth chakra is the **AjnA or 'third eye' chakra**, and if you know your Hindu mythology, you can guess where that is located. Yup, in the centre of the forehead, between the eyebrows, where Shiva's third eye is always shown to be! It is the seat of anger – remember how Shiva burnt the god of love, Kama, to cinders when he disturbed his meditation, by opening his third eye in anger?* – but also the seat of intuition, deep knowledge and awareness, which is why Shiva the enlightened yogi is shown to have a third eye in the first place; his AjnA chakra, associated with light, is unblocked and wide open.
7. And finally, the highest, greatest chakra, the **sahasrAra or the crown chakra**, connected to the one universal energy that pervades all things. SahasrAra literally means thousand-petalled, and the opening of the thousand-petalled lotus at the crown of our heads, which happens when we are able to pull our spiritual energy all the way to that level, signifies the attainment

★ Even the great Shiva did not get away scot-free for succumbing to a most unyogi-like rage against Kama, however justified he felt it had been. He lost much of the power that had accrued to him through his long and rigorous penances, and was forced to begin his austerities from scratch to regain them. Let that be a lesson to you, young 'uns !

of pure consciousness, when we do not think of ourselves, others, or anything else in the universe as bodies, minds, or breath, but as one vast, unified energy vibrating in harmony with everything else, and are filled with unending joy.

Are you feeling all starry-eyed, goosebumpy and overwhelmed right now? Can't wait to nourish your thousand-petalled lotus with your kunDalini energy and watch it bloom? That's wonderful, but hey, remember where the work to get there begins? That's right, the moolAdhAra, and all the tough, tough practices that Maharishi P has so kindly laid out. Back to base now, everyone, chop-chop!

Practice 8

To Invigorate Your Life Force, Regulate Your Breath

तस्मिन् सति श्वासप्रश्वास्योर्गतिविच्छेदः प्राणायामः ॥ २.४९ ॥

tasmin sati shvAsa-prashvAsayorgati-vichcHedah prANAyAmah

Once that (Asana) has been mastered, one must practise prANAyAma, by regulating the in- and out-breaths (2.49)

Have you noticed how some people simply seem to have more energy than others? While most of us are wilting after a long day at school or work and just want to slouch on the couch, there are others who will run to sports practice, finish their homework, bathe their baby brothers (okay, that's a stretch – substitute with something more likely), and still burn up the dance floor at a party the same evening. How do they do it? If you asked Darth Vader, the Sith Lord from the *Star Wars* movies, to explain the secret of that never-ending energy, he might have offered, 'The Force is strong with that one'. That's exactly what Maharishi P would have said as well. 'The prANa,' he might have said admiringly, 2,000 years before Darth, 'is strong in that one.'

There is a lovely story in the Prashna Upanishad that underlines the importance of prANa, the quintessential life force, for our ability to live a full and fulfilling life. It goes like this.

Once, in days long past, six men, all true seekers of the cosmic energy referred to as Brahman, decided to visit the great sage Pippalada. Each had one burning question to ask the sage, whom they had chosen as their guru. A year later, it was finally Bhargava's turn to ask his question.

'Bhagavan,' he said, addressing Pippalada respectfully, 'who are the gods that support life in the body? Which of them make a being "alive" to everything around itself? And which among them is the greatest?'

And Pippalada answered: 'The five elements, dear Bhargava – space, earth, fire, water, air – of which the body is made, these are the gods that support the physical body. But speech and mind, sight and hearing – they are the gods that light up the body, turning it into a self-aware, intelligent entity that can engage with the world around itself.

'Let me tell you a story about these four gods. As they appeared in the body, one by one, each boasted, "I, and only I, am what truly sustains and supports the body."

'Only after they had all spoken did prANa the lifebreath show himself. "Do not delude yourselves," he said. "Without me – the vital energy – neither the body nor any of you would survive. It is I alone, dividing myself fivefold,* who sustains and supports the body."

'"Ha!' mocked speech and mind, sight and hearing. "Show us!"

"'I will,' said prANa, and made as if to leave, proceeding towards the passage at the top of the head through which life enters and leaves a body. And the gods that light up the body, all four of them, found themselves being pulled upward, willy-nilly, in prANa's wake, just like bees are 'pulled' behind the queen bee when she leaves the hive.

"'Mercy!" cried the gods in alarm. "We believe you now. When prANa leaves, so do the other faculties – none can exist without the lifebreath !'"

★ For more deets on the fivefold prANa, see box 'Pancha PrANa: The Five Lifebreaths' on page 278.

***

Given how important prANa was considered to be by the ancients, Maharishi P was very clear that it would take up an entire rung – the fourth – of his eight-rung ashTAnga ladder to freedom. Just to reiterate, prANa is not the breath, it is what we may call 'vital life energy'. The two are very closely linked, however.

How do we ensure that our prANa is charged and vibrant and 'on' at all times (except when we are getting our full quota of shut-eye, which is a great prANa recharge in itself)? Since prANa is nurtured by the breath, it stands to reason that monitoring and controlling it, to ensure that it does not dissipate by pooling in blocked nADIs or by being used up in pointless pursuits, *must* involve monitoring and controlling our breathing. That is why breath regulation or prANAyAma –

in Sanskrit, AyAma means restraint or stoppage – is so central to yoga practice.

Here's the good news – even if your current level of prANa is nowhere near that of your naturally high-energy friends, the ones we talked about in the opening paragraph of this section, you can get to where they are as well.

How is that possible?

Aren't high-energy people born with a greater volume of prANa than ordinary folk? Not at all – they just choose to deploy their prANa better than others. Instead of frittering away their portion of prANa by letting it get consumed in their lower chakras, they use it for the more important things first – sports practice, homework, helping around the house. Because they are not constantly griping while doing their duties – 'This coach never gives us a break! Why does that teacher give us so much homework? Why do I have to do all these chores? My friends' parents never ask them to!' – and are doing them with good cheer instead, they manage to *conserve* their remaining prANa, so that there is enough left over to enjoy themselves at the party afterwards. See how that works?

You can do that too – and the practice of prANAyAma (remember to always do it supervised, with a good teacher) will certainly help you along that path. For, if restraining your passions and emotions helps conserve prANa, the vice versa also holds good. Restraining your breath, aka prANAyAma, will help you hold back your emotions and passions instead of letting them bubble out of you unchecked.

What does prANAyAma involve? Most of us would say that breathing involves only two steps – inhalation and exhalation, but Maharishi P and his ilk were equally concerned about two other phases of breathing – the brief 'no-breath' pause between inhalation and exhalation, when we are, for one beat, in what you may call suspended animation – we are alive even though we are not breathing – and the other no-breath pause between exhalation and inhalation. It was these two pauses that yogis were expected to work on, lengthening them gradually until a complete cessation of breath, the highest state of prANAyAma, could happen – do NOT try this at home! Apart from this, yogis worked on the inhales–exhales as well, shortening and lengthening them depending on the practice, but it was the pauses that were the Holy Grail.

Yogis believed, because they had experienced it for themselves, that by regulating the breath (prANAyAma), and 'locking' certain lower channels (bandha) to prevent prANa from leaking away, they could use their store of prANa more effectively. Specifically, they wanted to use their thus-conserved prANa to open up the sushumNA nADI, at the bottom of which lies the coiled serpent of kunDalini energy, so that it could then uncoil and begin to rise, suffusing them with its power.

Yes, it's a lot to take in at one go, but you don't have to bother your head too much with the mechanics of what actually is supposed to happen during prANAyAma. Suffice it to say that the Maharishi thought it was a very important part of the yoga practice, and what was good enough for Maharishi Patanjali is definitely good enough for us.

Just like he does not mention any specific Asana, saying instead that *any* posture that is comfortable and steady and effortlessly held is a good Asana, our Maharishi does not mention any of the standard prANAyAma exercises taught in yoga classes today, some of which you may be familiar with – bhastrikA, nADI shodhana, ujjayi breathing, pUraka, reYchaka, kumbhaka, bhramari and that most famous skull-shiner, kapAlabhAti – in the Yoga Sutras.

All he says is that prANAyAma comprises inhalation, exhalation and restriction of the breath, and that the breath in each case can be either long-drawn or short, expressive or subtle. What kind of breath is appropriate to a practice is based on time, or the duration of the breath; place, or the area 'covered' by the breath – for example, when you exhale, does a leaf a certain distance away quiver; when you inhale, do you send the breath all the way to your toes or do you hold it in your belly; when you are holding your breath, are the hairs in your nostrils motionless, and so on; and number, i.e., how many cycles of inhale–exhale–restrain you must do. Using these rather broad – and rather vague – guidelines, teachers who came after Maharishi Patanjali developed the prANAyAma routines that are taught and practised today.

And then, to round it off with a grand flourish, as per usual, Maharishi P holds out his golden carrot. Do your prANAyAma diligently, he promises, and the veil (of ignorance) shrouding your light (of knowledge) shall fall away, and your mind will be made fit and ready for meditation. Makes you want to stand up and cheer and start googling yoga classes, what?

Hang on a minute there, though. The Maharishi assures us that prANAyAma makes your mind fit for meditation, but are you sure *you* are ready for prANAyAma? Have you truly mastered the first three rungs on Maharishi Patanjali's ladder? Butbutbut, you protest, even though prANAyAma comes *after* Asana on your ladder, doesn't anyone who joins a yoga class do both, right from the first class itself? So can't we simply add the yamas and niyamas to this, and start all four at the same time? What's the actual point of the hierarchy of yama, niyama, Asana, prANAyAma, and all the rest of it, Maharishi P?

The Maharishi smiles into his long white beard. 'The thing is, young 'uns,' he says kindly, 'there is nothing, absolutely nothing, to stop you from leaping straight on to the fourth rung and beginning a prANAyAma practice today. Butbutbut, without first clearing your mind of junk – which is what the practice of the yamas and niyamas help you do – and without getting your body into the kind of shape that will let you forget about it, which is what I call Asana – prANAyAma becomes an in-out–in-out breathing exercise and nothing else, don't you see? To truly experience its mind-blowing benefits, you must do the work to make yourself *worthy* of it! No shortcuts, I'm afraid, that's just how these things go.'

Aaaaaargggghhhhh. Foiled again!

Pancha PrANa: The Five Lifebreaths

You know now that according to yoga physiology, there is a vital energy or prANa system in the body that runs parallel to all our other biological systems. This parallel system is responsible not only for keeping us alive (if prANa leaves the body, so do all the other faculties) but also for making us *feel* alive – the amount of energy we have to do the things we want to do depends on how well we are able to control our prANa, ensuring that it doesn't get stuck in dead-end thoughts or wasted in doing actions that are dishonest or hurtful or lazy or mean.

There is only one prANa, but it is believed to function as five separate breaths or vAyus in the body. One of them, the inward and downward breath, which nourishes the head, lungs and heart, is simply called prANa. Since the heart is the seat of the anAhata chakra (see page 266), a balanced prANa vAyu results in calmness and serenity.

Another vAyu is apAna, the downward and outward breath, which pushes out or evacuates stuff from the body. A robust apAna, associated with the moolAdhAra chakra, leads to robust excretory and reproductive systems.

Then there is uDAna, the upward vAyu, associated with the vishuddha and AjnA chakras, which nourishes the throat and diaphragm, and is responsible not only for a healthy respiratory system, but also for clarity of speech, a good memory and creative thinking.

The fourth is samAna, the equalizing breath, which churns like a whirlpool in the region of the navel and the maNipura chakra, at the point where the downward breath, prANa, meets the upward breath, uDAna. The churning motion, and its position in the body, associates samAna with digestion – a good samAna leads to great metabolism.

The last is vyAna, the vAyu associated with distribution, which takes the vital life force to every last cell in the body. If your fingers and toes don't freeze up on cold nights, your vyAna, and by association, your circulatory system, is doing very well indeed.

Right. Now, if you have done haTha yoga and prANAyAma in school or elsewhere, the teacher may have asked you to hold your hands in a particular mudrA, or gesture, while doing a particular prANAyAma routine. Can you recall what mudrA you are asked to hold while doing, say, kapAlabhAti? That's right – the apAna mudra. Why do you think that is so? kapAlabhAti focuses on exhalation, which is a downward breath, and helps to remove toxins, clear sinuses and evacuate waste from the body, all of which is aided by the apAna breath. Any wonder then that you are asked to hold the apAna mudra while doing it?

What about when you are doing alternate nostril breathing or anulom-vilom, also called nADI shodhana (or nADI cleansing), which helps to remove blocks and balance the prANa in the lunar (iDA) and solar (pingalA) nADIs? What mudra are you asked to hold your hands in then? Can you guess why?

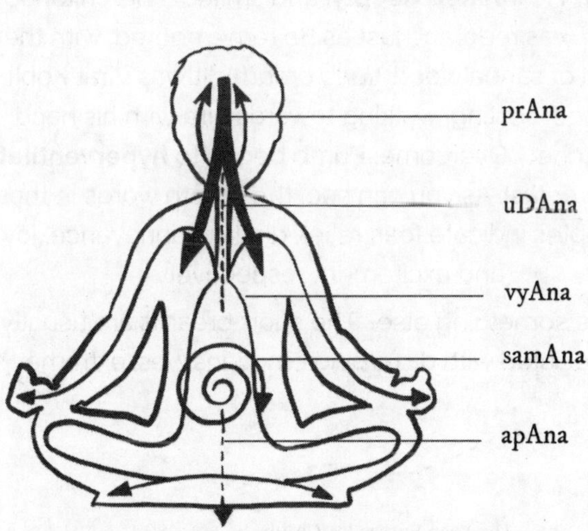

Think about it!

Brea-brea-breathe vs breeeeeeaaathe

It is said that each of us comes into this world with a limited and predetermined number of breaths, and that each person's complement is different from everyone else's. Some of us, therefore, are destined to live longer than others. But there's a catch – how you use those breaths, how long you make them last, is entirely up to you. What does that mean? Think about it. The pattern of your breathing changes with the emotion you are feeling. When you're fearful, anxious or angry, you tend to breathe fast and shallow. When you're calm and relaxed, you breathe long and deep. This breath–emotion connection is best reflected in language. 'She **gasped** in horror' (*short breath*), 'He gave a huge **sigh** of relief' (*long breath*), 'Their accomplishment is not to be **sniffed** *at' (short breath) and* 'She stormed out in a **huff** after losing the game' (*short breath*), 'He **inhaled deeply**, and smiled – his childhood home was redolent, just as he remembered, with the smell of sandalwood' (*long breath*), 'It was Virat Kohli himself, smiling, walking towards him with his hand outstretched. Overcome, Purab began to **hyperventilate**' (*short breaths*). As you can see, the breath words in these examples indicate fear, relief, disdain, annoyance, joy and excitement respectively.

Notice something else? The short breaths are usually associated with disturbing emotions (yes, extreme excitement is a disturbing emotion), the long ones with calm and joy. If you use up the breaths allotted to you for this lifetime (refer to para 1) by allowing yourself to be rocked constantly by disturbing emotions, your life will be much shorter than it would be if you practised being calm and equanimous in every situation, which would make each of your breaths long and s-l-o-w. If that isn't a good reason to just chill and get off the emotion roller coaster, what is?

Here's the good part. If the way you breathe is so deeply connected to the emotions you're feeling, shouldn't changing the way you breathe – i.e., slowing it down – transform your emotional state as well? Of course it does – that's what prANAyAma is all about. But prANAyAma is a long-term daily practice, to be done under the supervision of a teacher. What do you do when you are perilously close to a panic attack? Or so mad at someone you could punch them in the nose? Or so choked up and tight in the chest after a break-up that you feel that you cannot breathe? Here are some ideas.

1. When you begin to feel overwhelmed, take a step back, pause and become aware of your breathing. Sometimes, just watching your breath will make it begin to regulate itself, in a slightly embarrassed fashion, like a child caught doing something it should not have been.
2. Remove yourself from the scene, however difficult that may feel, however much you want some kind of closure in that moment. Summoning up the will to walk away uses energy, which will be diverted away from

the present emotional situation, starving it of some of the oxygen it needs to stay alive.

3. Force yourself to breathe deeply, to move from thoracic breathing or chest breathing, which does not entirely fill your lungs and does not involve your diaphragm, into what is called diaphragmatic breathing, in which you consciously and deliberately push your stomach wayyyyyy out as you inhale, and pull it fully in when you exhale.

4. Now begin to breathe to a particular count. Inhale for 5 seconds, exhale for 6. Do this 8 to 10 times. Then dial it up a notch – inhale for 8 seconds, exhale for 10. The deep, long breaths you are taking will themselves help to make you calmer, but there's something else going on here too. Counting breaths demands your attention; to do it, your attention will necessarily have to be drawn away from the emotion you are feeling. This is also why first-time meditators are simply asked to focus on their breath instead of on an object or something more abstract – your breath is always with you, you need no props, and it can be quite absorbing to turn your awareness to the ever-present inhale-exhale cycle.

5. Another technique to try, in a similar vein, is what is called 'box breathing'. Breathe in to a count of 4, hold your breath for 4, breathe out to a count of 4, and hold (i.e., don't inhale) for another count of 4. It helps to visualize a square box when you do this, seeing the inhale and exhale steps as the two opposite vertical sides of the box and the hold steps as the horizontal

sides. Visualizing plus counting will consume a lot of your attention, and that, as we discovered in the previous point, is exactly what is required.

6. Here's one last technique which is supposed to be very good at reducing anxiety. It is called pursed-lip breathing, and goes like this. First, inhale slowly for 2 to 3 seconds. Next, purse or pucker your lips like you were going to blow out a candle, and hold for two seconds. Finally, separate your pursed lips and exhale through them for 4 to 5 seconds.

You don't have to wait until you are overwhelmed to try any of these breathing techniques. You can do them any time during the day, to get back to calm, or simply to become mindful of your breathing.

All the best!

Practice 9

Hold Firm the Reins, and the Horses Will Fall in Line

स्वविषयासंप्रयोगे चित्तस्य स्वरूपानकारैवेन्द्रियाणां प्रत्याहारः ॥ २.५४ ॥

sva-vishaya-asamprayogeY chittasya swarUpa-anakAraiva-indriyANAm pratyAhArah

When the mind is withdrawn from objects pleasing to the senses, the senses follow its lead, withdrawing themselves from the same objects. This is known as pratyAhAra. (2.54)

ततः परमावश्यता इन्द्रियाणाम् ॥ २.५५ ॥

tatah paramA-vashyatA indriyANAm

From this arises the complete mastery of the senses (2.55)

Here we are, finally, at the fifth and last 'prep' rung of the ashTAnga ladder – pratyAhAra – before it zooms up into the rarefied heights of the deep absorption rungs of dhAraNa, dhyAna and samAdhi. This is the rung at which we take our leave of Maharishi P, leaving the explorations of the rest of the ladder for another day.

'Temptation,' said American businessman and humorist Arnold Henry Glasow, 'usually comes in through a door that has deliberately been left open.' Maharishi P would have agreed with that sentiment. 'If the horses of your senses stray this way and that,' he might have added sternly, 'don't blame the horses; blame the reins and the incompetent charioteer.'

But you knew that already. We succumb to the temptations of the flesh – delicious food, beautiful things, provocative music and visuals, not because of our wayward senses but because of our weak willpower. 'I really did want to wake up with the alarm and study,' you say, 'but it was so cosy in the quilt that my treacherous body would simply not move!' Or, 'I really should not be eating that extra wedge of apple pie, but it smells SO good that it's gotten me drooling, and you know there's no turning back after that!' Or even, 'I told you we would only focus on studying tonight – why did you have to tell me that the new season of XXX had just dropped? It's all *your* fault!'

See how good we are at this kind of thing? Friends, family, teachers, school, the government, content creators, the fragrance of pie – anything and everything will do as a peg to hang our excuses on, just as long as we do not have to acknowledge that the desire for whatever object that is at the moment pulling our horses towards itself originated not only in the horses' minds but also in the charioteer's. The horses only follow where the charioteer guides them; they go their own ways when he isn't holding the reins tight enough. The most insidious part? It is the devious charioteer, the higher mind, which is itself coming up with these excuses, playing victim instead of owning up to its weaknesses.

That's the problem with the mind. When it is well nourished with positivity and inspiration, when it is able to keep a certain distance from everything happening around it and does not take things personally, when it trusts that the universe is on its side, your mind is your most formidable ally. Then you can work hard and cheerfully, countering negative thoughts with positive ones, counting your blessings, hurting no one, pausing before you say or do something you may regret, being mindful about your every decision, practising self-discipline, and being the best version of yourself.

When its equanimity is disturbed by fear, however, the same mind turns into the kind of foe you would not wish upon your worst enemies. 'It's not your fault,' it will coo sweetly, when you transgress, 'it's other people, *they* are the problem. What else can you do but hurt them back? I mean, you're not a doormat, are you? They should know they cannot walk all over you! Well done!' In a darker mood, it will hiss in your ear, 'What else did you think would happen? You are a nothing and you know that. You will never get anywhere, never amount to anything, never inspire anyone. You are a burden to your family and an embarrassment to your friends. You might as well not exist.' Ouch.

How do we coach our mind to be our friend more often than our adversary? More importantly, how can we tell the difference between a mind that is genuinely being a cheerleader and one that is simply providing us excuses for our faults?

'How about we change the question?' jumps in Maharishi P. 'How about you simply ask me – *Maharishi P, how do we get to pratyAhAra?*'

'All right, Maharishi P, we will indulge you. How do we get to pratyAhAra?'

'Gotcha!' Maharishi P roars with laughter. 'You know that already!'

Indeed we do! We get to the fifth rung of Maharishi P's ladder by climbing past the first, second, third and fourth rungs, of course! And what exactly is that fifth rung? That blessed place where the mind is finally able to detach itself from the objects that appeal to the senses; when it is able to look dispassionately at all the beauty the world has to offer, and enjoy it to the fullest, without getting attached to any of it. In other words, that is the stage at which your mind becomes your best friend.

What does that mean?

That if some of the things you enjoy disappeared the next day – a sick grandparent moved into your home and you had to share your lovely room with them, or a new student began to top the class, taking away the position you had yourself held for a long time – you wouldn't fill your head with negative thoughts about your grandparent, your classmate, or yourself. Instead, you would immediately start thinking about how to enjoy your room in a different way with your new companion, so that it is a pleasant experience for them and you, and challenge yourself to work harder at your studies (if that is possible) without for a moment resenting your classmate's success. If you feel you are already giving your best to your studies, you will simply continue to work as hard as you always have, cheerfully accepting whatever position you end up with after the exams. Such a state of grace seems impossible to achieve for most of us, but as Maharishi P assures us, we will get there if we commit to the practice of the first four rungs of his ladder. That's a nice thought to snuggle up to when things are looking bleak, what?

What is it like, really, being at rung five? Think about it this way. Years and years of assiduously and mindfully practising the yamas, niyamas, Asana and prANAyAma have turned the mind-charioteer's hold on the reins of the sense-horses into a practised, firm one, and the horses themselves into obedient animals that have learnt to trust the light pressure of that guiding hand so much that they, incredibly, have come to prefer that pressure to haring after everything shiny and alluring within their field of vision. At long last, the charioteer and the horses are not pulling in opposite directions; instead, they are on the same team. In the ensuing calm, the mind is finally able to dream of the day when even the higher rungs will be within its reach.

What a state of absolute grace pratyAhAra seems to be! A calm, if not yet entirely still, chitta lake, a lessening of covetous desire for the things of the world, whether they be yours or others', a cheerful equanimity to face anything life may lob at us, a heart full of compassion for our fellow beings, an ability to live in the moment, free of anxiety and fear, and a grateful spirit that trusts in the universe...

In short, a calmer, happier, kinder, relaxed, more content, and more positive YOU – seriously, what's not to like?

CONVERSATION

Got to say, Maharishi P, you sell this whole yoga deal well.

Haha, thank you, young 'uns. I'm flattered.

Can't help feeling, though, that the sneaky agenda behind all the dazzling rewards of yoga is to make us behave...

Eh? What do you mean?

Well, we aren't allowed to lie or be mean or jealous or selfish or slouch or sleep until noon, forever and ever!

I mean, it's a choice, *you know. No one's forcing you to do it.*

Uff, how are you so good at making that sound exactly like its opposite?

Hehe. I'm talented like that.

Say It Right!

THE OFFICIAL (SORT OF) PRONUNCIATION GUIDE

The list below will help you in two ways:
(1) It will help you pronounce correctly the Sanskrit and Hindi names of people and books/texts mentioned in this book, which are written as they are usually written in English, and
(2) It will help you understand what the weird capital letters in the middle of certain words in the book mean, and how to pronounce those words correctly.

Try it and see!

a – a as in **a**long
A – aa as in f**ar**
ch – ch as in **ch**ain
cH – aspirated ch (छ)
d – soft d as in **th**em
D – hard d, as in **d**og
dri – soft dri (दृ)
dh – aspirated soft d (ध)
Dh – aspirated hard d (ढ)
eY – ay as in p**ay**
g – g as in **g**ame
h – soft exhalation through mouth. As in tapa**h**, written in Sanskrit as :
i – i as in tr**i**p
I – ee as in tr**ee**
jn – nasal gn sound (ज्ञ)
kh – aspirated k (ख)
n – soft n as in **n**ame
N – hard n (ण)
O – long oh, as in **o**nus
t – soft t as in pas**t**a (त)
T – hard T as in **t**ell (ट)
th – aspirated soft t, as in **th**under (थ)
Th – aspirated hard t (ठ)
u – u as in f**u**ll
U – oo as in gr**oo**m

Word	How to Say It
Adi Shankara	Adi shankara
Adiyogi	AdiyOgI
Agastya	agastya
Ananta	ananta
Anshuman	anshuman
Arjuna	arjuna
Asamanja	asamanja
Ashoka	ashoka
Ashtadhyayi	ashtAdhyAyI
Atharva Veda	atharva veYda
avidya	avidhyA
Bhagavat Gita	bhagavat gItA
Bhagiratha	bhagIratha
BhagIrathi	bhAgIrathI
Bhargava	bhArgava
Bhashya	bhAshya
Bhishma	bhIshma
Bhoja	bhOja
Dasharatha	dasharatha
Dhritarashtra	dhritarAshtra
Durvasa	durvAsA
Dushyanta	dushyanta
Ganga	gangA
Guru Govinda Bhagavatpada	guru gOvinda bhagavatpAda
Guru Granth Sahib	guru granth sAhib
Hariharananda	hariharAnanda
Hatha Yoga Pradipika	haTha yoga pradIpikA
Ikshvaku	ikshvAku
Ilan/Ila	ilan/ilA
B.K.S Iyengar	B.K.S. ai-yen-gAr
Katha Upanishad	kaTha upanishad
Krishna	krishNa

Krishna Dvaipayana	krishNa dvypAyana
Krishnamacharya	krishNamAchArya
Madhvacharya	mAdhvAchArya
Maha Upanishad	mahA upanishad
Mahabharata	mahAbhArata
Mahabhashya	mahAbhAshya
Martanda	mArtanDa
Nachiketa	nachikeYta
Narada	NArada
Narmada	narmadA
Pandu	pAnDu
Pandava	pAnDava
Panini	pANini
Patanjalatantra	pAtanjalatantra
Patanjali	patanjali
Pattabhi Jois	paTTAbhi jo-is
Pippalada	pippalAda
Rama	rAma
Ramanujacharya	rAmAnujAchArya
Ramayana	rAmAyaNa
Sagara	sAgara
Sama Veda	sAma veYda
Shakuntala	shakuntalA
Shantanu	shAntanu
Sivananda	shivAnanda
Tattva Vaisharadi	tatva vyshAradI
Trayi Vidya	trayI vidhyA
Trishanku	trishanku
Vachaspati Mishra	vAchaspati mishra
Vallabhacharya	vallabhAchArya
Vardhamana Mahavira	vardhamAna mahAvIra
Vashishta	vashishTha
Veda	veYda

Vishnudevananda	vishNudeYvAnanda
Vishwamitra	vishwAmitra
Vivarana	vivaraNa
Vivekananda	vivekAnanda
Vyasa	vyAsa
Yadava	yAdava
Yayati	yayAti
Yoga Sutra	yOga sUtra

PS: If certain Sanskrit/Hindi words in the book aren't included here, it means that they have to be pronounced just as they are written, following the Pronunciation Guide.

The YS READY RECKONER

When in Doubt, Check This Out!

What is Yoga?	The stilling of all the churnings of the mind. In other words, it is the NIRODHAH of the VRITTIS of the CHITTA.
What happens when you still the churnings of your mind?	The mud churned up in your chitta lake by all your emotion-waves and thought-waves settles. In that still, clear water, you are able to see your true reflection, not some distorted version of it, and you understand who you really are.
And who am I, really?	Not your body, certainly, and not even your mind, but an invincible, eternal, luminous spark of cosmic energy that is limitless in its intelligence, its power and its capacity for kindness.

Woohoo! Now, how do we reduce our thought-waves?

Learn to examine your thoughts and put them into different 'thought-buckets', so that you can start ignoring the unhelpful ones and focus only on the helpful ones. Eventually, the unhelpful ones will disappear.

Bucket 1: PRAMANA – Right Knowledge

Thoughts based on something you experienced personally (pratyaksha), deduced (anumana) or were told by someone or something (like a book of wisdom) that you trust complctely (agama). (Usually helpful)

Bucket 2: VIPARYAYA – Wrong Knowledge

Thoughts based on information whose authenticity is not confirmed, like hearsay, rumour, gossip, or data from a source that is not 100 per cent reliable. (Usually unhelpful)

Bucket 3: VIKALPA – Imagination and Fantasy

Thoughts that have no basis in reality but exist only in your mind (for e.g., anxiety or anticipation of events that may or may not be happening/may happen in the future). (Usually unhelpful, but some kinds are helpful)

Bucket 4: SMRITAYAH – Memory

Thoughts about good and bad things that happened in the past/people who existed in your past. (Usually unhelpful, but some kinds are helpful)

Bucket 5: NIDRA – Deep Sleep

Thoughts about nothingness. The only way to get to this kind of restful, dreamless sleep is to cultivate a calm mind, which comes from paying scant attention to viparyaya, vikalpa and smritayah. (Usually helpful)

How do I keep unhelpful thoughts from rising in my chitta lake and muddying it up?

By blocking negative, unhelpful thoughts with positive, helpful ones. You get better at this through practice, practice, practice (ABHYASA) and by not being too attached to people, things or the outcomes of your actions (VAIRAGYA). Remember that both have to be practised over a long period of time, consistently, and with great reverence.

How can I be sure that it will work?

It will, if you have faith (SHRADDHA) in the process, the courage (VIRYA) to walk the long, hard road to success, the constant memory (SMRITI) of why you have undertaken this journey and what awaits you at the end of it, a deep absorption (SAMADHI) in everything you do, and the discrimination (PRAJNA) to know which thoughts are useful and which ones are not, what works for you and what does not, and what is real and what isn't.

How do I get to a state of mind calm enough to begin this journey?

MAITRI: Cultivate friendships with cheerful, positive people.

KARUNA: Be compassionate towards those who are sad, confused or bitter.

MUDITA: Take joy in other people's joys.

UPEKSHA: Don't take people's mean and hurtful words and actions personally.

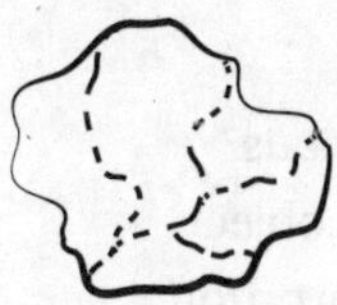

Right. Let's get started. Is there some kind of signposted map we can follow?

There is, and it has the eight legs (ASHTANGA) of the journey marked for you. But even before we look at the map, some essential prep is required. It's called KRIYA YOGA, and the Maharishi promises that committing to it will help you immensely on the journey.

Bring it on. What does Kriya Yoga involve?

Three elements, all of which are game changers.

TAPAH – Discipline, which will transform you from the inside out. Without discipline, you cannot bring about the changes you wish to in yourself.

SVADHYAYA – Introspection and reflection. Spending time with your thoughts gives you a great insight into the kind of person you are and where your challenges lie.

ISHVARA PRANIDHANA – Devotion to God. Chant the primal syllable Om, which is Ishvara's name, and ask for grace.

The ashtanga map now, please!

Here you go.

YAMA – Be good to others: do NOT practise the things on this list.

NIYAMA – Be good to yourself: DO practise the things on this list.

ASANA – Make your body strong and flexible.

PRANAYAMA – Increase your vital energy by controlling your breath.

PRATYAHARA – Stop thinking about the things you want; focus on what you need.

DHARANA – Focus intensely on an object, develop concentration.

DHYANA – Observe an object minutely, learn to meditate on it.

SAMADHI – Where the separation between you and the object blurs and disappears, and you become part of everyone and everything else, the Great Undivided, or ADVAITA.

THE YAMAS
(WHAT NOT TO DO)

AHIMSA – Do not commit violence, in thought, word or deed.

SATYA – Do not lie. Always speak the truth, but gently.

ASTEYA – Do not steal. Not people's things, not their dignity, not their peace.

BRAHMACHARYA – Do not fritter away your energy; channel it into good, meaningful work.

APARIGRAHA – Do not be greedy for what others have or envy them their successes.

THE NIYAMAS
(WHAT TO DO)

SHAUCHA – Keep your body and mind clean.

SANTOSHA – Learn to be content, count your blessings, be grateful.

TAPAH – Stay committed to your path, make the sacrifices it requires.

SVADHYAYA – Set aside time each day to spend with yourself.

ISHVARA PRANIDHANA – Trust in God, pray for grace.

Oh, also, any particular obstacles I should watch out for on the way?

You bet. These are the five main KLESHAS or obstacles. Beware of them!

AVIDYA – When we cannot see that we are whole and complete in ourselves, and believe that we need other people or things to make us feel good.

ASMITA – When we feel we are different from everyone else, and treat 'our people' and 'our things' differently from 'other people' or 'other people's things'.

RAGA – When we constantly feel desire for something and can't rest until we have it, and then can't rest because we fear we will lose it.

DVESHA – When we feel hatred, anger, jealousy, resentment for what other people have and are.

ABHINIVESHA – When we are so fearful of death that we cannot live joyously and freely in the world.

ACKNOWLEDGEMENTS

Like most people, I came to yoga through asana practice. Like most people, I had no idea that yoga was far, far more than postures and pranayama. It was only during the COVID lockdown, when time hung heavy on my hands and technology afforded me the luxury of connecting with the world in ways hitherto unexplored, that I first made my acquaintance with the Yoga Sutras. In the course of a wonderful lecture on the subject, renowned Yoga and Indian psychology scholar, Dr Vinayachandra Banavathy, unpacked the stunningly simple proposition of the ancient text – calm your mind, and all the riches of the world will be yours.

I was instantly intrigued. The YS's conviction that this was indeed the truth, its pithy but crystal-clear instructions on how to, slowly but steadily, get to calm, and its ruthless clarion call – 'No exceptions! No excuses!' – seemed exactly what a fragile world riven by anxiety and self-doubt needed as a guiding light in our Age of Continuous Distraction and Easy Cop-outs. Even as I told myself I would explore the subject further 'when I have the time', the algorithm (or the universe – who knows?) threw up a series of engaging talks, on YouTube, by Edwin F. Bryant, professor of Hinduism at Rutgers University, USA, and the author of a recent, definitive book on the YS. It felt like a sign.

Inspired, I plunged into the task of researching and writing a book for the young on the Yoga Sutras with great enthusiasm.

I could not have completed it with any level of confidence, however, if not for the support and encouragement of a number of people, to all of whom I owe a great debt of gratitude.

To my yoga teacher, Mala Bhat, for the invaluable gift of her expertise, dedication and friendship. Thank you for keeping me honest – no excuses! – these past three years, and teaching me, as I wobbled in vrikshasana and struggled with chakrasana, that real transformation waits, patiently, on the far side of fear.

To my COVID-time Sanskrit teacher and now-time friend, the passionate Sanskritist, polyglot and bundle of good cheer, Dr Anuradha Choudry, IIT Kharagpur, for unlocking portals into dazzling new ways of seeing that I was entirely unaware of, through the unified philosophy that underlies Indian Knowledge Systems, including Sanskrit and yoga; I will return soon for the advanced level Sanskrit course, Anu – no excuses!

To Prof. Edwin Bryant, for his exhaustive but wonderfully accessible tome on the YS, which served as my primary reference, and for the alacrity with which he responded, in the affirmative, to a cold-call mail I wrote him to ask if he would review the manuscript of this book. Thank you, Professor, for your warm endorsement.

As always, to the brilliant Prof. Bibek Debroy, for his immense generosity in casting a critical, meticulous eye on the manuscript despite everything else he had going on, and suggesting edits and additions in his unfailingly polite – but unfailingly firm! – manner. I am over the moon that you approve of this book, Prof. Debroy – thank you so much.

To Sayan Mukherjee, for the beautiful, beautiful cover and all the illustrations inside. This is the third of my books that your work has illuminated, Sayan, and I could not be happier or more grateful. We should seriously make plans to meet irl (as the kids say) – no excuses!

To my endlessly supportive, eternally hard-working, unfailingly wonderful editor, mentor and friend, Vatsala Kaul Banerjee, who would certainly disapprove of so many adverbs in one sentence, the biggest hug. This year marks three decades of us working together, Vats, but who's counting? Suffice it to say that we ain't never gonna stop – no excuses!

To my publisher Thomas Abraham, and his entire team at Hachette India – especially Riti, Somu, Sini, Medha and Raghunandan – for their unstinting warmth, support and cheerleading over the years, and for always having my back. I'm thrilled to have you all so firmly in my corner.

And finally, to the mysterious Maharishi P, for doing a deep dive into the mind and the psyche to reveal to us, in so few words, one of the great secrets of human existence – control your mind, young 'uns, and *ta-daa!* you control the universe!

SELECT BIBLIOGRAPHY

Bryant, Edwin F.: *The Yoga Sutras of Patanjali*, Macmillan, 2018.

Iyengar, B.K.S.: *Light on the Yoga Sutras of Patanjali*, Thorsons, 2002.

Paramahansa Yogananda: *Autobiography of a Yogi*, Rupa Publications India, 2017.

Sri M: *Yoga Also for the Godless*, Westland Publications Private Limited, 2020.

Swami Prabhavananda and Isherwood, Christopher: *The Yoga Aphorisms of Patanjali*, Vedanta Society of Southern California, 1953.

Swami Satyananda Saraswathi: *Four Chapters on Freedom*, Yoga Publications Trust, Munger, Bihar, 2013.

Swami Vivekananda: *Patanjali's Yoga Sutras*, Om Books International, 2020.

Swami Vivekananda: *The Complete Book of Yoga: Karma Yoga, Bhakti Yoga, Raja Yoga, Jnana Yoga*, Prakash Books India Pvt Ltd, 2021.